Legend of Hollow Wood

Lost in Pain

By: J.J. Dice

ISBN-13: 978-0692276075 (J.J. Dice)
ISBN-10: 0692276076

Published by Legend of Dice

www.JJDice.com

CONTENTS

This book is dedicated to the Dice Family.
Thank you for your love and support.

Prologue

It was a brisk autumn eve at Hollow Wood Manor. The wind carried a light rain, and the weeping willow on the front lawn danced with each gust. The large estate's labyrinth of rooms concealed its secret treasures. Peter Frederick had tucked himself away in a study hidden within the walls of his mansion. The room was filled with maps, worn books, handwritten journals, and ancient artifacts.

His faithful butler, Gavin, walked through the manor's halls, contemplating why Peter had chosen this particular study to conduct his research in. There were dozens of rooms within Hollow Wood Manor and each held hundreds of books and journals with no particular organization that Gavin had ever detected. He had spent most of his life traveling and adventuring with Peter, acquiring only a small portion of the available knowledge. During his time living in the mansion, he had tried to familiarize himself with as many books as he could, but it had taken Peter more than four lifetimes to collect the massive library, and he knew he would never come close—mostly because a large number of the books were written in ancient languages that Gavin was unable to translate on his own.

Peter sat at his desk with the flickering flame of his oil lamp casting shadows on his hand as he scribbled. He analyzed maps and books before writing in the blank journal before him. Charts of his travels were strewn across the floor surrounding him, and books were stacked waist high next to the desk. He whispered to himself as he frantically took notes.

"Ahem. Master Peter, Master Jack has been waiting in the dining hall for over an hour. Would you like for me to reheat your meal?" Gavin asked, as he stood tall in the doorway with his hands clenched firmly behind his back.

Peter glanced at him, but only for a moment. "Not now, Gavin. I am so close." His voice was strong and deep. His hair had flipped in front of his eyes as his head had whipped around. His long, thin fingers pulled the rogue strands of hair back in place.

Gavin watched his beloved friend fret over his life's research. "If I may point out, you have already worked through dinner every night for the past few weeks. Jack is concerned, as am I."

Peter continued to write in his journal, muttering, "Something is coming. I must decipher when and where it will arrive." He pulled open another book and shuffled the maps about, his focus unwavering.

Gavin's concern grew; he had never seen Peter in such a state of madness. "What is coming?" he asked, picking up a book from a stack surrounding the desk. He flipped through the pages to identify its importance, but it was written in another language, one that he was not familiar with. He could not begin to translate it, and there were no sketches or handwritten notes.

Peter's eyes rose briefly to meet Gavin's. They were bloodshot and glazed over from exhaustion. "I don't know. But we must be prepared."

Slamming the book shut, Gavin put the book back on the stack. He sighed and urged, "Mayhap it is time to speak with Jack. He could be of value. Isn't it time he knew?"

"The boy is not ready!" Peter snapped. "I will handle this threat, just as I have kept him safe in the past." His voice was strained from exhaustion and stress.

A three-dimensional map of a distant land was built into a wooden table with a glass case surrounding it. The terrain rose and fell with mountain peaks, cliffs, and valleys. Gavin could recall his journeys there as if they had happened yesterday. As he studied the map more closely, he noticed strange markings he had never seen before. Thin metal pins of a colorful variety were pegged across the map. His head cocked to the side, his attention was drawn back to Peter.

"What would you need of me?" he asked, sincerely offering his assistance. He peered across the desk to catch a glimpse of what Peter was obsessing about.

"Nothing," Peter replied harshly. "If I do not return, you will have to train him when the time comes." His voice softened and trailed to a whisper as he stared off across the room.

His words stung Gavin. In all his years of traveling and working for Peter, he had never been spoken to in this way. Peter usually confided in Gavin with all of his plans, even when Gavin was to remain in Hollow Wood and look after young Jack. What could be coming that had Peter in such a nervous state? He sat down in a large brown leather chair and began flipping through old books stacked high on a round glass table next to him. They had tattered bindings, and the letters on the covers were barely legible. The first book contained ancient lore of the Arctic Circle; another described a nasty-looking green creature with pointy ears and sharp, pointed teeth in a mischievous grin; another held enchantments and spells. Gavin tried to put the pieces together, reminiscing of another world.

Looking over to Peter's frantic writing, Gavin asked, "Do you need my assistance with your research? I could help you sort through it if I knew what you were looking for." His anguish was audible in his voice.

"No." Peter never even raised an eyebrow.

Desperately searching for something that would spark Peter's interest in explaining what this was all about, Gavin blurted, "Does this have something to do with—"

Peter grunted and slammed his hands down on the books and maps canvassing his desk. Sweat dripped from his brow. Utterly annoyed, he bellowed, "The only thing I need from you is to prepare my bags for travel. I will take my car and leave in the morning. You must stay and protect the boy."

"He's not a boy anymore, and how will I know when it is time to train him? He should hear it from you," Gavin persisted.

Peter looked up from his map with his brows crossed and a contentious stare, but then he smiled. "Oh, yes, yes. I'll speak to him soon, old friend." There was something in his eyes that told Gavin he was lying.

Chapter I

Awakening

Here I stand in a dirty alley, over this poor man's body. How did this happen? He continued to stress his memory, but the more he tried, the more he realized he couldn't remember anything. *I can't remember my name. How can I not remember?* he thought, in the cool, damp alleyway. He stared down at the body, and it glared back at him in turn with lifeless yellowed eyes. The body was of a middle-age man, heavyset but not obese, wearing an expensive suit. His skin pealed back exposing muscle tissue with blood oozing from the lacerations marking his neck and wrists, and his clothes were saturated in blood.

"Who are you, old man? Why are we here? Who—what did this to you? Could it have been—could I have really. . . ?"

A miniscule sound triggered the confused young man's attention like a rifle shot. He jumped back into a dark corner behind a dumpster. Slowly, he peeked back around from his shadowed hiding spot to investigate the noise only to realize nothing was there, not even the body that he had, only moments before, been inspecting.

"Did I imagine it all? Was it really all in my head? It all felt so real, and here I am in this dark corner talking to myself."

The young man emerged from hiding, confident he was no longer in danger, though even more confused. He had come out of what felt like a deep sleep to find himself quite awake, standing over a mutilated dead body which then disappeared without a trace.

He made his way down the alley toward the side street it branched from. He looked down the street both ways to see if he could find a public restroom but didn't see anything besides residential apartments and homes. The hustle and bustle of cars and people came from off in the distance, and his instinct guided him toward the higher traffic. After walking down a few quiet streets, he found himself on Main Street, a beautiful cobblestone road lined by red brick buildings with signs all over the front windows advertising sales, discounts and special offers.

His basic knowledge seemed intact, but he was still unable to grasp the life he had lived before this point.

Golden brown leaves tumbled past his feet in the brisk air as he made his way into the first door he came to. He found himself in a small diner with only two waitresses and three men in back preparing food. A few customers sat at the bar and tables, chatting among themselves. As he approached the bar he took notice of a patron's face, distorted and mangled. His jaw seemed to ghostly dangle as if no longer attached and his eyes appeared to be drooping from their sockets. The young man rubbed his eyes in disbelief, wondering why no one else seemed to notice.

****

Jessi, one of the waitresses, noticed the young man quietly entering the diner. He looked about twenty, and his thick black hair gave him the look of an unblemished man having the worst day of his life. He had dirt on his hands and face with stains down the front of his light blue button-down. Even though he was covered in dirt and looking ragged, she felt the urge to stare. Their eyes met for only a moment, and her heart jumped, filling her with thoughts of intimacy and the illusion of love. She attempted to shake the infatuation.

A nice shirt to ruin, Jessi smirked to herself as she continued admiring his face. She had been staring at him for several moments before she finally blurted out, "Welcome to The Sea Shack Diner. Take a seat anywhere, and I will be over in a minute to get your order, sir."

"I'm just looking for a restroom, please," replied the young man in a gentle and polite tone.

"Down the hall to the left, door's on your right after the kitchen. Honey, you'll have to buy something. Customers only."

****

The man patted his pockets, realizing he hadn't explored his own effects yet. He found a wallet containing many bills. Still distracted from the repulsive faces surrounding him, he pulled one out without looking and set it on the bar.

"Just some eggs over easy, toast, and bacon please," he said, though he didn't feel hungry. He was dwelling on his awakening, trying to wrap his mind around the horrific images unsuccessfully. The waitress looked puzzled as she nodded in the direction of the bathroom. He strode down the hall, closed and locked the door behind him.

"It looks like I slept in a stable last night," he said aloud as he washed the dirt from his hands and face. Leaning closer to the mirror, he placed his hands on the sink and began to explore his reflection as if looking at a stranger.

"Who are you? I don't know. Who *are* you?" He pulled the wallet back out to investigate further. Opening it from the top, he inspected the money. The wallet was full of hundred-dollar bills. Tucked inside he found a small plastic identification card. He saw the picture of the man who was dead in the alleyway. In a panic, he slid the card back down into place before reading the name. Knees weak, he dropped the wallet and caught himself on the sink. His blood ran cold. Only one thing was certain: the dead and vanished man was real.

He was submerged in his own thoughts and continued staring in the mirror at the stranger's face. His face. After a few more minutes, he quickly stuffed the wallet into the back pocket of his gray pants and took in a deep breath through his nose.

Footsteps started down the hall to the restroom. Not wanting to confront one of the crooked customers, he quickly dried his face and unlocked the door. It swung open to the horrific sight of a ghastly face, unnerving him with a small jolt. The disfigured face was covered in boils, seeping pus. The young man attempted to shy away, but the monster leaned in closer.

"Are ya alright boy? You look like ya seen a ghost," his face was dripping with secreting purulence.

"Excuse me," he said before slipping past him pressed against the door. He returned to the bar, sitting upright and still, intently staring at the countertop.

"Sir, it's only eight in the mornin'. We can't break a hundred-dollar bill this early!"

"Keep the change, ma'am," the young man said, trying to sound as pleasant as possible while avoiding eye contact.

"Sorry sir, but the meal you ordered is only six dollars."

He looked up in an effort to assert his demands, only to discover the radiantly beautiful face before him. The waitress was smiling brilliantly, drowning out his confusion with purity. Their eyes met for only a moment before she blushed and bolted for the kitchen. Returning quickly with two plates in her hands, she plopped his order on the countertop.

"We gave you an extra plate of bacon," she said proudly.

"Thank you, ma'am."

The smell of the bacon teased his nose. Five minutes earlier he couldn't even think about eating, but the smell of the meat made him realize how hungry he was. When had he last eaten? He started devouring the bacon as fast as he could.

The waitress looked at him, bewildered by the change of manners in the young man who said *please* and *thank you* and tipped ridiculously well but stuffed food in his mouth as if he were raised by wolves.

When all the bacon was gone, he ripped off a piece of the toast and pushed it into the egg yolk. As he raised the yolk-covered toast to his mouth, his stomach curdled and lurched. He put the toast down until the nausea passed. He picked up the toast again, and the same nausea occurred. He pushed himself up from the counter and turned for the door.

"Was it not to your liking, sir?" the waitress asked, obviously confused why anyone would spend a hundred dollars on a few pieces of bacon.

"The bacon was so great, thank you. It seems to have satisfied my hunger. Have a nice day, ma'am." He made his way back to the door and onto the street.

"What a strange man," she said under her breath and moved on to her other tables.

The young man stood outside the diner looking around, unsure what to do. Unable to remember who he was, he didn't know where he belonged. His mind began rattling with questions. *Do I have a home, a family? Are they missing me? Where do I go now? Did I murder an innocent man? Who am I?* Frustrated, the only thing he could do was walk.

He walked east down Main Street toward the water. He wasn't entirely sure how he knew he was facing east, but he did. He tried to keep his mind from exploding in rage by looking through the windows of all the shops along the way. Everything seemed so bright, so lively. He inhaled as much salty, fresh air as he could taste in his mouth, allowing him to calm his mind into coherent thoughts. Gusts of wind blew past him bringing with it the sounds of crashing waves and sea gulls squawking in the distance. The brightness of the busy street kept bringing him back to the darkness of the alley, the birthplace of the man he now was, the first place he could remember ever being. He continued east for several blocks and then passed through an open courtyard with large brick buildings on both sides leading up to the seaside docks.

Down on the docks, several benches faced the water. The ocean was tranquil with small swells rolling toward the shoreline. Birds flew overhead and on occasion dove straight down into the dark water in search of fish.

"Maybe the calmness of the ocean will help me clear my head," he said aloud, hoping to convince himself. The benches were chilled by the cool autumn breeze coming off the ocean as he sat there watching the sun move from its early morning position to directly above him. Sitting in silence, he racked his brain trying to remember anything about himself: his job, his friends, his home. But most of all he tried to understand the body he had encountered in the dark alley. The man on the ID in his pocket.

The sun had moved to the afternoon sky when he finally stood up from his uncomfortable wooden bench on the dock. He ran back up Main Street where he had seen a phone booth not far from the diner. He looked around cautiously as he approached it, taking note of a tall man wearing a suit and glasses talking on the phone. The man's face appeared angry and lopsided. He leaned against a wall in view of the man in the booth to wait his turn.

After several minutes, without even an acknowledgement from the man on the phone, he stepped forward and politely knocked on the door. The man whipped around with his middle finger sticking straight up. His decaying face twisted and flapped as he yelled, "Up yours. Wait your turn!"

He had not expected such a response, and it infuriated his every bone that someone could be so rude and ugly. He grasped the metal frame with both hands and shook out his frustration and fear of the creepy man. Blue light surged through the veins in his arms as he tipped the whole phone booth, rocking it on its mount. After being violently shaken, the man on the phone stared at him in terrified awe.

"Freak!" the rude man yelped as he dropped the phone and ran down the street without even saying goodbye to the person on the other end. The booth's frame was slightly twisted after being dropped back into place but the connecting wires were intact.

Looking down at his arms, the young man couldn't figure out how he had summoned the strength to shake the whole booth or why he had seen a blue light flash through them. He shook his head, trying to stay focused on the first mystery he was attempting to solve, even though this one was equally exciting but less frightening. He shut the phone booth door behind him and leaned against it, making sure it was secure. The wallet fell to the ground as he fumbled through looking for the identification card with the name and address. *Peter Fredrick, 13 Hollow Wood Lane, Braxton, ME.*

The young man pulled out the phone book from under the pay phone labeled *Braxton Greater Area* and searched for the name and address successfully. He tore out the page, folded it up, and stuffed it into the wallet. Now all he needed to do was find some change. He wondered how he would break a hundred-dollar bill as he exited the phone booth with a slight feeling of accomplishment. He now knew where the body from the alley lived and had the phone number of his residence.

Remembering the stains covering his shirt, the young man walked back down the busy street to a clothing store he had passed on his walk toward the docks. He quickly picked out a short-sleeved, black button-down to compliment his gray pants, black belt, and shoes. As he approached the checkout counter, he saw a gray brimmed hat with a black strap around the base hanging on the wall behind the clerk. Eager to make his call, he quickly requested the hat to add to his sale, paid the cashier, and asked for coins in his change.

Now he was starting to feel as if he were making progress in discovering himself. He had a clean new shirt and a hat that could hide his face enough if he pulled the brim down. As he approached the phone booth, it was again occupied. He tapped on the window to signal his urgent need to use the phone. The waitress from the diner turned in the phone booth with a scowl until their eyes met. She looked up at him, the scowl immediately turned to a smile, and she nodded as she put her index finger up to signal she was almost through. Moments later she exited the booth and apologized.

He paused to take in her pure beauty, forcing him to smile. He thanked her politely and entered the booth as she walked away. She looked back at the intriguing, stunning young man, but he was already occupied with his call. His hands were sweating as he dialed the number from his torn page and the phone began to ring.

"Good afternoon, Fredrick's residence," a woman answered with a Spanish accent.

"Hello, is Peter home?"

"I'm sorry, sir, he wasn't home when I arrived to work this morning," she informed him.

"Is this Mrs. Fredrick?"

"No sir, I am the housekeeper."

Thinking fast, he poured every ounce of persuasiveness and authority he could into his tone. "I was expecting to be staying with him, and he thought he would be home when I arrived to town. Do you suppose you could leave the back door unlocked for me? I will have no place to sleep tonight if he doesn't arrive home today."

There was no reply at first, but after a long pause the woman answered, "I suppose it would not be the first time Mr. Fredrick would have guests without his presence."

"Thank you, ma'am. Mr. Fredrick will be pleased to have my company, I assure you." He lied so easily, and she believed every word. Though his conscience buzzed about lying, his need for answers overwhelmed his scruples.

The young man hung up the phone and stepped back out. The sidewalk was crowded with shoppers, making him uncomfortable. Every face he looked upon seemed broken, tarnished, sad, distorted, or just evil, as if each person was wearing their soul on the outside for him to see who they truly were. He tipped his hat down and headed back up to the diner. As he entered, he instantly spotted his waitress, who, unlike most, was beautiful with an aura of purity, her features untarnished, sitting at a booth eating lunch. He approached her with a smile and asked politely if he could have a seat. She obliged.

"I was wondering if you could help me with directions. I'm looking for Hollow Wood Lane," he asked while uncontrollably staring at her, her kind heart radiating in an unearthly manner.

"Why would you ask such a silly question?" the waitress replied with a mocking tone.

"Excuse me?"

"Why are you asking me a question you already know the answer to?"

"I don't understand, ma'am," he replied honestly. The booth squeaked and groaned as he adjusted his position and nervously looked around the diner and out to Main Street, avoiding eye contact.

"I saw you down by the old Hollow Wood Manor last night. I live in that area, and I've always wondered who lived there." She dropped her gaze to the table with a puzzled look.

He paused, looked down at his hands on the table, and said, "I don't know how to say this, but I can't remember anything from before this morning, when I was here for breakfast. Will you please help me?" He feared her laughter and disgust with such a preposterous request.

After a momentary pause, she replied, "Sure thing, honey, my shift ends at three, and I'll be passing by that way anyhow."

"Thank you so much. You don't know how much this means," he said. He wasn't sure why she decided to offer a ride when he was simply looking for directions, but the thought of spending more time with her made him smile. In an effort to hide his excitement, he kept his gaze on the table.

"Honey, it's the least I can do after your breakfast this morning." She smiled sweetly at him. "My name's Jessi. Do you have a name, stranger, or did you forget that too?" She chuckled flirtingly, but he just stared at her flawless smile.

"Yes," he replied softly after a pause. Her cheerful gaze quickly turned to a nervous glare. After a moment of awkward silence he said, "Ma'am, if you don't feel comfortable. . ."

Though his words made Jessi feel uneasy, her emotions pushed her fiercely in desire to spend every moment she could gather staring at him. She interrupted his insecure mumbling. "Nonsense, I won't leave you to walk nearly twenty miles when I'll be driving out that way. You seem very sweet." She began to blush as if she let on to her unexplainable desire. "Don't go forgetting again, and you'll get your ride in a bit."

"Thank you again, ma'am. I suppose I'll walk down to the docks and admire the ocean while I wait."

"That sounds fine, honey, and please call me Jessi. Ma'am makes me feel old. I'm only twenty-five," she said with a grin as she stood up from the booth, putting her apron back on.

At the end of Jessi's shift, she counted out her tips and hung her apron in the kitchen quietly, distracted from closing out by thoughts of the strange man. Replaying all the conversations in her mind, she anticipated the forthcoming events with giddiness. Had he noticed her the way she noticed him? She worried she had fabricated his signs of affection in her mind. His eyes drew her in, and his smile captivated her. She thought him arrogant for throwing money at her, but he had an innocent charm that made the arrogance easy for her to look past. Over all else, there was something strange pulling her to him. Her heart pounded, and she craved him every moment since they first made eye contact. When he was near her, she couldn't escape the urge to ravage him on the spot.

Pushing back her emotions for a moment, she stuffed her tips into her purse and walked out onto the cobblestone street, turning right toward the ocean. Though the docks were quite far down the street, she could see the figure of a man in a brimmed hat sitting on a bench, still as stone. Just knowing that the shadow of the man was him, her heart began beating like a drum, and her smile pulled back so wide it hurt. She began her descent down the shallow incline of the street toward the docks.

Chapter II

Forced Impulse

The young man sat on the docks for what seemed like days, mulling over every detail of the only day of his life he knew. Jessi's face kept coming back into his mind to relieve his pain and confusion but only for moments at a time. His body felt like ice, except for the back of his neck, which felt as though the heat of the sun was warming through the top of his spine and tingling to the back of his skull. Sitting there on the bench like a statue, he closed his eyes. Though his body did not budge, images rushed through his mind.

Standing in the dark alley again, he saw the man being attacked right in front of him, but he could not see what was attacking him. Nothing was there. The man appeared to have lifted off the ground, his toes barely scraping the pavement, kicking back and forth, trying to touch ground again. His heart began racing intensely at the vision of the man being torn and ripped apart in front of him as if he were possessed by demons that could not be seen. The skin around his neck and wrists started separating as the man struggled to grab at his throat. He was trying to scream, but no sound emerged from his pale lips. The blood spread rapidly on his clothes, pooling on the pavement as the young man stood motionless watching, reliving the horror his mind had tried so hard to repress.

A hand rested on his shoulder.

"My shift is over, honey, if you're ready to take a ride down to Hollow Wood Manor," Jessi said softly.

The young man gasped, jumping forward off the bench and spinning to see her. His face was pale with wide eyes, and his jaw dropped.

"Are you okay? It's just little ol' me," she said, startled by his reaction and noticing the bewildered look on his ghostly pale face.

"Yes, I'm fine, ma'am. I must have fallen asleep." He paused to take a deep breath, relaxing his shoulders. He wiped beads of sweat from his forehead and the color was returning to his face. "And I was having an awful dream."

"You weren't moving in the least. You were sitting up straight on the bench the whole time. I could see you from the diner. You must have just been daydreamin', honey; no one can sleep sittin' up." She mocked him slightly, trying to lighten the mood and ignore the infatuation this man instilled in her. "Do you want to talk about it? Talk about the dream? Maybe it will help ya remember about yourself."

"No!" he snapped at her, then smiled and continued in a much gentler voice, "No, it was nothing important, just a nightmare."

"Okay," she paused a moment as they stared at each other. He smiled softly as she examined him. Jessi broke the moment of silence. "Well, my car is back up behind the diner in the main lot. Shall we?"

"Yes, thank you again. You don't know how much I appreciate you helping me. I am a complete stranger, even to myself, it would seem. I truly have no place to go."

Jessi and the young man started back up the street. She couldn't keep her eyes off him. His face was strong but young, his skin holding onto youthfulness as if he had never had a moment of stress, though the expression on his face seemed as though he would never smile again. Glistening in the afternoon sun, she gazed at his blue eyes with gold flecks striking out from his pupils. With his hat in his hand, his thick black hair fell perfectly in order on his head and into his face in a fantastic mess. His jawbone appeared to be strong enough to chew through steel, and his lips were calling to her sweetest senses. He was the most beautiful and mysterious person she had ever laid eyes on. Her heart pounded in her chest as she stared at him out of the corner of her eye. She didn't want him to notice her admiring his face.

As they walked side by side up the street, Jessi caught herself biting down on her lower lip, attempting to hide her pleasure. He still seemed to miss or ignore her affectionate gaze. She looked away, realizing she was being carried away by lust for a complete stranger who appeared to be in intense pain.

After a long and nearly silent walk, they turned down a side street behind the diner leading to the main lot. As they finally approached Jessi's car, they both advanced to the driver side. She slid the key into the door and unlocked the car with two twists clockwise. She straightened up and turned to the young man who was still standing behind her. Their eyes met. His face cleared of pain as a smile broke on the lips she was still coveting. He reached past her hip and pulled the door lever, opening the door for her like a gentleman. When his arm brushed against her and he leaned forward, adrenaline rushed through her.

"Ma'am," he said politely, gesturing her to the door he had opened.

"Please, call me Jessi," she replied softly, still staring into his eyes. The young man smiled as he walked around and opened his door. Her eyes followed him around the car, turning her body against her open door.

Grasping the rusted roof of the small white sedan and still smiling, "Shall we?" He sat down in the passenger seat and closed his door with a thump. Jessi had been staring at him with that stupid look a nerdy schoolgirl gives the quarterback when he speaks to her for the first time. She shook her head, ashamed of herself, and slid into the car.

"Sorry," she murmured under her breath just loud enough for him to hear.

"Sorry for what, might I ask?" he inquired as if he were playing a game.

"Never mind. Let's get you to Hollow Wood Manor," she said defensively, hoping he really hadn't noticed her giddiness. She put the car in reverse and backed out of her parking spot. Her hand trembled on the shifter as she attempted to put the car in gear, but instead a loud screeching sound curled both of them.

The young man glanced at Jessi with an inquisitive smirk, "Are you new to driving stick?"

"No, I just—I feel . . ." she tried to explain, but she didn't even know how she was feeling or at least she didn't understand how she could possibly feel in love with him.

"I understand, I am a complete stranger to you. You must be nervous, but please believe my only intention is to get to thirteen Hollow Wood Lane." His words were comforting, and she was relieved he had interrupted her confused stuttering.

"Yes, so I will take you there now." She returned his smile. She made a second attempt to put the car in gear. Sliding the stick, she let off the clutch smoothly, and they were on their way.

The young man sat next to Jessi quietly. He struggled to prevent the nightmare from taking over his mind again. To keep himself otherwise occupied, he began staring at the beautiful woman who was clearly infatuated with him. He gazed at her long, straight, brown hair. Most of it she had pulled over her left shoulder, but a few strands stayed strewn across the right side of her face, exposing her neck to his eyes. Her skin looked as soft as satin and had the remnants of a tan from the summer. Her lips were full and forced him to wonder how they would feel pressed against his. Her eyes were dark blue and radiated the color magnificently. She wore very little makeup, if any; her face did not need to be hidden. He wondered how he hadn't noticed her physical beauty earlier. Had it been the apron or the stress he'd been under?

****

Jessi glanced at him for a moment only to see he was staring at her. It made her smile and blush. Inside, that nerdy schoolgirl was screaming in excitement that this man she barely knew but couldn't seem to get enough of recognized her. She began fishing for his emotions, hoping to find out why he was staring at her with that gentle smile of his.

"What are you looking at?" she asked with a flirty grin.

"Oh, I was just wondering how long the drive to Hollow Wood is," he replied, letting her down on her hope he would pay her a compliment.

"Wow, are you so eager to be rid of me?" She tried to hold back her disgust with him and her childish crush.

"No, not at all! I was hoping you would say it would take hours," he exaggerated with a grin. "I could ask the question more appropriately, I suppose. How much more time do I get to spend with you?" His eyes stayed locked on her as she stared at the narrow, winding, heavily wooded road ahead.

"You're sweet," she smiled, "but in less than an hour, you will be on the doorstep of Hollow Wood Manor." She paused for a moment, trying to decide if she could interrogate her passenger further; she had to know more. "I'm sorry to pry, but if you don't remember who you are, or anything at all, how do you remember to go to Hollow Wood?"

"Uh, well—"

"I'm sorry, it's none of my business, and I'm sure when you get there you won't want to see me again. No reason for you to talk about it."

"Nonsense, I don't think I could get enough of you. When I close my eyes, I'm greeted with only nightmares, but when I look at you—" He stopped his own sentence in fear he had indulged too much in the conversation, not knowing what kind of danger he could involve her in.

"Yes?"

"When I look at you, I can smile again. You are a complete stranger to me, but your beauty is stunning in and out. It seems to dispel this demon that haunts my thoughts. I know it sounds crazy, and maybe I am. I really couldn't tell you."

She smiled and blushed even more intensely than before. "I must be dreaming. Guys like you pay no attention to girls like me." Her guard was back up; she clearly believed her own false words.

"What is that supposed to mean? I am here. I may not remember anything prior to this morning, but I am real, and I am telling you the truth," he exclaimed in an attempt to break through her barrier of doubt. "All I know is something terrible has happened to me, and you make the pain go away."

"Please tell me—tell me why you are going to Hollow Wood Manor," she inquired softly but firmly.

"It's not that easy. I don't know how it all happened or how I ended up where I was, but it doesn't look good for me, and I would truly hate to scare you off before I can figure it all out," he confessed honestly.

His evasion was intended to be comforting, but instead she found herself intrigued. She didn't dare to look away from the road at him for fear his eyes would trap her again. "I need you to try, and I promise I will try not to freak out if it really is that bad," she said.

"It *is* that bad," he quickly replied, looking away from her for the first time since they got in the car. The look of pain swarmed back over his face as the radiant foliage mesmerized him.

For the next few miles, they both sat in silence. The young man started falling back into his nightmare with his face leaned against the glass.

This time his eyes stayed wide open as the trees flew past his unmoving gaze, but all he could see was the man, all the blood pushing its way through his neck and wrists, being held up by who knows what.

Jessi took her hand off the shifter and wrapped it in the young man's hand, sitting palm up on his leg. Her action drew his face from the window and his attention back on her. She glanced away from the road for only a moment to share a smile with him. He smiled back through the pain in his mind, but this time the smile seemed forced.

All of the fears Jessi explored in their silence turned into only one fear: she worried she wouldn't see him again after this car ride.

"You seem so sweet. You are not the bad guy." She paused collecting her thoughts. "You continue to call me ma'am, and you open doors for me because I'm a woman." Choking on her heart-felt words, she continued in a whisper, "Please tell me, and I can make the car ride longer as you wished earlier."

She watched as the young man's smile was completely lifted again. Something about her was so pure, as if he was speaking to an unblemished spirit. He drew a deep breath and released it with a sigh of anguish.

"The first thing I can remember is standing in an alleyway this morning. A man lay before me. He was fatally wounded, and I don't know how. I don't know how it happened to him or how I ended up there with him, but it gets even stranger."

"Maybe you were right, maybe I shouldn't know," she said with a frightened look, attempting to retract her hand.

"Please, you must believe what I am about to tell you." He pleaded, squeezing her hand gently to signal his desire to hold it still. "Something or someone moved behind me, so I jumped behind a dumpster nearby. When I looked to see if I was still alone, I was—completely alone. The man who had been lying there was gone. No sign of him, not even a single drop of blood."

"So you were having one of your nightmares, and none of it was real," she speculated.

"No, the nightmares are about him, how he died, but they don't make any sense. Also, you asked me how I know where I'm going. I have the man's wallet, and I have no memory of taking it from him."

His words did not fall easily on her mind. She pulled her hand back slowly from his and placed it on the steering wheel.

"Are you going to hurt me?" she asked in a fearful tone.

"No! I could never imagine hurting anyone, especially not you. You are the only person in the world that I know. I hardly know anything about you other than you make me smile. You are the most beautiful person I can imagine."

Silence crept over the car as Jessi flicked her turn signal and pulled into a long driveway leading up a steep hill to an enormous house. A massive cast-iron gate crossed the bottom of the driveway with the golden letters *HW* engraved in oval plates on each side. The gate was over eight feet tall, and the cast-iron rods transformed into vines as the posts crawled to the top, intertwining and weaving throughout the peak of the gate.

"Please, Jessi, come with me to the door at least. I told you I don't know what happened, and you are all I have in the world right now."

"If he's not home, I can't say I won't jump back in my car and leave your ass here," Jessi snapped back at him, feeling like she had been tricked into bringing him here. In her mind, she really knew the reason was her schoolgirl crush on the young man, who was undoubtedly even younger than her.

"That's fine, and I will completely understand, but you need to know I am not a killer." He seemed to be trying to convince himself as well.

The gate remained closed as they approached it. They stopped at a control panel. "What now?" Jessi asked.

He took a deep breath before reaching across the driver's seat, extending his arm out the opened window. He only had to press a single button before the gate began to open. They looked nervously at each other with blank expressions before they continued up the rest of the driveway and parked at the front door. The young man jumped out of the car and walked around to Jessi's door. She was still gripping the steering wheel. The car was already off, and she was staring at nothing.

He opened her door, offered his hand, and spoke gently, "Jessi, are you okay?"

She nodded and started lifting herself out of the car, ignoring his hand. She accompanied the young man to the front door and rang the bell herself. A few moments went by with no sound of movement, no sound at all. No birds or crickets, no wind, only the sound of her own heartbeat stuck in her throat. Her hand trembling, she reached out and pressed the doorbell a second time. Still silence. Jessi turned to the mysterious young man she had started this adventure with.

"He doesn't seem to be here," she said with sorrow in her eyes.

"Are you going to 'leave my ass here' then? Or should we try the back door? I spoke to the housekeeper on the phone; she said she'd leave it open."

"Oh yes, breaking and entering," she said sarcastically. "Or maybe I will ring one more time." She looked up at him, her face full of fear, hope, skepticism, and a peculiar sadness. Her trembling hand raised a third time to ring the doorbell, but before she could, a black car came up the drive way. The black luxury car pulled up next to Jessi's car and came to a halt, the dust settling around its tires. The windows were tinted too dark to see anything inside. The rear door swung open, and one foot stepped out onto the driveway in a shoe more expensive than Jessi's car. The second foot landed next to the first, and a dark figure emerged. Jessi's heart was beating harder now than it had all day with the added excitement of her new friend, who at this point seemed solid as oak, standing tall, strong, and handsome.

The man exiting the black car stood up, and the young man's mouth dropped when Mr. Fredrick's face peered over the open door. His face appeared horrifically clouded and disfigured as had the other people in town, but the young man dismissed the similarities in relief that he was still alive.

Mr. Fredrick gave the young couple a strong glare, slammed the door shut, and patted on the roof of the car to signal the driver to pull away. Mr. Fredrick started toward Jessi and the young man and stopped within a few paces of them.

"You're alive!" exclaimed the young man, feeling a weight lifted from his chest.

"Of course I am, Jack, why the hell wouldn't I be?" Mr. Fredrick replied with a nasty snarl.

"Jack?" the young man inquired.

"That is your name, isn't it?" Mr. Fredrick's words cracked out like a whip.

"Sir, I'm sorry. I don't remember anything from before this morning, and I seem to have your wallet."

"That's complete nonsense. I have my wallet here, m'boy. Now are you going to help your uncle with his bags, or are you going to stand there holding on to that sweet little thing you have neglected to introduce?"

Jack was knocked back by this whole greeting. He didn't understand any of it, though Jessi smiled as she stepped forward to greet Mr. Fredrick.

"My name is Jessi, sir. So you are Jack's uncle?" She was grinning from ear to ear.

"Yes, m'dear, and it seems Jack has lost his manners." He shook her hand.

"Sir, he's really lost his memory. I've just met him this morning, and yet somehow he convinced me to bring him here. I'm quite pleased he did."

"Please call me Peter, and if he's lost his memory, how would he know to come back home?" The look on his face indicated he already knew the answer to the question, as if it were a test.

"Peter, I have your license. It was in the wallet in my pocket. I believed it to be yours," Jack explained.

"Ah, yes, the store clerk in town had checked my ID for purchases but I left it behind. You ran to fetch it while I attended my business meeting. Gavin and I waited for an hour before we figured you must have been preoccupied in your own affairs. I can see we were right," he gestured to Jessi. "Now, if you don't mind helping me inside with my bags, I must rest before traveling. Jessi, it was a pleasure, but I must be so rude as to not invite you inside." Holding his briefcase in one hand and a small bag in the other, Peter mounted the stairs and made his way to the door past the couple.

"I understand, sir. I should be going anyway. Jack, will I see you again?" Jessi asked, concerned the man she had spent the day fawning over was too rich and too good for her.

"My uncle seems to need rest, so I should be out of the house anyway," Jack replied with a grin. Jessi smiled and blushed, hoping that he had been fishing for an invitation.

"Help your uncle with his bags, and then, if you would care to, you may accompany me home. You could scare the shit out of me with more ghost stories. I would be most delighted." Her grin widened as Jack's eyes stared into her soul, pulling her into a soppy mess of emotions again.

In a hurry, Jack hoisted two bags in each hand and jogged to the door, yelling, "I'll be back later, Uncle!" He only waited a moment for a response.

"I said call me Peter! Now let me sleep!" Peter's voice echoed sharply from somewhere in the gigantic house.

Jack burst out of the front door, still confused but overwhelmed with happiness that the man he had seen dead in an alleyway turned out to be very much alive. To top it off, Mr. Fredrick was his filthy-rich uncle whom Jack gathered he was living with.

Jessi was leaning against the car facing the house. Jack took one look at her stunning smile and tripped down almost every stair. She giggled at his excitement. She swiped a few strands of hair from her face and tucked them with the rest behind her ear. Jack was admiring every bit of her even though she was still wearing her work clothes, a white button-down tailored around her stomach to accentuate her breasts, especially once she undid the top three buttons when she got off her shift, and a black pencil skirt that formed to her perfect hourglass figure. He was so full of confidence after all of the tension between him and Jessi that, once he got a solid footing, he walked to where she was standing and ran his hands along her hips. Staring at her, trembling, he leaned in closer as she stared back at him with pink cheeks. Her eyes closed, and they kissed. It was long and sweet. Jack stood up straight, still smiling down into Jessi's eyes, but when their eyes met, she looked shyly away.

"What's wrong, Jessi? Was it not a good kiss?" Jack pretended the day was normal and okay.

"It was amazing, too amazing. I met you only hours ago, and I feel like I'm falling for you, and who are you? You are insane! You have nightmares during the day, and you hallucinated this morning a terrible death for your uncle, who at the time you did not know was your uncle. And now I've invited you to my home without even thinking about what's right."

"I don't need to go with you. If you would like, I will stay here and wait for my uncle to wake up so I can quiz him on who I am. I am sorry you feel this way, and I am terribly sorry I frightened you. All I know is being with you is all I want, whether it is right or wrong." Jack pleaded for her to see he wasn't insane. There had to be a logical explanation, considering his uncle was alive and well. "This explains why I got up from behind that dumpster in the alleyway! The body was gone, and there was no blood. I must have been jumped and hit over the head with something hard enough to make me lose my memory. It wasn't a hallucination, simply a vivid dream that ended with me coincidentally in the same place I hid."

"Wouldn't your head hurt? Wouldn't you have a bump or cut? Why didn't they take all that cash you're carrying?" Jessi reasoned with him, still with an accusatory tone, but at least she could look him in the eye again with a smile on her face.

"I don't know what happened, but Peter made it very clear he is not in the mood for discussion, and the only thing I can think of is what I know, and I only know what has happened today. I would much rather spend the rest of this sideways day with you. You are the only good I know. The rest is a nightmare, literally."

"You are so cute when you beg. How can I leave you here to suffer your own insanity? Get in the car, Mr. Jack, before I'm forced to kiss you again and waste the whole day not learning any more about you."

Her sassy manner made Jack grin. Being left alone would be worse than any torture, watching his uncle be torn apart by an invisible villain.

They both got back into Jessi's beat up little white car and drove off. They only drove for a few minutes before arriving at Jessi's home, a small trailer that once may have been called a motor-home parked on a meager piece of land left to her by her late parents. The tires were flat, and she told Jack how the engine had been stripped out by thugs a year ago when she had traveled home to see her dying mother. Without a pause in the conversation, they moved from the car to inside her home. She did most of the talking as Jack didn't have any memories to share. He listened to her voice and watched her lips move as she spoke, admiring her gorgeous eyes as they sparkled in delight as she told stories about her family and her childhood.

"You've told me so much about your brother and your father. You mentioned your mom passed away from cancer last year, but what happened to them?" Jack asked, still eager to learn everything he could about this amazing girl. He felt like she should have been with him all along. The question echoed in silence, and her eyes darkened and swelled.

"They were murdered behind a truck stop on their way to visit me in school," she said quietly, her voice sputtered through the tears hidden in her eyes.

"I'm so sorry, Jessi, I didn't mean to pry," Jack said sincerely, his gut wrenched with the guilt of asking her such a personal question.

"But you did. It's okay, I like you, Jack, and if I didn't want to tell you, I wouldn't have. The worst part about the whole thing is whoever did it framed my kid brother to have killed his own father and then himself, but I know my brother could have never hurt anyone—he cried when his pet frog died. My father was good to us, especially to him. He was the perfect son, and they were best friends. That's when I dropped out of college and started working at the diner so I could be there for my mom until she was moved to a cancer clinic. Enough of the sad stories. Do you want a drink? I think I need something strong."

"No, thank you, I'm happy as I am."

Jessi stood up from the couch and went to the kitchen only steps away. As she reached for a bottle of cheap whiskey in the cabinet above the fridge, she felt his hands wrapping around her waist, and he pulled her away from the liquor cabinet she was grasping. He kissed her neck as she brought her hands down to his and spun herself in his arms to kiss him.

"How do you make me feel like this?" she whispered and put her hands on his stomach, pushing him backward down the short hallway into the bedroom, still kissing him.

Not understanding the feelings that took over every time her eyes met with Jack's, she pressed him onto the bed and started unbuttoning the rest of her shirt. She kicked the door shut behind her and crawled slowly onto the bed over Jack's body.

Her face was no longer sad but glowing with a sensual smirk as they gazed into each other's eyes. As she moved along his body, she removed his shoes then unbuckled his belt and unbuttoned his pants while she kissed his fit stomach. Sitting over his knees with her shirt unbuttoned, she slid her hand under his shirt, caressing up his stomach toward his hard chest, bringing his shirt up with her arms. She carefully pulled the shirt over his head and threw it to the floor. Her back arched as she slid her body against his. She kissed his lips and allowed his hands to explore her body. He started at her shoulders under her shirt and easily slid the shirt off her back and down her arms; his hand returned to the center of her back to unclasped her bra.

She sat up on him and held her shoulders forward, allowing gravity to let the undergarment fall freely from her perfect form. He gazed at her astonishing body and gasped for air, but all the blood in his body had left his head. She smiled softly at him and slid his pants off with her feet, bracing herself up with her arms, looking down at him with her gorgeous smile and beautiful eyes. Jessi's heart screamed in her chest, and an animal side took hold when she felt her well-endowed lover's excitement pushing against her, pleading for entry. She leaned forward, guiding him in. Pain and pleasure alike took over Jessi's face. Soon it would only be pleasure.

Hours later, Jessi and Jack lay in her bed, exhausted. He was sprawled on his back with her head resting on his bicep, her hands feeling his beating heart through his chest.

"Are you hungry?" Jessi asked.

"No, I am just fine right where I am," Jack replied honestly. "I am really tired now. I think I'll close my eyes."

"Please be here when I wake up," she whispered in his ear.

A smile came over his face even with his eyes closed, and he let himself drift off to sleep tangled up with the woman he most desired. At least he could not imagine desiring anything more than having her in this moment. He didn't know how, but he was intensely in love with her.

Chapter III

Nightmare

The next morning, Jack woke early, sweating from another nightmare. Jessi had rolled off him in the night and was curled up on the other side of the bed. He quietly stood up, pulled his boxers and pants back on, and crept out of the bedroom, closing the door behind him as gently as possible. He explored her small living space. On his left was a petite closet, and to his right was the bathroom he so desperately needed. Past the closet on the left was the fridge then a countertop with an embedded stove and sink. Cabinets hung above the stove and sink. Across from the kitchen was a simple couch made of an old cushion mounted to a plywood seat that he lifted to expose more storage area. Beyond the kitchen, at the other far end of the trailer, there was a dinner table with bench seats. Above the table was a top bunk for extra sleeping space.

After making his observations of her home, Jack used the bathroom, emptying his bladder for what felt like five minutes. He used his extra time to replay the past evening in his head and could not help but smile and feel giddy. He felt like jumping up and down and screaming, "I'm in love!" He refrained from doing so for two reasons: mostly he didn't want to wake Jessi, but he also didn't want to expose his true feelings, worried he may scare her away. He came out of the bathroom after washing his hands in her tiny sink and approached the fridge.

When he opened the door, little was in there other than leftover food from the diner, a half-gallon of milk, and a few small containers of pre-cut fruit from the market. Jack had planned on making Jessi breakfast in bed, but found himself at a loss with the lack of ingredients. He quickly checked the cabinets; he found cereal—the box was almost empty—and some crackers.

"This won't do," he mumbled to himself as he rummaged through her kitchen. Jack crept back into the bedroom in silence, picked up his undershirt and the black button-down he bought the day before. Tossing them over his shoulder, he then leaned down and kissed Jessi on her forehead and snuck back toward her front door. She showed no sign of waking. Pulling his clothes on quickly and quietly, he grabbed the keys to Jessi's beat up little car and left the trailer, closing the heavy door behind him as quietly as possible but, unfortunately, with a thud and a loud click.

He stopped for a minute and listened outside the trailer to see if there was any sign of her disturbance, but he heard nothing. Jack smiled and made his way to the car. He sat down in the driver's seat, put the key in the ignition, and cranked the engine. A vision of fire exploded in his face, pushing him back against his seat. He gasped and tried to brush the fire off him for only a moment before he realized it wasn't real.

He put both hands on the wheel of the idling car, his eyes wide with confusion, his knuckles white. He looked down at the radio clock and realized it was only five-thirty in the morning. The sun was barely peeking through the trees, giving the sky an illusion of a cloudy day even though there wasn't a cloud in the sky.

"Wow, I must be overtired. Pull yourself together, Jack!" he scolded himself, trying out his own name for the first time. He put the car in gear and drove off down the only streets he could remember, leading him back in the direction of his uncle's street. He had noticed a twenty-four hour market on their drive the day before. His trip was short but successful; he bought eggs, bacon, milk, orange juice, and pancake mix. He returned to the trailer by six o'clock, proud he would easily be able to sneak back inside.

After he got the groceries out of the back seat, he carefully pushed the car door closed, leaning his body against it to make sure it was shut completely. After sneaking around all morning, he felt quite adept at being stealthy. He headed inside and began preparing breakfast as quietly as possible. The bacon crackled and popped in the frying pan, and the smell of it toyed with his nose. His stomach growled as the meat sizzled, but he refused himself the satisfaction, wanting to eat his breakfast with Jessi in bed.

When he was finished preparing a feast of pancakes, eggs, a glass of juice, and the full pound of cooked bacon, he was ready to wake Jessi. He balanced the plate on his left forearm while holding the glass of juice in his left hand and turned the short distance to the bedroom door. It resisted opening at first, and the handle felt hot to the touch but not scalding. When the door came free it made a sound like Velcro pealing apart, and a substance with the consistency of melted cheese strung between the door and the door jam. He couldn't see Jessi or much in the shadowed room.

"Jessi!" he shouted in a panic, "Jessi!" He took a step back from the door and kicked it in, the melted orange substance allowed the door to break free with a loud ripping and crackling sound. Upon closer inspection, the goo appeared to be more like molten lava devouring the room, covering the walls and floor. The glass of juice and plate fell, shattering at his feet as he stared in awe. Tears fell from his eyes, but not one sound escaped his mouth. Jessi's hands were glued to the ceiling above the center of the bed with the scorching material. Her feet were pulled back to the wall above the head of the bed, also stuck, forcing her lifeless head to dangle over her naked chest, which had been flayed open and tacked to her back with sharpened bones. Under her, the bed was saturated with her blood and organs; nothing remained inside her torso but bone and air. Jack fell to his knees, tears flowing. The only noise his throat could gather was a squeal followed by a deep bellowing cry barely resembling the words *no* and *Jessi*.

"It's okay, honey," Jessi's voice said from the ceiling. Jack looked up at her dangling body to see her head lift up and blood dribble from her mouth as she repeated, "It's okay, Jack."

Jack sprang out of bed in Jessi's perfectly neat bedroom, aside from their clothes strewn about from the night before. Jessi sat up and stared at him with concern. She was very much alive.

"Are you okay, Jack?"

"You—you were—it was so real," he tried to explain, but the images still flashed in his memory vividly, making him flinch away from her.

"It was just a dream, sweetie, and you don't have to tell me about it if you don't want to, but I think you must have seen something yesterday morning, something terrible. The stress of what you saw is what repressed your memory, and now it's trying to force its way out through your dreams."

"You don't understand. It wasn't a dream, I was there, and you were—you were there, too. I made breakfast for you, and . . ."

"That's how I know it was dream. My fridge is empty," she mocked with a cute smirk.

"I know, there's a half-gallon of milk, some leftover food from the diner, and some fruit. I went to the store and bought the stuff to make breakfast, and when I brought it in to you—you were—"

"I was dead?"

"Yes, but it was awful!" he exclaimed and proceeded to tell her about the dream in detail.

"Well, just because you guessed the contents of my fridge, you can clearly see I'm fine and very much alive. Now get over here and kiss me," she said flirting with him, hoping he would let go of the nightmare. He obliged her demand reluctantly at first, but her beauty took over him quickly.

Jessi stood up from the bed after their long and passionate kiss, still naked from their fantastic evening. She started toward the bathroom, but when she reached the bedroom door, she turned and looked back at Jack, smiling.

"Will you join me for a shower?" Her seductive voice tickled Jack's loins.

"Absolutely," he replied, jumping out of bed to join her in the shower, where he made love to her again.

When their shower was over and they had both dressed, they sat down at the little table with coffee and stared at each other, smiling. Jessi enjoyed the company, but they were mostly silent with the occasional giggle from Jessi. It had been a long time since she had dated, much less been to bed with, anyone, usually being quite the prude. Jack was the first person she had even kissed before a second date, and all she could think about around him was extremely emotional or sexual. She adored him, but suddenly realized the time.

"I wish I could take you to work with me, Jack. You are something else." She looked down at her coffee. "What do you want to do today while I'm at work? I mean, you are more than welcome to stay here so I can have you when I get home, but there isn't much to do."

"No, I think I should try to talk to Peter," he replied, though the idea of being there waiting for her sounded great to him. He still had so many unanswered questions. "And I will wait there for you to pick me up after you get out of work," he said eagerly, revealing how much he wanted to be with her.

"And you will spend the night again?" she asked, her expression showed signs of doubt and worry.

"For you?" He tried to sound skeptical for a moment just to see her face drop. "I'll stay as many nights as you will have me." He enjoyed watching her smile lift again.

"It's a date then, but we really need to get going if I'm going to get to work on time."

The two lovers left the trailer, Jessi only pausing to lock the front door while Jack waited at her car door to open it for her. They both settled in the car with Jessi driving and Jack sitting shotgun, his eyes glued on her beauty, mesmerized by the purity that radiated from her. Jack could see she could feel his eyes on her, and he smiled every time she glanced at him on their short drive back to Hollow Wood Manor.

He continued smiling at her, which made her blush and ask, "What?"

He simply replied each time, "You," or, "Still you," in a sweet and content voice.

The ride was quick, but for the two who wanted nothing but to stay together, the drive felt faster than a blink. As they pulled up the driveway, Jack turned to Jessi, "I was just wondering, how is it that a trailer park came to be right around the corner from the manor?"

"My grandmother use to tell me stories of her grandparents who lived in the trailer park when it was new, although it was more of a gypsy camp back then with dozens of wagons and nightly parties spread throughout the camp. I'm rusty on the details, but what I can remember is there was a time of great despair, a famine or monster or something; there were so many stories. Anyways, when they finally triumphed, the owner of the park had the manor built and promised land forevermore to all whose families had survived. I suppose I'm the last of any bloodline that once lived here because it's just me and my trailer there now. That's why I've always been so curious about who lives in Hollow Wood."

Jack assumed her grandmother must have passed some time ago and did not want to force Jessi to tell another sad story of her family members passing. "That is a fantastic story!" Jack said. "I wonder what Peter knows of this. He can't be much older than forty, but he may have unlocked some secrets when he moved into the manor." Jack continued staring at Jessi for a minute before she spoke.

"Sweetie, as much as I hate to kick you out, I don't want to be late for work." She leaned toward him, signaling for a kiss. Jack accepted the kiss, smiled, and jumped out of the car. He made his way to the driver-side window, which Jessi had opened in the time it took him to walk around the car. He bent down and put his head in to kiss once more the beautiful woman he had shared such an amazing evening with.

When he pulled away, only inches from her face he whispered, "Don't forget me."

"Trust me, I won't. I'll be here before four p.m.," she replied as Jack stood up. She smiled at him and said, "See you," then drove off, leaving Jack in her rearview mirror, waving.

Jack shook the daydream of his new girlfriend out of his head and turned to the giant house before him. The house had a double front door. The first was a light door made of glass with a golden lever that twisted with ease. Past the glass door was a second, giant solid door with no windows that seemed to be oak wrapped around steel. Jack attempted to open the second only to find it locked, so he rapped on the door with three hard knocks. He then listened intently but heard nothing for a few moments. Once he realized the house might be too big to hear his knocking, he tried the doorbell, which chimed inside like a church bell. A middle-aged man came to the door and greeted him.

"Ah, Master Jack, how good to see you remember where the doorbell is," the man said in a dry but witty snip. Jack recognized his Uncle's driver.

"I'm sorry, Gavin, right?" Jack replied, feeling confused and out of place.

"Forgive me, Master Jack, but is it not too early for heavy drinking?"

"I haven't been drinking. I have amnesia, and the only reason I found my way here yesterday is because I had Peter's ID card."

Gavin gestured him to come inside so he could close the door.

"Is my uncle home now?" Jack inquired as he looked around the entryway to this enormous house. The ceilings had to be more than fifty feet high in the entrance foyer, which housed only a giant winding staircase, a long dark oak table against a wall, and four balconies that served as a large landing at each floor.

"I'm afraid Master Peter is still in bed at this hour. You can find your room on the top floor at the far end of the hall, in case you've forgotten, sir."

"Thank you, Gavin. I think. Will you please let me know when Peter wakes up?"

"Splendid, sir." Gavin turned and walked away with his nose up.

Jack started up the stairs, all the way up to the fifth floor, running his hand along the railing of the balcony that overlooked the entranceway, amazed by the immensity of the house. After he climbed the five flights of stairs, he was bewildered by the hallway before him. He could see the door to his quarters described by Gavin. It had to be a hundred paces from the balcony to his bedroom, with five doors on each side of the hallway. Jack ran down the hall, his footsteps silent on the soft rug even at a full sprint. He felt like a little kid exploring a great castle, excited to find a treasure at the end of the hallway.

The treasure he was seeking was the answers his bedroom might grant him. He hoped when he saw his own belongings his memory would return with a flash. He approached the door, breathing only slightly heavier from running down the corridor and climbing the stairs. He expected to be exhausted but was only enthused. He walked into the room to behold a sight that took his breath away.

His bedroom was more of an apartment, or even a small house. He walked into a small entry room with a big kitchen to his right. All the cabinets were dark wood, all the appliances were stainless steel, and the floor was slate. Beyond the kitchen was a bar that separated the kitchen from a large living room with a black leather sectional sofa against the wall. The couch sat on a dark rust-colored plush rug, and a huge flat-screen television hung on the opposite wall. Past the couch, large glass sliding doors led to an outside balcony overlooking the backyard and garage.

To his left was a doorway into a large dining room with a table that could seat twenty. The floor was the same tile as the kitchen, and the walls were painted in the same dark red as the living room rug. The table was decorated with silver candleholders, red candles standing erect and unused in each. At the far end of the dining room another door gaped parallel to the one he peered through. Instead of exploring in that direction, he continued down the hallway.

Past the length of the dining room, the corridor bent to the left. He assumed the unexplored door in the dining room must exit to this hall. On the right side stood two doors. Jack opened the first to find a bathroom that Jessi's entire trailer could fit in. It had a giant tub with at least ten water jets, a marble counter against the wall with four sinks, and a massive mirror that spread the distance from counter to ceiling. Four other lightweight slatted doors lined the back wall. The door farthest to the left wall was a closet with a stacked washer and dryer, the second and third door concealed toilets, and the last door was a standing shower.

Jack smiled to himself in disbelief that he could have forgotten these things. He left the bathroom and turned right to inspect the next and last room in this hallway, a bedroom with white walls, two empty bureaus, an empty closet, and a queen-size bed neatly made with an ugly pale green comforter on top. Jack could not believe his suite came complete with so much, even a guestroom. He exited the guestroom, turning right once more out into the hallway and followed it to the end where it bent to the left. Following the corridor around he was faced with another short hallway, a door on the left that would clearly be the dining room, and a staircase. He mounted the staircase. Here he found the first room that really felt like him, like a place where he belonged.

The ceiling's woodwork was exposed as in an unfinished attic but was fully caulked and stained, giving a log-cabin look with cedar floors that filled the room with their beautiful smell. The back wall had a windowed wooden door that led out to yet another balcony above his downstairs balcony but was inaccessible from any point other than this door or dropping from the peak of the roof twenty feet above the balcony. In the bedroom was a king-size bed with a dark red comforter, dark stained oak bureaus and table, and a large walk-in closet. Jack started rifling through the two bureaus, hoping to find a stash of memorabilia, old pictures, anything that could help him remember, but he only found endless shirts, pants, shorts, socks, and underwear. He moved on to the walk-in closet still seeking personal items only to find hats, suits, sneakers, shoes, and sandals.

Disappointed, Jack gathered a pair of blue jeans, a white t-shirt, boxers, socks, and a pair of white sneakers that appeared to be brand new and headed back downstairs to use his shower, for what seemed to him the first time.

The shower helped clear Jack's mind. He realized he had overlooked the desk upstairs. Hastily dressing, he ran back upstairs to the desk and pulled on the top center drawer, but it did not yield. He tried each drawer, and each gave the same response: nothing.

"Why would I lock my desk, and where would I keep the key?"

****

Jessi was still glowing. She was serving the restaurant floor with one other waitress, Carla. At a quiet moment during their shift they sat in the break room together chatting, glad to have a minute to relax.

"Darlin', you've been bouncin' around this diner with a liveliness I haven't seen in you before," Carla started prying.

Jessi's cheeks became hot, no doubt hinting to Carla she was on to something.

"It wouldn't have anything to do with Mr. Money Bags who came in yesterday and gave you that big tip, would it?"

"Maybe, maybe not," Jessi said with a smile that likely betrayed her.

"Jessi, you better tell me every detail. Honey, men come in here drooling on themselves for you, and you don't even notice. Then this guy comes in as if he doesn't even notice you, devours some bacon, and tips you nearly a hundred dollars. Tell me, did you kiss him? Was it good? Are you seeing him again?"

Jessi just stared at her with the stupid smile she couldn't get rid of all day.

"Well are you going to tell me? Wait. You slept with him, didn't you?" Carla exclaimed.

Jessi's face flushed hotter. "Carla! That's none of your business!" Jessi shouted, still unable to stop smiling. Jessi expected to feel ashamed about her promiscuous actions, but even without Jack there for her to look at, she still felt fully indulged in him, as if she belonged to him, a notion she was completely satisfied with.

"Mhmm, and it must have been good too, because, honey, love is dripping off you, and it's disgusting."

"Is someone jealous?" Jessi snipped, her smile turned only for a moment into a cruel smirk.

Carla grabbed her server rag, used for picking up hot plates, wound it so it looked like a rope and used it as a whip on Jessi's butt.

"Damn right, a man like that, I would have taken him home too," Carla confessed in a sassy attitude as she left to check on her tables.

Jessi sat there in her daydream of Jack while she was staring at the clock that seemed to be stuck at ten. She couldn't wait for this afternoon. She wondered what Jack was doing and if he had the chance to catch up with his Uncle Peter.

Chapter IV

Unknown

Jack was sitting in his living room, wondering if he would ever get to speak with his uncle. Peter was obviously extremely busy his whole life to be able to afford this luxurious lifestyle. Just then a knock came on the front door of his living quarters. Jack jumped up and rushed to the door, hoping to find his uncle.

"Greetings, Master Jack. Master Peter has instructed me to give you the new keys to the house and garage, as you have lost your set; I have changed all of the locks. He has also instructed me to inform you that you are welcome to use anything in the garage. The keys to all the cars are labeled in a lock box just inside the back door. He also sends a message that he is terribly sorry to leave you in such a condition, but he must depart immediately for an urgent business matter on which I, as always, will be accompanying him. Oh, and don't be worried if you hear anyone moving about, the maid is in daily."

"Can I not speak with him for a moment?" Jack desperately begged.

"I do apologize, Master, but he is already waiting for me in the car," Gavin replied in his dry tone.

"Thank you for the message, and please call me Jack," he replied in a saddened voice.

"As you please, Jack. I must take my leave now."

Jack shut the door as Gavin turned away from him in the hallway. Feeling frustrated and neglected by his uncle, he tossed the keys onto the bar on his way back to the couch, where he sat down for only a moment before curiosity grabbed him.

"What's in the garage?" he exclaimed aloud, feeling excitement overcome his disappointment. Jack rushed to the bar, grabbed the keys, and burst out his front door into the massive hallway. He looked at the first door on the right, labeled *Elevator*. Through the door was a small lobby with two elevators. He pushed the button and waited only a moment before the elevator dinged and the doors opened. Looking at the floor selection, he pressed G, and the elevator descended to the bottom floor. The doors opened, and he was staring at a long ramp that led up to the garage. The floor, walls, and ceiling were all cement. He jogged his way up the ramp, which in his excitement felt never-ending. When he reached the top of the ramp, he stood and looked at the back door and the lockbox mounted to the wall to its right. To his right, the room expanded into a ten-car garage. He opened the lockbox and picked out the first key. Jack didn't care much about which car he would drive, since they all appeared to be very expensive and most of them fast.

The key he chose appeared to be a small black box with four buttons embedded in it, one with a locked symbol, one with an unlocked symbol, one that was just red, and a chrome button that, when pushed, shot the key out from the small box like a switchblade. He pressed the red button and one of the many cars started beeping and flashing its lights. The car had no logo on it, but it was glossy black with black tinted windows, black rims with red brake calipers, and a body style that intrigued Jack. This was the car he was going to visit Jessi in today.

He pushed the red button a second time to stop the alarm, then unlocked the car. He climbed in the driver's seat, shut the door, stuck the key in the ignition, tried to turn it, but it wouldn't budge. He looked around and lifted a small, almost invisible black latch that blended in with the black dashboard to reveal a small green button. With the key in the ignition, he pressed the green button, and the engine roared. The starting of the car with its unique starter felt like déjà vu.

Jack was pleased with himself and his choice of car. He opened the garage door with the control pad on the visor. He went tearing up the driveway, around the side of the house, and down to the street. He didn't know what kind of car this was, but it was fast, and it was fun. He spun the tires entering the street and gave it full gas, watching the smoke behind the car. He was on his way back to Main Street, a forty-five-minute drive through winding country roads he planned to make in twenty, and he did.

As he approached Main Street, he slowed down and looked for the lot Jessi parked in. When he found it, he pulled in and parked in the spot next to Jessi's beat up little white car. He locked up with the push of a button and began to walk toward Main Street, twirling the key on his finger with a smile on his face. He was so excited he was about to see her. Jessi made him happier than any car could.

As he walked through the door of the diner, Jessi's eyes lit up, though she seemed to keep her emotions under control.

"Welcome to The Sea Shack Diner. Take a seat anywhere, and I will be over in a minute to get your order, sir."

"I'm just looking for a restroom, please." Jack replied with a grin on his face, this time much cleaner than his visit the prior morning.

"Down the hall to the left. Door's on your right after the kitchen. Honey, you'll have to buy something, customers only," Jessi replied exactly as she had the day before, but this time the words came out through a grin she attempted to hide.

"I just want to buy you lunch." Jack's voice caught Carla's attention. Turning so fast to see the man who was speaking, she dropped the order out of her hands. The plates shattered on the floor as Carla simply stared at him. Jack's attention was fixated on Jessi, smiling, waiting for a response.

"Honey, I'm skipping lunch so I can get out at two o'clock, but you're welcome to sit at one of my tables for the next two hours so I can look at you," Jessi flirted in return.

"Hell, you can sit at one of my tables if you want to, sugar. I'll wait on you all day," Carla blurted.

Jack couldn't take his gaze off Jessi's eyes. He needed her, and would wait forever if he had to.

"I would hate to be a distraction," he said, "but don't leave without me. I'll be back by two, not a minute later. Then I want you to come see my place. It's amazing; I can't believe it." He tried to conceal his excitement, but he was like a child waiting to show a friend his new fort.

"Two o'clock sharp," Jessi replied through the permanent smile. She watched him walk out.

Jack strolled away from the diner, looking down the street to the bench he had occupied on the previous day. He had only sat a short while when that perfect voice shouted his name. He turned around just in time to catch Jessi as she threw herself on him for a kiss. He held her feet off the ground and spun with her momentum, kissing her passionately until her boss, the cook, followed behind to find out what had happened to his employee. The cook was a short, obese, greasy toad of a man.

"Jessi! What the hell do you think you're doin'? Get your ass back to work; it ain't two yet!" The cook screamed at the two kissing as if they couldn't hear him only a few yards away.

Jack set her back on her feet, and they smiled at each other warmly as she slowly backed away from him to return to work.

"Move your ass, girl!"

Jack hated hearing a man speak that way to any woman, let alone Jessi. Jack's face turned red, and he followed behind Jessi without her realizing it. Once Jessi passed the cook and reentered the diner, Jack stopped the cook from following her with an icy grip on his shoulder. The cook spun to see Jack with his teeth clamped shut and his face burning red. The cook's eyes widened. Jack grabbed the cook by his throat and slammed him against the diner door, shutting it tight with the cook's fat body and blocking any view of Jack from inside.

"If you ever speak to her that way again, I will come back here, cut your balls off, and feed them to the fish down the street. You get that, fatty?" Jack growled through his teeth in blind anger, spit spattering from his lips with the words.

"Yes, sir, it won't happen again. I'm sorry, sir," the fat cook replied frantically as if he were trying to escape the grasp of a monster.

Jack released his neck, spun himself away and back onto the sidewalk to prevent Jessi from seeing the outburst. He was sure she would have been mad at him for this altercation, as he could have cost her the job at the diner. Luckily, the cook was smarter than that.

Jack strolled down to the bench on the dock and sat to look at the water. It was calm and beautiful, shimmering under the afternoon sunlight. This time, instead of nightmares popping into his head, it was Jessi. The way she made him feel was something he imagined everyone was searching for.

****

Quite a mess lay behind the counter at the diner due to Carla's clumsiness when meeting Jessi's new boyfriend. She had only glanced at him during his first visit because she had a full set of tables to attend to. She was the type of girl who loved to stir up unnecessary drama any way she could to amuse herself, so naturally, after learning about the events of the previous night from her coworker, she took full notice when the man walked into the diner.

She expected a cute guy but instead saw a familiar face, a beautiful one she had chased once before with no luck. That rejection was unusual for Carla; she was beautiful, with dark skin, big brown eyes, tight curls in her thick black hair, narrow waist, and a fit body. Most of the guys she chased weren't much of a chase at all, but this one not only got away, he hurt her pride by ignoring her completely.

The sight of him alone was enough for her to choke up, but when she realized he was the guy Jessi had been with the night before and all morning, she stumbled, dropping three full late breakfasts for her table. Immediately, the cook started screaming from the kitchen about how this is his diner and he didn't remember hiring any stupid people, demeaning Carla over the accident. She remained quiet and cleaned the mess, mumbling the rant she would love to yell at the cook and just quit, but she needed this job.

While Carla was sweeping the broken plates to the side, Jessi followed Jack out the door. The cook watched her out the pass-through window, still grumbling to himself about the stupid girl who can't handle a few plates. He switched his focus to Jessi, chasing behind her out the door, complaining about how she thinks she can run around outside on his clock.

Carla left the swept pile of broken plates up against the wall under the broom and returned to the table that was supposed to be eating the food that was dropped.

"Folks, I'm terribly sorry for your order being ruined, and now the cook has stepped out. Would you like to wait or have me clear the check and let you drink free coffee and eat free muffins?" The table nodded happily to free coffee and muffins.

Minutes later, Jessi came skipping back in to the diner with a heart full of love. Her hair bounced with her, and her smile was bright with happiness. The door closed tightly behind her; she was oblivious to the conflict between the cook and Jack.

"Don't be so smug, Jessi," Carla snapped at her happy fluttering. "I've seen him before, and he's no good for you."

"Carla, I've known you for too long not to know that means you tried and failed, and now your pride is hurt. But you know what?"

"What?"

"Jealousy is the only thing that doesn't look good on you, so just be happy for me, okay? Don't ruin this for me," Jessi finished with a whip of sass.

"You're right, completely right. I still want to meet him. Maybe I'll swing by tonight, unannounced, and say hi." She laughed to lighten the tension, but Jessi knew she was serious.

"That's a great idea." Jessi paused as she rummaged through her pockets. "I'll give you a key so you can let yourself in," she said agreeably, although she had already made plans to go to Jack's house that night, so she wouldn't be there anyway.

"Seriously, you'll let me do that?" Carla asked, shocked by the ease in receiving an invitation.

"Yeah, just make sure you don't tell him I gave you a key for this. Just play it off like you've had it for emergencies," Jessi explained to gain her trust so Carla would fall into her harmless prank.

By the time the two girls were done conspiring, Carla had the broken plates and spilled food cleaned up. The cook was back to sweating over the stove but, for once, doing so in silence.

Carla's only table was getting up to leave. It was almost two o'clock, and the lunch crowd had gone back to work. The only table left was one man sitting by himself with a newspaper propped up in front of his face. He was sitting in Jessi's section, but Jessi was getting ready to leave.

"Carla, please take this. It's only one guy, and I'm off the clock in ten minutes. Please?"

"Yeah, I'll get this one. Just get his order for me and grab his drinks, and I'll take care of the rest," Carla agreed.

"Thank you, thank you!" Jessi kissed Carla on the cheek and ran out to greet the man with her happy and upbeat attitude.

"Good afternoon, sir, how may I help you today?"

"Just coffee for now, thanks," a stern voice sounded off as if the man did not want to be bothered.

Jessi poured the coffee and left him alone. She set the coffeepot back on the burner when Carla came up close, putting her lips to her ear, and whispered.

"Go out the back door. I'll clock you out; it's only five minutes."

Jessi's face lit up, but she remained quiet and moved through the kitchen to the break room, quickly gathering her belongings. She stood by the door of the break room, hesitating; if she tried to sneak out, the cook would only have to turn to see her leaving. Just then, Carla started yelling.

"You know what, you fat bastard? Cook! I'm talking to you!"

The cook glared at Carla through the kitchen window. Jessi snuck past him and around the corner to the back door used mainly for taking out trash. It opened onto the back lot, but as she opened the door as quietly as she could, she heard something she never expected to hear the cook say.

"I'm sorry, Carla. I was out of line," he apologized as if it was his first time ever uttering the word *sorry*.

"What did you just say to me?" Carla gasped. Today's insults were not nearly as bad as others. "You're lucky I don't just walk out on your fat ass most days! And today you say you're sorry for this?" Carla continued ranting to make enough noise so Jessi could shut the back door.

****

Jessi was glad to be away from that conversation but even more so to be on her way to see Jack. She skipped back to the parking lot. She stopped to admire the extremely expensive-looking sports car parked next to hers.

"What snob drives this beautiful car?" she wondered aloud.

"That would be this snob. Would you want to go for a ride in this beautiful car?"

"Jack!" Jessi yelled before she could even turn around to hug him. "Is this really yours?"

"No, it's my uncle's, but he's gone away on business. He left this morning and gave me the keys to everything. So how's about that ride?"

"I'd love to. What are we going to do with my car?" she asked, not worrying about the car as much as how she would get to work the following morning.

"Jessi, I will bring you here in the morning, and I'll bring you home now to get clothes and whatever you need. Then I'm taking you to Hollow Wood to see something awesome." She smiled at his sweet gestures. He seemed too perfect to be real.

Jack led Jessi to the passenger side of the car, opened her door for her, then walked around and got in. He stuck the key in the ignition, flipped up the latch, and pushed the green button. The engine roared as it started. "All blacked out, secret buttons, and sounds like it has a monster under the hood. I'm in love!" Jessi exclaimed with joy. "I don't know much about cars, but I love this one, Jack."

"You love it now? Just wait," he said with a sinister smile as he gripped the wheel. Jessi was excited to find out what he meant.

Chapter V

Old Friends and New

He pulled out of the parking lot slowly and drove down the side street leading away from Main Street. He signaled right as they approached the back road that led out toward Hollow Wood Manor and dropped his foot on the gas. The tires spun and screamed, spewing smoke over the road behind them.

In less than twenty minutes, they were passing his uncle's mansion and quickly approaching Jessi's trailer.

"Just wait right here; I'll be two minutes," Jessi said, already halfway out of the car before he could come to a complete stop. She ran to her door and went inside. Only moments later, she came out with a small handbag full of clothes and essentials, locking the door behind her. As she approached the car, Jack leaned across her seat and opened the passenger door. She slid herself back into the seat, closed the door, and smiled at him.

They drove back the couple miles to Hollow Wood Manor, and Jack pulled the car down into the garage. He returned the key and took Jessi's hand to lead her down the ramp to the elevator.

"Oh my, an elevator in a house?" she asked, sounding annoyed.

"Yeah, it's a little much, but wait until you see what they call my bedroom," he replied with a snicker.

The elevator came quickly to the call, and they boarded promptly. Jack reached down and pressed the five key, then turned to Jessi and pulled her by the waist against him.

"This is all so new and exciting. I'm so glad I found my best friend on the first day I can remember," he said staring down into her eyes with pure honesty. Jessi started to blush again; he loved that about her. She was so beautiful already, but something about her insecurity made her more than perfect as she stared back up at him with her innocent smile and red cheeks, her eyes glistening.

The elevator reached the top floor rapidly. Jack's bedroom door was to the left. Thankfully he found the elevator so Jessi didn't have to climb the five flights of stairs and trek down the long corridor.

"Well, here is my bedroom, or what Gavin calls my bedroom," Jack joked and opened the door. He held the door for her as she stepped into the entry of his quarters.

"This is a bedroom?" she asked. Her trailer could fit five times just in the living room.

"So they tell me. Looks more like a house to me. Make yourself comfortable. I don't know where anything is, so feel free to touch anything you like," he said with a smile.

Jessi giggled. Jack could sense her thoughts were elsewhere, but they continued to explore this immense "bedroom" that consisted of more rooms then the house she grew up in as a child.

"You don't have any family photos up anywhere, and there is nothing personal in here at all. I wonder why that is." She hoped to find something to help Jack have a clue to who he had been before she met him, especially since Peter seemed less than willing to help Jack remember his past.

"I wonder if something terrible happened to my parents, and that is why I am staying here with my uncle. That might also explain why I wouldn't have any family photos to remind me of the pain I experienced."

"That's really sad. I hope it turns out to be a happier story, like you moved in with your uncle who is ridiculously wealthy so he could help fund your genius inventions of awesomeness." Jessi desperately tried to give Jack hope, but she began remembering stories she had read in the paper. She wondered if one of the terrible accidents that had occurred in the past few months may have had something to do with Jack.

"Jack, what was your uncle's last name?" she quizzed him, masking her investigation with curiosity.

"Fredrick. Why do you ask? Did you find something?"

"No, just being curious. I don't seem to remember hearing anything about a Peter Fredrick doing anything the media picked up on," she replied honestly, as the name didn't spark any lead in her mind.

Jack led Jessi to each astonishing room. When they finished the tour of his accommodations, they returned to the large sectional sofa and sat down, wrapped up in each other.

"The bathroom is wondrous. Maybe we should take a bath before we go to bed tonight," Jessi's suggested, grinning wider.

"Anything you want," he said, smiling, willing to bend to her every desire but intrigued by the idea himself.

"Well, what should we do now that it's just past three o'clock?" she asked, filling an uncomfortable silence as both lovers were preoccupied with their own thoughts.

"Well, I'm new in town, and I don't know what there is to do anywhere around here. I only know how to get to the diner, the market, your house, and this house."

"This house is something else, we could probably have a lot of fun just exploring your colossal palace." Jessi offered the first thing she had on her mind. She had been driving past this house for a long time, never knowing who lived there, wondering what marvels lay within, and now she was on the top floor inside with Mr. Perfect.

"That actually sounds like a great idea. We could act like little kids and chase each other around for hours." He laughed out loud until Jessi smacked him playfully.

"You're it!" She bolted for the door to the hallway with Jack pursuing her.

"You saucy little minx!" Jack trailed her with a big smile on his face.

Jessi ran down the corridor to the staircase balcony, turned left into a door, and shut it in Jack's face to slow him down.

"Are you even trying?" She hollered through the door, "You have to be faster than little ol' me."

Jack was holding back to let her win for a while, then he swung open the door to another hallway. Five doors were strung along each side of a passage even longer than the one that led to his room.

Jessi was nowhere to be seen in the corridor; she had to have gone into one of these doors. Jack wondered what he would have done had he been the one running to hide. He ran down the hall as fast as he could to the third door on the left. The distance should have left him gasping for breath, though his stamina seemed inhuman with Jessi near. He slowly cracked the door open to reveal a room in complete darkness. As he opened the door wider, the lights suddenly turned on automatically.

"She can't be in here or the lights would have already been on," he thought out loud as he backed out of the room slowly, still peaking around to see if maybe his slick and sneaky friend was possibly hiding in there anyway. Something caught his eye, and he stepped forward into the room for only a moment when one of the other doors in the hallway swung open.

His attention was immediately diverted to Jessi exiting one of the earlier doors in the hallway. She ran back down the corridor, giggling. Jack slammed the door shut and bounded down the hall behind her as fast as he could.

She slipped out of the door that led them into this passageway back out to the main fifth-floor hall. Turning to her left, she made her way to the balconies and the massive, winding staircase. The door she had fled from shut, and she heard Jack's footsteps following the same direction she had gone.

"You can run, but you can't hide," Jack yelled loudly with a grin. He couldn't imagine getting away with being so childish with any other adult. His silly banter made Jessi giggle, and Jack's attention was brought to the stairwell. Bouncing down the steps, skipping every two to three stairs, he launched himself over the last six to the fourth-floor landing. He kept his momentum down the hallway with haste and a smile on his face.

He cautiously entered the hallway, trying to quickly cover the vast distance and detect his hidden playmate.

"Boo!" Jessi leapt out from her corner at the front of the hall as he passed her undetected. The startling noise sent a shockwave up his spine, and he jumped from the excitement. He spun with force and grabbed her as she laughed uncontrollably at her success in scaring him.

"I got you!" she snickered, as he held her arms behind her back so she couldn't get away.

"No, I've got you."

"And what will you ever do with me now that you have me?"

"I can think of a lot of things I could do to you." His head lowered, bringing his lips closer to hers. She lifted her chin to try to capture a kiss from him, but he pulled away and smiled. "You won't get me that easy."

She said nothing but continued to stare at him with her big beautiful eyes that were saddened by him teasing a kiss. He smiled down at her and came back in to kiss her for real this time. Just before their lips could meet, with everything around them starting to fade from reality, a loud bang sounded from the floor above. It sounded like it came from the hallway in which Jessi first hid. The two looked at each other with wide eyes.

"What was that? I thought we were alone." Jessi whispered nervously.

"I'm not sure, maybe a door slamming. Did we leave any ajar? I thought I saw something in the first room I looked in, hoping to find you. When I heard you burst out of a different door, I dismissed it as nothing and went after you," he replied. His mind was envisioning his nightmares coming to pass.

"What was in that room? A small zoo, I hope, with cute and cuddly animals." Her expression was glazed, deep in thought, clearly anticipating something worse.

"There were some tall tables full of who knows what, covered by sheets as if someone was hiding something or just keeping the dust off. There were also a few bookshelves, like a small library."

"Are you scared?"

"I am, but I am also fast and very strong. I should check it out if we are going to be spending the night. I would like to know you are safe here." He intended his words to surround her like a security blanket for a small child.

"I feel safer just being with you, Jack," she said gazing up at his perfect face. Jack took her by the hand, and they walked back up the winding staircase to the fifth floor. They approached the first door on their right and re-entered the hallway to investigate. Jack led with Jessi's hand in his; she followed close, peering around Jack's broad shoulders. The hallway was clear; there wasn't a sound other than the two trying to breathe as quietly as possible, which still sounded like thunder in Jack's paranoid mind.

Jack slowly and silently proceeded down the corridor to the third door on the right. Jessi's hand felt cold and clammy wrapped in Jack's warm, steady hand.

Still holding her hand, Jack slowly opened the door with his free hand. The lights were still on. He slowly analyzed the room from corner to corner. Nothing was visibly moving, but there were a lot of blind spots behind each sheet-covered table and bookshelf. There were no signs that anything had toppled or moved out of place since the few moments in which he had investigated the room earlier. He stepped forward into the room with Jessi still latched to his hand and following on his heels.

Suddenly a sound caused Jessi to jump, "What the hell is that!" she screeched.

It sounded like something was chewing, gnawing, and scratching. The sound was coming from behind one of the covered tables. Sheets dangled to the floor around every angle of the table, making it impossible to investigate from a distance.

Jack advanced toward the noise; Jessi began resisting his motion. He looked back at her with calm eyes, strength radiated from him. He brought his index finger to his lips gesturing for silence as he gently retracted his other hand from hers and held it up to signal her to stay put. Turning back to the table, he leaned over it to catch a glimpse of the intruder, moving closer and closer to the sound. He paused at the sound of a deep and fearsome growl, but only for a moment. He pushed himself forward to gaze upon his foe.

Jack jumped back and gasped. Jessi screamed at the top of her lungs, and in a black flash a giant beast jumped on top of the table, spilling books from under the sheet, each making a loud thud on the floor. Jack started laughing at the sight of a fluffy black dog wagging its tail with a bone clasped in its jaw. At first Jessi looked disgusted that Jack had gotten her back for scaring him earlier. Her eyes met with Jack's, and she let out a sigh of relief.

The dog was pure black with one bright blue eye and one bright green eye. It was tall; standing on the table, it had no trouble licking Jack's face repeatedly. He laughed with joy, relieved the household pet was so friendly.

"Who's a good boy?" he said in the demeaning tone dogs seem to love. Seeing Jack turn into a child again at the sight of the adorable, fuzzy dog with tall, pointy ears made Jessi chuckle. She approached Jack while he petted the dog and it continued bathing his face in kisses. When she stood beside Jack, she slowly extended her hand, palm up, for the dog to sniff. It sniffed a few times, looked up at her, sniffed more, looked up at her, and then backed away, jumping off the table, running behind the bookcases.

"That's so strange; dogs usually love me." In reaction to her words, the dog peered back around the corner at her, growling and barking. It took a step forward with a snarl. Drool began foaming up at its mouth.

"We should just leave it be, I think," Jack said as he backed Jessi away from the angered dog.

"And to think you were just letting him lick your face—he could have just as easily eaten your face right off!" She tried to lighten the mood as they retreated. Jack was unable to recall who cared for the pet while his uncle was traveling, so he assumed Gavin would have made the appropriate accommodations for the fuzzy beast and closed the door behind him.

"Can we just stay in your bedroom for the rest of the night please?" Jessi begged.

"We can do anything you want to, but I think I will cook you dinner tonight, so let's run to the market first."

They made their way back to the garage using the elevator. Jack followed his previous steps, selecting the same sports car he drove earlier.

"Wow. I didn't get to take this all in earlier." Jessi stood with her mouth open at the sight of all the beautiful and expensive cars lined up in the garage.

"I had the same reaction," Jack laughed as they got into the sleek black vehicle. He put his left hand on the wheel, shifted the car into gear, and grabbed Jessi's hand with his right.

"I haven't felt this close to anyone since my mother passed away last year," Jessi said. "I shut everyone out other than Carla, the girl I work with."

"I don't have any recollection of ever being close to anyone, but I know I want to be close to you for as long as you let me." She smiled at him as he drove, focused on the road.

The drive to the market took less than ten minutes. Jessi filled each second with stories of her past while Jack listened intently, smiling at the sound of her voice. When they arrived at the market, they held hands through the parking lot and throughout the store. She grabbed ingredients to prepare the dinner Jack had chosen from a cookbook. They both felt like they were living in a fairy tale, skipping over the action straight to happily ever after. As they strolled through the parking lot, a hand on his shoulder pulled him around. A girl grabbed him and kissed him. Jack turned away, but she pulled him into an embrace. Jessi was infuriated. She squeezed Jack's hand so hard it brought Jack's attention to her with alarm, and her other hand clenched into a fist.

"Jack?" The beautiful young woman said. "I have been looking everywhere for you!"

"Uhh—." He watched as Jessi turned her head to acknowledge the person speaking. She had long straight blonde hair, bright blue eyes, and a body almost as fit as Jessi's, dressed in clothes Jessi couldn't afford even if she saved up for five years.

"Jack! Where have you been, and who is this little tramp?" Jack pushed away, all happiness gone from his face.

"Her name is Jessi, and she's more than you could ever hope to be," he snapped, not recognizing the woman in the least. In his perception the woman's face seemed wrong and evil, as if seeing her inner self displayed over her physical beauty. "And why would someone like you be looking for me?"

"It's me, Jack, Anna. We've been dating for five years. Why are you acting this way?"

"I've been having a memory—issue the past few days, but I'm very happy where I am. I'm not who you think I am." He turned back around to ignore her and Jessi followed. He gently squeezed Jessi's hand and smiled at her warmly.

The girl spouted off more insults. "Are you kidding me? You're going to take some poor, pathetic trash over me? Since when have you been about charity?"

Jack took a deep breath, ready to scream, but before he could even realize what was happening, the blonde was trying to get off the ground, and Jessi was shaking the pain out of her knuckles. Jessi had decked the girl hard enough to put her on the ground with a swelling and soon-to-be black eye.

"Who's the tramp now, bitch?" Jessi taunted then grabbed Jack, kissing him passionately while the wounded girl sat on the pavement crying.

Many people gawked as the events unfolded, but no authorities were called to the scene. When they were back in the car, Jessi was in a deep thought with a small smirk on her face.

"I'm sorry I punched your girlfriend in the face."

"You're my girlfriend now, not her," he replied.

"Oh am I? I don't remember agreeing to that," she said sarcastically.

Jack slammed on the breaks, yanked the car off the road, put it in park, and turned to her. Staring in her eyes, he took both her hands in his. Jessi looked worried, as if she thought he was going to kick her out of the car and tell her to walk.

"Jessi, will you be my girlfriend, my lover, my only friend?"

"I could agree with that, I guess, but how do you know it's me you want when you can't remember anyone else? That Anna girl seemed to—"

"Jessi, you have given me a chance when even I didn't know who I was. I may never know who I was, but at least I know who I am now, and you fit me perfectly. Every minute I have with you is happier than the minute before." He explained flawlessly, but she still wasn't satisfied completely.

"She is so beautiful," she said, looking away. He placed one hand on her face and gently pulled her back, their eyes meeting once again.

"Jessi, she is nothing next to you. One look at her and you can tell she is fake. Money buys her everything, and it has tarnished her personality. I could never be with someone like her." His passion began pushing Jessi's doubts aside with more ease now. "So, Jessi, will you have me be yours, and will you be mine?"

"Yes, Jack. I've been yours since you walked into my diner yesterday," she confessed, blushing again. She started to look away again, but Jack pulled her back for another kiss then looked her in the eye.

"Good. I couldn't be so happy anywhere else than here with you," he said. "Now I better feed you before you beat me up too." They laughed as Jack put the car back into gear and took off down the road. Just before he pulled into the driveway, Jessi spotted something further along the street toward her home. It appeared to be the black dog that had been on the fifth floor with them earlier. The dog was simply trotting down the street away from them; it either didn't notice them at the distance or didn't care.

"Should we go after him?" Jessi asked, concerned for the dog but also concerned to have the dog that seemed to hate her sitting behind her in the car.

"No, I can't imagine it's the same dog, unless the one we met earlier has learned to open doors. I'll tell my uncle if he escaped after we investigate that room again to be sure he's there."

As they got out of the car and started down the ramp to the elevator, Jessi was quiet, lost in thought again.

"What if that girl could have helped you learn about your parents? She could have had answers, and instead of letting you speak with her like adults, I socked her in her rude hole."

"I wouldn't have believed a word that came out of her mouth anyway. I'm not sure I want to know too much about my past now, knowing I was dating such a snob. What if I was a snob like that too?" he added as they entered the elevator.

"You couldn't have been all bad. You turned Carla down. She recognized you today when you came in to say hi. That's why she dropped the plates. You are one of very few men strong enough to turn her down, and it sounds like you just ignored her."

"Carla knows me?" he asked, wondering if he could find out anything about who he was from her.

"Not really. Like I said, you just ignored her. She hit on you and was probably trying to get you to take her home. She's a bit aggressive."

"She's not my type."

"Oh yeah? And what is your type?" Jessi asked, digging for a compliment.

"I imagine her to be a waitress in a small diner, and her name would *have* to be Jessi." He enjoyed watching her cheeks go red again. "Oh yes, and she'd blush every time I complimented her, even when she was digging for it."

Jessi wrapped her arms around his neck just as the elevator doors opened. Jack gently grabbed her waist, lifting her off the ground as they walked out of the elevator, kissing. He turned to his door, swung it open, and carried her over to the couch where they sat down, still passionately entangled.

Jessi sat up, pulling her face away from him with a disappointed look.

"We forgot the food in the car," she reminded Jack.

"No worries. I'll run down and grab it. You stay right here." He was already halfway to the door before he finished speaking.

"Hurry back," she demanded softly, smiling at him with conspiring beautiful eyes.

Jack moved as quickly as he could, thankful for an elevator. He ran to the car, back to the elevator, and within a few short minutes he was walking back through the door to his living quarters. He placed the bag of food on the counter next to the fridge and looked around the living room. Jessi wasn't sitting on the couch anymore.

The bag she had packed earlier at her trailer still sat on the bar where she had left it.

"Jessi?" he called out, wondering where she had run off to, but there was no reply. He walked down the hall to the bathroom and knocked on the door.

"Jessi, are you in there?" Still no reply. He twisted the handle to find it unlocked, and the room was empty. He continued down the hall, looking in the guest room. Empty.

"Jessi, are you hiding on me?" A scuffling sound up in his bedroom reminded him of the sounds they heard from the dog earlier. His heart sank, remembering the dog's attitude toward Jessi. He flew up the stairs in a panic. As he reached the top of the stairs and turned to the room, nothing could have prepared him for the sight he beheld. His mouth dropped in awe.

Jessi stood in the center of the room wearing a short, dark red dress that was tight against her goddess-like figure and black high heels with straps that wrapped around her ankles and halfway to her knees. She was smiling, her hands folded together in front of her with her head tilted down slightly, just enough to look up at him flirtatiously.

"You look stunning," he gasped, trying to keep his composure. So far he had only seen her in work clothes and naked. Although her naked body was perfect, wrapped in this dress, which fell only partially down her thighs and amazing cleavage, her curves teased his mind, driving his sensual being insane.

"You like it?"

"I love it. I should change too, though. I'm in blue jeans and a t-shirt, and you—you are perfect." He stuttered the words like a scared little boy as she stepped toward him, swaying like a dream. Jack's knees went soft. The blood left his head, and he began thinking he was going to fall, though somehow he kept upright. She strutted all the way to him and threw her arms around his neck again.

"Where were we just before you went back to the car?" she asked in a sexy, soft voice that drove Jack crazy. She started kissing him again for a moment then pulled away, placing both hands on his stomach to secure a distance between them.

"Go change if you need to, but I'll be downstairs." She smiled, walking past him with the irresistibility of a siren.

****

Carla ended her shift around three o'clock, relieved by the scheduled dinner servers. She punched out and hustled about town on errands buying herself dinner since she lived alone.

When she finally arrived home, thinking of her plans to interrupt Jessi and her new boyfriend in Jessi's trailer, she quickly got herself ready. She put her single-serve dinner in the microwave for five minutes, kicked off her shoes, and stripped down on her way to the bathroom. Wrapping a satin bathrobe around her naked body, she turned the faucet on in the tub, letting the water warm up, which took about five minutes because the water heater in her rundown apartment was old. She left the bathroom with the water running down the open drain and returned to the kitchen, where she flipped through a magazine while she waited for her food to finish.

The microwave eventually beeped, and she closed the magazine and brought her dinner to the bathroom. She pulled off the robe, letting it slide down her back. She plugged the drain, slid into the tub, and began eating her small meal while the water filled around her.

It didn't take long for her to eat the small amount of food that comes in a single-serve meal. Once finished, she enjoyed the hot water and soap she lathered on herself. After turning off the water, she laid her head back against the tub and spread a wet washcloth over her face to block out all the light.

Just as she felt herself drifting off to sleep, a loud knock came to her door. She sat up quickly splashing water on the floor. She sat for a moment listening, hoping maybe she had fallen asleep and no one was really trying to interrupt her much-needed afternoon bath. Then it came again—three hard knocks on her door.

She lifted herself out of the tub, grabbed a towel, dried herself, and wrapped her satin robe over her soft, fresh body. Another set of three knocks sounded off as she reached out for the doorknob, causing her to jump back. She quietly moved her face to the peek hole to investigate the impatient knocker.

Through the hole, she saw the face of an older gentlemen, weathered by cigarette smoke and sun exposure masked only by his facial hair. It was a familiar face, the man Jessi had left at her last table whom Carla so graciously took responsibility for so she could go off gallivanting with Jack. Smiling in triumph, she swung the door open to her side, holding one hand on the edge of the door up high, leaning her body against it while rubbing her foot against her leg anxiously.

"I didn't think you'd actually come," she said coyly, adjusting her robe to be slightly more revealing.

"I would have driven all day to follow a firecracker like yourself, darlin'." She reached out and grabbed his shirt, tugging him inside.

"I see you dressed up for me," he joked, staring at her flawless figure in her tiny bathrobe.

"I really wasn't expecting you to come tonight for a double date with a complete stranger, but seeing as how you *did* come, I can only think of one way to thank you before we catch up with the other couple," she said with a sultry smirk as she ran her hand on the inside of her bathrobe, exposing her chest to the complete stranger.

"I will take that offer happily, miss," he said as he slipped his hand inside her robe along her hips, pulling the half-tied robe loose and exposing her full front to him. He tossed her on the couch behind her, pulled down his trousers, and took Carla in ways she had never experienced.

When the stranger was finished, Carla lay almost paralyzed from the pleasure of the multiple orgasms this bearded man had inflicted upon her.

"Wow, you should come over every day," she teased, still out of breath and feeling weak as her new friend pulled his pants up from his ankles. "You got a name, honey, or should I just call you Dynamo?"

"My friends call me Tei, but Dynamo is a new one. Whichever you please. Now I'm wondering, Carla, what kind of girl sleeps with a man she just met without even knowing his name?"

"A bad one, honey,"

"Oh yeah? How bad?"

"For someone as handsome as you? As bad as I have to be to please you. Now take a load off, and I'll be ready to leave shortly."

Twenty minutes later, Carla came out of her bedroom wearing a tiny strapless green dress that barely clung to her breasts enough to conceal her nipples. The neckline was cut so deep that, were she to bend down, she would reveal all.

"So, whatcha think?" She pranced about the living room in front of Tei, swinging her hips back and forth with her hands up in the air.

"You look delicious. I can't wait to get back inside your skin tonight," he said abruptly.

It was almost creepy, but Carla figured her actions had provoked him to assume a different personality to better match her. She suspected he was really just some lame and boring guy who was lucky he got an invite to her home. She hoped he would crave her self-proclaimed perfection.

Chapter VI

Dreams Come True

Carla tugged Tei off the couch and held his hand as she walked to the door. He kicked it shut without bothering to lock it. Carla had the key, and she was three steps ahead of him, still tugging on his hand like an excited child trying to show her mother something she wanted in a toy store.

They made their way down to the car. Carla was driving because Tei didn't know where they were going. They drove the fifteen minutes without speaking to each other at all. Tei glared out the window, rubbing the beard on his chin as if it were new. Carla had the radio on and was attempting to sing along to a song she said was her favorite but didn't know half the words to. She sang loud and proud, but her voice was like nails on a chalkboard; the words she didn't know came out as incoherent sounds.

When they pulled up in front of Jessi's trailer, Carla pulled in fast, the tires locked, slipping to a stop on the dirt driveway. She swung her door open and jumped out of the car, slamming the door shut as she hurried past. She walked as quickly as she could in her stacked wedges, dragging in the dirt with every step.

She sorted the keys to find Jessi's door key and stuck it in the door. She then turned around to check on Tei. He stood and stepped around the car door as she looked. He looked toward her with a blank expression, pushed the door shut with his fingertips, and started forward the few paces to catch up to Carla.

"Hello?" she hollered as she walked in. Tei stepped in and shut the door. She moved in further toward the bedroom at the end of the short hallway. Tei moved his hand back down to the door and locked it inconspicuously.

"Jessi, if you're back there, I'm coming in!" Carla blared through the door as she reached down for the bedroom doorknob.

"You said they would be here!" Tei snapped and growled.

"Aw, honey, are you scared of a little trespassing?" she mocked him, still misunderstanding his intentions.

She swung the door, exposing only an empty bedroom with the light off. She flicked the switch on to see that her eyes weren't lying to her. She turned back to Tei, who at this point had moved up right behind her. When she turned, his chin was only an inch from her forehead. His teeth were clenched and lips pulled back.

"What is your problem, psycho?" Carla fearfully yelled in his face. His expression was so fierce it froze the blood in her veins.

"You said they would be here!" he bellowed in a thunderous voice, emphasizing every syllable through teeth that did not unclench. His eyes became dark, even the whites clouded with a deep black. His incisors grew longer with sounds of snapping sinews and breaking bones.

Carla stepped backward into the bedroom, unable to speak, wishing she could scream, but the blood had run so icy cold it burned with every motion as she retreated. Her eyes were wide, filled with terror, fixated on Tei's teeth and black eyes. His mouth opened, exposing bottom incisors that had grown to a fearsome size, as sharp as the fangs on top. When his mouth opened, only an inhuman roar, deep from his throat, could be heard. Tei grabbed Carla by her neck and lifted her off the ground as if she were weightless.

"See, Carla, I am not here for you. When I devoured this old man yesterday I believed I was finished, but he had a secret." He paused for a moment as if he were waiting for Carla to show interest in what he was saying, though she continued to squirm in his inhuman grip. "I am here to take what is mine, and all is mine. But there is a prophecy of a man with the power to stop me hiding in a place far from my home, here, to be precise. So I came. But it is not a man. Instead I find he is practically a child. A child I have already been face to face with, and somehow I am unable to track his whereabouts. His power has kept him secret from me still. Now I know, after wearing his caretaker's skin for far too long, I know his secrets."

The back of Carla's legs had been pressed against the foot of the bed when Tei lifted her from the floor. He stepped forward with her throat in his hand. His arm fully extended pushing her up by the neck toward the low ceiling. With his free hand, he grabbed Carla's wrist and held it to the ceiling, smiling disgustingly as his black eyes peered into her soul. The skin from the back of his hand split down the middle; each side peeled into small strips that seemed to stand straight off the back of his hand. His skin and blood melded together, forming an adhesive substance of an orange-red color. The small strips slapped down around her wrists, securing her to the ceiling. By the time the morphing skin had left his hand, brand new skin was healing over the wounds. Within a few seconds her whole hand and wrist was glued to the ceiling with the orange substance. Tei switched hands on Carla's throat, grabbed her dangling arm and held it up to the ceiling, repeating the creation of restraints.

Carla fell into a state of shock after seeing Tei's eyes and teeth morph. When he grabbed her throat, it jostled her so violently her body was rendered limp, and she was no longer conscious.

Twenty minutes later, she began moaning, and Tei watched as her eyes slowly blinked opened. Once her eyes adjusted, her mind became her own again. Extreme pain radiated from all of her major joints, and she was staring down at the center of the bed. Her arms stuck straight up to the ceiling and her feet were immoveable halfway up the wall above the head of the bed.

She tried to open her mouth to call for help, but it wouldn't open. Tei had laid one finger across her lips, sealing them tight with the orange flesh glue. She could only give a muffled moan and squirm unsuccessfully. Then she heard a dark, evil chuckle directly in front of her. She struggled to lift her head to see down the short distance to Jessi's fold-out dinner table across the trailer where Tei sat, watching, waiting for her to regain consciousness for his theatrical horror. He stood up slowly and walked down the hall; each footstep fell like thunder. The veins in her forehead bulged as she tried desperately to scream.

Tei took her chin in his hand, lifting her head for visual contact. "You're going to feel every inch of your failure to me," he hissed in her face with eyes as black as his soul and the teeth of a canine. He raised a hand with one finger out. The nail at the tip of his boney finger was long and razor-sharp. He pushed it into Carla's chest just under her throat. As the nail broke skin, Carla moaned, and tears flowed from her eyes. Slowly he began pushing his blood-covered appendage down the center of her torso, slicing through her sternum effortlessly. Blood spewed onto the bed and covered Tei's clothes. He looked up at Carla for her last moment of life and revealed his trick. "And now your soul will be mine, and I'll have some fun in your sultry skin while I finish my work here."

****

In the smallest and highest corner of Hollow Wood Manor, Jack sat in his bedroom suite. He had changed into a dark red button-down tucked into a pair of black slacks, a black tie loose around his neck and pair of black shoes that felt as comfortable as sneakers to his feet. He came downstairs to his living room by five o'clock to start preparing for dinner with Jessi.

The new couple stood elbow to elbow in the kitchen, slicing vegetables and peeling potatoes. They reminisced and laughed about all they had done already in such a short time. Jessi thanked him for being her hero, valiantly saving her from the savage beast, the fluffy dog down the hall. Jack thanked her for giving an odd, forgetful stranger a ride to Hollow Wood Manor.

Jack paused, the smile fading from his face, detaching from the conversation for a moment while deep in thought as he peeled another potato. "What does it feel like to wonder about who someone else may be when they themselves don't remember?" Jack had been spending so much time wondering who he had been, especially after meeting that wicked woman claiming to be his girlfriend. He wondered what type of man he would have to have been to impress a girl like that.

"I told you already, I don't care who you were. I see who you are now, and you are a good soul. You have opened every door for me since I met you. You held my hand as we walked through the market, and when that girl kissed you, you didn't even think about kissing her back, and she was beautiful." It was clear she had not spent as much time thinking about the situation the way he had been. She had noticed each and every little thing he had done for her, how his hugs warmed her, how his kisses were genuine and never rushed, and how simply making eye contact with him made her go crazy with lust in an impossible, even magical manner. "Jack, you take so much care in being a gentleman, so much care for how I feel. Most people I've ever met only think of themselves."

"Yeah, I guess you could be right." He smiled at her politely. "But I feel like I'm capable of great destruction. Earlier today, something happened outside the diner. I got angry about the way your boss was talking to you—"

"I get angry at him every day. I'm not a bad person, am I?" she joked, filling in the pause Jack took, knowing he had tried to hide it earlier.

"Well, I may have pinned him to the door by his neck and told him I'd cut his balls off. But I wasn't just angry; I felt rage. I moved him with one hand as if he were literally empty inside. Honestly, the guy is big, and he weighed nearly nothing to me. The words came through my teeth instead of my lips, and I meant every word. If I wanted to, I could have snapped him in half."

"Well that explains why he was so nice after you left. I thought his doctor must have called and told him he was dying or something," she said chuckling.

"I could have made you lose your job or, worse, killed a man, and you're not mad?" he asked, still feeling guilty for putting her in jeopardy.

"First of all, you didn't kill a man when you could have easily, as you said. And second, I couldn't be mad at you. Every time I look at you, my heart melts, and I'm just yours. Besides, if you got me fired, then I'd just have to come live with you," she said with sass, a hint of demand in her voice that fell out with a smile. Jack stared at her beautiful face, every expression she made. He knew exactly what she meant when she said her heart melted every time she looked at him because he felt the same for her.

"I guess I'll have to find a better way to get you fired then," he said, still smiling. She gazed up at him with an annoyed look behind a forced smile.

"You can't say that stuff to me, Jack. You are driving me crazy with your gorgeous face, your flawless hair, opening doors for me, and saying everything just right. You can't be real. If you are, I'll help you get me fired. But please don't say things you don't mean." Jessi let out her small rant. She had bought every single word Jack had said so far, investing everything into the new relationship instantly, but for all she knew, he could have even been lying about the memory loss. She had been only hoping these past two days were real because they felt like they were out of a fairytale.

"Jessi, you are the most beautiful woman inside and out that could possibly walk this planet or any other, for that matter. You helped me when I had no one. You convinced me no matter who I was that I am good, and that's the most important thing I need right now." He looked into her eyes, speaking from the depths of his heart. "And every time I look at you, I feel the same as you do. You're the only person I know, and, to be honest, when I have you, I have no interest in anyone or anything other than seeing you smile. So when I say something like, 'I'm trying to get you fired so you'll live with me,' it's simply because I don't want to sit around tomorrow waiting for you to finish work when realistically we could be together playing tag."

"I don't want you to feel stuck with me; I can't just quit my job after knowing you for two days," Jessi replied with a hint of skepticism in her voice. Her expression briefly showed disgust with his overbearing childishness, but she looked up at him, and her expression became loving again.

"I don't feel stuck with you, I feel stuck without you. But I understand. I'm sorry I offended you."

"I'm not offended. Now shut up and kiss me or cook me dinner," she demanded, pointing the knife she had been chopping carrots with at him. Jack pushed the knife to the side and kissed her for a few moments then got back to making dinner.

He turned to the fridge and pulled out a large cut of beef. The smell rushed to his nose causing his mouth to begin aching and salivating at the thought of just eating the roast raw in his hands. He shook his head, trying to shake the urge, which went successfully for the most part. When he turned back toward the counter next to Jessi, he began cutting the meat into small cubes. The smell of the cut meat intensified his urge. He plucked a few of the bigger cubes and popped them in his mouth quickly, trying not to bring any attention to himself, but was unsuccessful.

"Did you really just eat that raw?" Jessi asked, astounded.

"Maybe," he replied as he stuffed a few more cubes of the raw beef in his mouth.

"Ew, stop! That's so bad for you!"

"I can't help it. I can't eat anything but meat without getting nauseous. I don't know what's going on with my diet, but I haven't eaten much other than the bacon yesterday," he tried to explain himself without coming off too disturbing, but hearing himself say it out loud gave him an eerie chill.

"That's a little concerning, don't you think?" she pressed.

"Not really. It's not like I'm going to eat you in your sleep. If I were, I think I would have last night," he finished with a chuckle.

"That's reassuring."

"Sweetie, I have no craving for people. Although I will confess, that dog smelled really tasty yesterday, but he was so cute I paid my hunger no attention." He popped a few more cubes of the raw meat in his mouth as he finished his sentence. "I do crave you though. Every moment I'm near you, I crave your lips and the feeling of your skin on mine." He turned to her and embraced her, seducing her again. "But your smell is enticing only to my sweeter emotions. A hunger for passion." He continued in a deep and silly voice, "I'm not monster!" He stuck his hands out in front of him and moaned a few times while Jessi laughed at his impression of Frankenstein's monster.

"Well then we have something in common. I can't stop thinking about last night. No one has satisfied me for so long, and every time we touch, even when our elbows bump while we cut these vegetables, you leave me wanting, starving for your affection. I, too, am not monster," she giggled.

Jack smiled, beginning to scoop up cubes of meat, potatoes, slices of carrots, onions, peppers, and cabbage, tossing each pile into a large pot full of water. He moved the pot to the stove and turned the burner on high. Jessi placed the rest of the bigger slices of potato on the cookie sheet with the others and put them in the oven.

Jack leaned against the counter they had been cutting food on, staring at Jessi's backside as she bent down to put the potatoes in the oven to roast. He bit down on his bottom lip and sucked air in heavily through his nose. As Jessi was completing the task, she had been wondering to herself why her last comment left the room silent. When she stood up and turned back to Jack, pleasure and desire radiated from his eyes with the same lip-biting face she had caught herself making when they got in her car for the first time together.

He held out his hand to her. She took the three steps across the kitchen to take it. He lifted her arm above her head, pulling gently, spinning her around to dance. He wrapped her arm around her front, pulling it down to her hip and reeling her in backward. His excitement pushed against her as he brushed the hair from her neck, kissing her gently. Her blood went hot, and her mind was crazy with sensual thoughts but also fears of him disappearing.

He kissed along her neck to her earlobe and whispered, "I never want to live a day without you in it."

The words coming from his lips tickled her ear, filling her with confidence and pleasure. She felt herself falling completely and irreversibly in love with him. She let herself fall freely, trusting this perfect stranger whom she had only known for two days as if she were being held captive by magic.

"I've tasted your love, and you have all of mine now, Jack. My love is yours, and no one could ever match the feeling you've given me. I love you, Jack, unconditionally. Even if you eat me, I will still love you," she said quietly with his cheek resting on hers.

He chuckled loudly at her joke, but pulled her closer. He wondered if, meeting with his memory intact, he would have dropped his whole life for her as he had. He was confident he would have.

"And I, you," he replied, whispering in her ear.

She pulled his hand away and turned in his arms to see the unflinching honesty in his gaze. For a few moments, there was only stillness as they stared into each other's eyes, filled with thoughts that struck like lightning, one after another, each more beautiful than the last. This evening would be full of magic for both of them. Everything was perfect, and their lust for each other was satisfied repeatedly through the night.

****

Tei stood in Jessi's bedroom, still in his beast form. He reached down into the bloody mess of Carla's organs on the bed and lifted out her car keys. With one finger strung through the key ring, he stuck the bloodied keys in his mouth and sucked the blood off them. When he pulled the keys out, he smiled a sinister grin, staring at Carla's lifeless open eyes.

"Oh, Carla, so easy, so tasteful. I will have your heart." He reached back into the mess strewn on the bed and lifted out her heart. He raised it to his mouth and bit into it like an apple. His razor-sharp and canine-like incisors ripped through the muscle, blood dripping from of his lips into his beard and splashing on his cheeks. He devoured the whole heart in only a few bites.

He left the trailer and looked around to be sure no one could be witness to his lethal and vile extravaganza, certain his mess would be left behind for Jack to find. The area was quite clear of witnesses as the trailer sat on a remote lot just off a winding road hidden by tall trees at every angle with only a small dirt driveway that could fit maybe three cars side by side.

Tei dismounted the trailer's single step and threw Carla's keys deep into the woods. He looked up at the sky and smiled. He took a huge breath through his nose and braced himself for extreme pain. Then he opened his mouth, letting out a roar that covered simultaneous bone-cracking sounds as his body began to jolt and twitch, his bones rearranging under his skin. He tore off the bloody shirt and let it drop out of his hands. His elbows snapped and rose on his arms as did his wrists, knees, and ankles. He dropped to his hands and knees as they shrunk. His fingers snapped and folded under his skin, retracting as the bones shrank. Thick black hair began sprouting over his body taking a shape that matched his teeth. When the transformation was complete, he had turned himself into a large black dog with fluffy fur. He shook his head, sending the fur shaking all along his body, spattering blood on the side of the trailer and Carla's car and dispatching the mess as if by magic. After disposing of the evidence outside the trailer, he howled to the stars one last time and bounded off into the woods.

Chapter VII

Unnatural Qualities

Early the next morning, Jessi woke smiling, tangled in Jack's arms and legs, wrapped in red satin sheets. It was still dark, but the moon shined brightly in the bedroom windows, allowing her enough light to look around. She rolled herself on top of his naked, sleeping body, kissing his neck and cheeks. By the time she made it to his chin he began to wake. He lay on his back, looking up at the woman of his dreams as she pushed her hips back and forth slowly, having her way with the sleepy man, smiling down on his waking face. He smiled back, and she watched as he blinked repeatedly to focus his eyes as she rocked back and forth on him. He let out a gentle moan followed by a gasp and a grunt. She trembled as she lay down flat on top of him with him still inside her.

"Good morning, sleepy head." Jessi said, happier than she had ever been able to imagine since the tragic events of her past. His eyes gave less resistance to the light shining through the window, and he smiled up at her.

"I thought you'd had enough last night," he said in a surprised but pleased tone.

"I don't think I could have enough of you. Besides, I'm working all day. I wanted that satisfaction before I have to be away from you for over eight hours."

She crawled off him, walked down the stairs to the bathroom, and started the shower. Jack lay in bed for a few moments while his mind came to grips with reality. The thoughts of the previous evening were running rampant in his mind; even as they occupied separate rooms, they both remained smiling. Jack hugged his pillow, giddy like a schoolboy with a crush. Jessi danced in the bathroom to the music of love that flowed through her.

He whipped the covers off and made his way to the bathroom. The water had finally warmed enough for Jessi to be stepping into the shower.

"Room for one more?" he asked, hoping he could be ready quick enough to drive her to work showered and clean.

"No, there's only room for another half," she said smirking at him through the open glass door even though the shower was easily large enough.

"I suppose I will have to stay close enough to you to make us a whole," he quipped as he stepped into the shower anyway.

They showered quickly, pausing only for a few moments here and there to kiss each other when they couldn't resist. Once they were both showered and clean, they stepped out together to dry off. Jessi exited the bathroom wrapped in an enormous towel, which hung low enough to be a terrycloth dress. Jack watched her from the bathroom as she went to the living room to retrieve her small bag.

In the living room she waited for Jack, who exited the bathroom with his towel secured around his waist and his hair combed back. Hand in hand, they climbed the stairs back to the bedroom, where they got dressed.

Jessi quickly threw on a clean set of work clothes and began brushing her hair. Jack stood in his walk-in closet while he dressed himself with the door open in Jessi's direct view. He wore blue jeans again and the white sneakers. He rummaged through a few piles of logoed t-shirts on hangers at the front. His hand grasped a black t-shirt with a small white skull on the sleeve and the same skull again on the back shoulder on the opposite side.

"I like that one," Jessi said. He picked it off the hanger and pulled it over his head. The fabric was snug around his chest, showing off his strong upper body.

"This is the one I liked too. You have good taste in my clothes," he joked, arousing a giggle from her. Jack led Jessi downstairs for breakfast; she followed, still brushing through her beautiful silky hair. She took a seat at the bar facing Jack in the kitchen while she finished fluffing her hair, watching him intently as he concentrated on making breakfast. He pulled a carton of eggs, a pound of bacon, and the butter from the fridge. He turned to Jessi to realize she had been staring this whole time as she brushed her hair, taking him by surprise slightly enough to give him a turn to blush. She giggled at him as his cheeks warmed; he stared at her like a deer caught in headlights.

"You were doing something, weren't you?" Jessi said with a light laugh.

"Yeah, I was, but someone got me all distracted," he snapped sarcastically, trying to keep a straight face unsuccessfully. He bent down to the left-most cabinet under the bar and pulled out two frying pans.

He turned back to the stove, placed the pans on the burners, turned them on medium, opened the pound of bacon, and started filling the entire large pan with as much as he could fit. He pulled out a few strips from what was left and stuck them in his mouth raw, moaning with pleasure as he chewed. He cracked open two eggs in the small frying pan and turned around to use the sink at the end of the bar to wash off the egg that spilled on his hands. Jessi's eyes stayed fixed on him as he stared at the soap on his hands, smiling to himself.

"You seem really happy," she said to him softly. His head tilted sideways, bringing his eyes to meet hers.

"Well if I am, it's your fault." Jessi adjusted herself in the chair, crossing her legs, placing her hands and brush in her lap, feeling just as happy.

He turned back toward the stove, opened the bag of bread, and slid two slices down into each slot of the toaster, pressing the lever down. He opened a few drawers throughout the kitchen looking for a spatula, finding it eventually. He returned to the front of the stove with his spatula and flipped the eggs first, then the bacon.

While he waited for the food to finish, he took what was left of the bacon and turned back to Jessi. He set the raw bacon on the counter in front of him and started eating it. She cringed, unaccustomed to watching him eat something that would make most people sick.

"I know I said I'd love you even if you ate me, but please don't, okay?" she said jokingly.

"Really, you're not my type when it comes to a meal. I just crave animal meat, like I was raised by a pack of dogs or something." He tried to reassure her, but it bothered her that he was still avoiding saying that he loved her out loud. He sensed she may have been hoping for her statement to dislodge the words that she, even he, wanted him to say. "You are, however, my type for everything else," he said, granting her some satisfaction as he stuffed more raw bacon in to his mouth.

"You're so sweet and charming all the time until you start eating. Then you're like an animal!" she blurted, not disgusted really, but amused watching him eat raw meat. His savagery made her want him more, made him almost godly when he was so gentle, tender, and loving for the rest of the day.

He stuffed the last few raw slices in his mouth and smiled at her. As his lips rose in a smile, her smile vanished and she sat back in her chair, stiff. She felt a ball of anxiety beating in her chest as her face lost all emotion.

"What's wrong? You're so pale, like you've seen a ghost," he said franticly and started to look around behind him. Her eyes seemed to be fixated on him, and she had just been laughing about his eating habits, so it couldn't have been that.

"Your teeth, Jack—they grew when you smiled at me," she said quietly, her hands shaking. "You are going to eat me, aren't you? You're like a vampire or something and you've been toying with me this whole time."

"That's nonsense. My teeth didn't grow, Jessi! You're imagining it." He turned to grab the toast that had just popped and saw his reflection in the shiny chrome. Grabbing the toaster up with both hands, he saw his incisors had grown disturbingly large and sharp. He had felt the pain in his mouth briefly, but the pleasure of the bacon had numbed it completely. He dropped the toaster to the counter, and the toast flopped out.

"How is this possible?" Jack shouted, the nightmare of his earliest memory returning—his uncle's mutilated body in the alley. "I'm a monster!"

"Look at me, Jack, please," Jessi pleaded in a loud enough voice to grab his frantic attention. "Are you still hungry?"

"No, well, I still want to eat the bacon that's cooking, but other than that, no."

"Do you want to try a bite of me?" she asked seriously, though a minute ago that question would have seemed ridiculous.

"No, I still just want to kiss you every time I look at you. I could never hurt you, Jessi."

"Well then it's settled. You are scary, but not dangerous, at least to me, anyway." She forced a smile, color settled back in her cheeks as her breathing notably slowed and Jack's aura took control of her again. "Could you come over here and let me look closer?"

"Yeah, let me get your breakfast first, sweetie," he said with a bewildered, painful look on his face. He turned to the stove again, pulling a plate from the cabinet. He flipped the two eggs onto the plate, buttered the toast and lay four strips of bacon across the eggs and slid the plate onto the bar in front of her. Again she was smiling at him intently, overlooking his freakish new quality.

He quickly tuned back to the stove, grabbed another plate, filled it with the rest of the cooked bacon, and carried it out of the kitchen around to the bar to sit next to Jessi. He looked at her with a concerned expression.

"Sweetie, calm down and smile, please," she said, feeling quite calm after the little fright. He smiled, revealing the enlarged incisors. She extended her hand out to his face and let her palm rest gently on his cheek, slowly moving her thumb to one of his teeth to touch it. He snapped at her finger as if he wanted a bite, and Jessi jumped back, screeching.

Jack burst out laughing, "I'm so sorry, I couldn't resist! Really, you are safe. You don't look or smell like food," he assured her, begging forgiveness for his insensitivity, "Go ahead, you can touch them. I promise I won't do it again."

"Ugh! You are such a jerk!" She smacked his arm, laughing slightly to acknowledge the humor of the prank. "You're lucky I'm so in love with you." Her hand returned to his face, rubbing her thumb gently along the tip of his upper incisor. The slightest prick peeled the skin back on her thumb, even though she had been gentle.

"Wow! That's sharp. Remind me never to feed you bacon before bed," she said with mock seriousness. The comment repeated in Jack's head, making him laugh.

Jack devoured the plate of bacon before Jessi was halfway finished with her breakfast, then he sat back in his chair and watched her eat. His feeding frenzy was over for only a few minutes before Jessi frowned thoughtfully.

"How strange," she started. "Your teeth, Jack. They're back to normal." She paused for a moment as Jack placed his thumb over his own teeth. "How is this happening?"

"I don't know, but I don't need to eat in front of you again if it makes you uncomfortable," Jack said, feeling sympathetic to the fright he caused her, considering it had even scared him.

"Don't be silly, Jack. You can do anything that pleases you in front of me," she said with a smile back on her face. His smile returned as well, his insecurity pushed away by her reassurance.

When Jessi finished eating, they headed out. Jessi took Jack's hand in hers, placing her other hand over the back of his as they waited for the elevator to arrive at the fifth floor. Jack was still thinking about the transformation he had experienced without his consent. His hand was warm and accepting of Jessi's clutch, but his eyes had a preoccupied glaze. When the elevator reached the garage level, they stepped out onto the long cement ramp hallway. Jessi turned her body weight against Jack, pushing him against the wall.

"Don't dwell on it. You will find your answers. I will help you every step of the way," she said as she propped herself on her tiptoes to kiss him. She kissed him soft and long, all of the feelings she had inflicted on him over the past two days rushed through his body, warming every part of him. "I love you, and I can't stop it. I won't stop it. Please just smile and be happy since you have me."

His smile returned as they continued up the ramp to the garage, into the same black car Jack had coveted since he laid eyes on it. Jessi pulled down the sun visor above her seat, pressing the garage opener. When the door had only opened halfway, Jack tore out of the garage, barely clearing the rising door. Jessi let out a delighted *woo* in excitement as the car revved out of the garage.

Once they were on the road with the car cruising in high gear Jack offered his hand to Jessi, who happily accepted it.

"I think you must have magic," she said.

"What do you mean?"

"You have completely taken me over in only two days as if by magic. Your teeth grow when you devour meat, and you seem to move with an inhuman quickness and finesse that I noticed first in my bed and again when you returned to the car last night to get the groceries we forgot. I mean, the garage ramp is really long, but you were back before I could rip my clothes off and get into my dress, and I was rushing the process so I could be waiting for you downstairs. Plus, your stamina in the bedroom blows my mind! I could have had a heart attack!"

"I have noticed I sometimes move quickly, but magic?"

"I bet you'll spend the day trying to move stuff with your mind while I'm at work," she joked.

"You're probably right," he smiled, laughing with her.

The whole drive to her work was full of laughter, giggling, and flirtatious glances. When they arrived in the back parking lot, practically empty this early in the morning, Jack was able to park next to Jessi's car. He jumped out of the car and was opening Jessi's door before she could pull the handle to open it herself.

"Maybe there's something to this magic thing," he conceded, acknowledging another unnatural talent. He held out his hand to help Jessi out of the car, which Jessi accepted and kept as they shut the door, walking toward the diner. When they approached the diner's back door, Jessi wrapped her arms around him. As her grip loosened, she lifted her face from his chest and leaned up, where he met her halfway for another soft, tender kiss.

"I love you, Jack. I'm going to miss you," she said with wide, love-filled eyes, the same beautiful eyes that engulfed every fiber of Jack's being. Her lips quivered as the words escaped them; his knees went weak again.

"I love you, Jessi, with every piece of me. I have half a mind to sit out here until your shift ends," he said, trying to keep air flowing through his stifled throat. "In fact, I mean not to leave, not quite yet, anyway."

"Oh? And what will my handsome prince, who loves me so, do if not leave and return to his castle?" she said in a cute, bubbly voice, noticeably giddy from hearing the words come from his mouth.

"The water seems calming, and I quite enjoy sitting on the bench on the dock. It seems I have no responsibilities in life other than to you, to whom I choose to give myself." The latter half of the statement drew the flush back to Jessi's cheeks, and he adored it, so he kissed her again without thinking.

"Okay, I have to go to work now. If you're still around by noon, I would love to share my lunch with you." She backed away from him slowly, holding onto his hand, allowing it to slowly slide away from her as the distance became greater than their reach.

"Then at noon I will be here," Jack replied with one last smile before she turned and entered the kitchen.

Carla was late, like most mornings; she usually didn't show up until just before the diner opened. Jessi always wiped down the surfaces, swept the floor, and made all the preparations for the morning rush.

Most mornings, the cook had nasty comments, sometimes rude and sometimes just raunchy, but this morning he was silent and acted as if he hadn't noticed Jessi's presence other than saying good morning to her as she entered the back door.

Now the diner was clean; it was time to open the front doors to let the folks waiting outside in for breakfast, and Carla still hadn't shown up for work. Jessi's first thought was that Carla was mad at her for the prank she had played the night before, giving her the key to the trailer so she could walk in on her date with Jack while she was at Jack's place, safe from interruption.

Four tables filled with people immediately, and Jessi was hard at work, taking orders, filling drinks, and balancing plates as she swooshed through the diner like the wind. Her emotions held her so high, nothing could bother her with Jack still planted firmly in her mind. She moved swiftly, gracefully, and with more poise than ever. Drinks were served to her tables, their orders all hung in the cook's window. With a free moment, she slipped out the front door to peer down the street to see if Jack's silhouette was on the bench. The sun was rising over the water to the east where Jack was, sure enough, sitting with perfect posture as he watched the water. To Jessi, he appeared to be a tiny shadow of a man sitting; she needed to make a canopy with her hand over her eyes to see him, but just from the sight of the shadowy character sitting on the bench, she knew it was Jack. Butterflies tickled her stomach. Her smile widened more than it had already been since they had separated from each other less than an hour ago.

She went back into the diner after only being gone for a few moments. The only thing her mind could possibly stress over was wondering where Carla was. Carla, who had been her only friend for the past year, must be really mad at her and punishing her with a busy morning's work to do alone.

"Have you talked to Carla this morning, Jessi?" the cook asked her through the kitchen window.

"No, but I kind of ditched her last night, so she's probably mad at me," Jessi replied. "But I'm sure she will be in soon."

The cook rolled his eyes, but spared Jessi his usual rant and aggravated insults. Jessi smiled smugly to herself, knowing why he was being so nice. "Have you tried anyone else to see if they can pick up a shift?" the cook questioned pleasantly.

"Jen can't get a babysitter, and Emily and Kat are still in school," she replied promptly before getting back to work.

Jessi had single-handedly waited on every table for the first two hours of her shift, but when Carla hadn't shown by nine o'clock Jessi began to worry. The diner had a phone the cook would only let people use in absolute emergencies. She asked the cook if he could cover for just a moment while she ran down to the phone booth to try to call Carla. The cook chopped his hand down next to him onto the phone; the handset of an ancient pushbutton phone popped up into his hand with elegance. He handed it through the kitchen window to Jessi.

"I'd say this is an emergency. You've been busting ass for fuckin' hours, and that little bitch is probably sitting on some useless asshole's face," the cook snarled with his usual attitude he reserved for Carla.

"Thanks, Cook," she said as she grasped the phone, confused about who the cook was and how he had possibly turned into a man she might one day learn the name of. Until now, patrons and employees alike just called him cook or the cook because he was such a rude, arrogant insect.

Jessi dialed Carla's number. It rang three times before the answering machine picked up:

"Hey, you've reached Carla. I'm not in right now. Leave a message if you love me."

"Carla, it's Jessi. Where are you? I'm sorry for lying to you yesterday. Please pick up!" Jessi paused and waited for a moment, but Carla never came to the phone. She pushed the disconnect button under the earpiece, held it for three or four seconds, then released and pressed redial. When she got the answering machine, she tried one more time and handed the phone back through the window to the cook.

"No answer. I hope she's okay," Jessi said, concerned for her friend.

"Like I said—"

"I don't want to hear that!" Jessi shouted through the window. "I know Carla, and she would never leave me stranded for some guy!"

The cook's face went blank as he looked back down at the food simmering in front of him. Jessi felt accomplishment; for the first time she had dared shout back at the cook, and he seemed frightened by her anger. She knew it was because of Jack, and she smiled as her mind returned to him.

Jessi continued successfully waiting on every table that came in through the morning, making it the most lucrative day she had ever had. It was almost noon, and Carla was still missing. Jessi worried she would have to cancel lunch with Jack, and just as she had the thought, he pulled the door open and their eyes met. Jack could instantly see something was wrong. Her hair was disheveled, and her face was sad. Her eyes looked tired and worn, and her smile was forced.

"Are you okay, Jessi?"

"I'm okay, but Carla never showed up to work this morning. It's just me waiting tables, and I can't take a lunch."

Behind Jessi, the cook was staring at Jack with a face as white as the whites of the eggs he was frying.

"Hey, buddy, how are you?" Jack asked him pleasantly to allow him to settle and not be alarmed.

With a genuine smile and one hand up giving a stiff wave that allowed the cook to breathe again, Jack's attention immediately returned to Jessi.

"Can I do anything to help?" he asked, hoping to save her.

"I've called her phone a few times, and there has been no answer, so she's either not home or somehow still sleeping, but I'm worried something worse has happened to her. She's never done this before in the year I have worked with her."

"May I occupy one of these empty tables and eat bacon until you get off your shift, then? I hate seeing you upset, and if you need me to do anything, just tell me."

"Of course you can, honey, but if you really wanted to help me, you could put an apron on and help me bring out all of these orders that are about to be in the window," she said jokingly.

Jack followed her into the kitchen and grabbed an apron. Then he looked at the cook, who had taken notice of Jack's approach to working for him for the day.

"Are you okay with me helping Jessi, sir?" Jack asked politely.

"Yes, thank you very much," the cook replied sincerely. He had acquired the business from his father, for whom he had worked since childhood. His father would be hurt if customers were unhappy, though Jessi had been doing a perfect job running every table so far.

Together, Jessi and Jack ran the diner smoothly with plenty of extra time to hang out in the break room snogging and flirting. Jessi took all the orders, and Jack brought the plates and drinks. The last few hours of Jessi's shift went by quickly. The night shift servers arrived by quarter of three, relieving the couple of duty. Jessi clocked out by three after she and Jack hung their aprons. The cook offered Jack money for the help, which Jack declined respectfully as his wallet was stuffed with hundred-dollar bills. Jessi had made over three-hundred dollars in tips from the shift, which she attempted to share with Jack, but he refused.

After exiting the diner through the back door, they walked back to Jack's car, where instead of opening Jessi's door for her, he spun her toward him and pressed her against the car to kiss her for a few moments.

"I believe I could get used to working at the diner. It seems so magical."

"I've been working at the diner for a long time, and today was the first day it felt magical at all because you were there with me," she said grinning, lifting her head to accept another short kiss. "Mmm," she moaned quietly, "I love you so much. You saved me today."

"I would have been there earlier had I known," he said in an apologetic tone. He pulled her away from the car and up against him as he opened her door for her. Before she could get in and close the door, she heard Jack's door closing.

"How do you do that?" she asked with a smile.

"I don't know. I just think about how much I want to be next to you, and I am." He smiled.

Jack started the car and drove toward their homes. For most of the ride they sat hand in hand, talking and smiling with love that would make most people either jealous or nauseous. As they were approaching Jack's home, Jessi's mind went back to Carla.

"Jack, can we please stop by Carla's too? She lives about fifteen minutes past my house, but I need to check on her," she asked, trying not to put him off, which would be impossible, but she considered his feelings nonetheless.

"Of course. Anything you want," he replied simply. "Just tell me where to go after we pass your place."

"Thank you. I'm really worried about her."

"Then so am I."

They passed Peter's mansion and were approaching Jessi's trailer. She had given Jack simple directions to Carla's apartment complex further down the curvy rural road. Jessi was looking out her window as he drove through each bend of the road. Her hand was still wrapped in his, caressing it with her thumb.

"Jack, stop! That's Carla's car at my place!"

Jack slammed on the breaks, securing Jessi in her seat with his free arm. The car slid sideways off the road and into the dirt, coming to a stop within inches of Carla's car. Dirt and the smell of burnt rubber filled the air from the sudden stop.

Chapter VIII

Crumbling Sanity

Jack and Jessi walked to Carla's car and began looking through the windows. The doors were unlocked, but nothing was out of place, so they left the car untouched, continuing on to the trailer. Jessi pulled her keys out of her purse, put the key in the lock, and heard the tongue click into place. So Carla had not only left the door unlocked, but the latch hadn't closed all the way.

Jessi turned the handle without turning the key, and the door popped open. As it opened, a rank smell rushed out of the trailer, causing Jessi to grab her face.

"Wow! I know she must have been pissed, but what did she *do* in here?" she asked, disgusted with her friend. Jessi stepped up into the trailer, looking at the floor. She immediately turned to her right and looked under the table first, then on her tip-toes to check the high bunk bed. Jack stepped in behind her, looking straight down to the bedroom, but the door was shut. He moved for the door, with his face uncovered, evidently unbothered by the smell. Jessi followed behind him, expecting to find some animal carcass in her bed. He reached out for the handle and gave it a twist. The door swung open, and a swarm of flies attacked them. They flinched away for a moment. Jack was the first to recover and look into the room.

"No!" he screamed, seeing his nightmare in reality, but with Carla's body hanging instead of Jessi's. "No!"

The shouts brought Jessi's head up quickly to her friend's hands pinned to the ceiling and her feet stuck to the wall with strange orange goo. Her body had been ripped open, her skin pinned to her back with small sharpened bones. All of her internal organs lay on the blood-saturated bed. Jessi turned away and ran to the sink to vomit. Jack pulled her hair back away from her face and soothed her as she leaned into the sink.

When Jessi's stomach was empty she went into shock from the trauma of seeing what had happened to her friend, led to her death by a prank. Her eyes were wide as she stared blankly at the walls. Her thoughts raced through how she could have prevented this, how this could have been her, should have been her instead. Had she been the intended target? She thought over every person that could have done this sick thing, but not one person came to mind that was so sadistically evil; it must have been a random attack. Jack scooped her up in his arms, carried her outside, and placed her in the passenger seat of his car. She could not even utter a single word but exhaled a hushed, raspy moan. He reclined the seat as far as he could, kissed her forehead, and whispered into her ear.

"I love you. I'm so sorry you had to see my nightmare."

The words connected with Jessi through her shock. She looked up at him with the saddest eyes.

"You dreamt Carla would die this way?" She trembled.

"No, Jessi. I dreamt you would die this way and I would be ruined. I have loved you since the moment I met you. I thought my dream was just a nightmare of losing what I desired most."

Jack closed the car door with Jessi lying down inside. He returned to the trailer to inspect it one more time before they called the police. He opened the door, preparing his nose for the foul smell of decomposing flesh, but he could only smell the sweet scent of Jessi. He cautiously entered the trailer, even more confused than he had been before, and looked down the hallway into the bedroom. To his amazement, Carla was gone. There wasn't a drop of blood anywhere. The bed was made, and there was not a single buzzing fly. Jack left the trailer, bewildered. The whole situation reminded him so vividly of seeing his uncle's body mutilated in the alley.

Jessi had brought her chair back up and made eye contact with him as he emerged from the trailer looking confused beyond belief. Jack proceeded to the car and sat down in the driver's seat, closing the door tight.

"She's gone," he muttered.

"I know, I saw," she said, fighting back tears.

"No, Jessi. I mean your trailer is perfectly clean, and the bed is made," he tried to explain to disbelieving ears. Jessi pushed her door open, ran to the trailer, barging through the door. She peeked her head inside without stepping in all the way, hoping she would not vomit again, but she could see the bedroom clearly from there. It was exactly how Jack described. She shut the door slowly, her hand lingered on the door for a moment, and she looked down at her feet, trying to understand the phenomenon she had just encountered. Exactly like the story Jack had divulged about his uncle.

Jessi moved herself from her trailer door and slowly back to Jack's car, returning to her seat.

"I'm sorry I didn't believe you, Jack," she said sadly.

"It's okay, I understand you needed to see for yourself."

"No, I mean I didn't believe you about your uncle. I thought a part of you must have been insane."

They sat in the car bewildered, unable to comprehend what had happened.

"I don't want to stay here. I never want to come back," Jessi whimpered.

"You don't have to. You can always stay with me. Go pack your bags. I will keep watch out here."

Jessi exited the car again and entered the trailer cautiously. Jack began looking around, inspecting the surroundings of the trailer. Closely looking for anything out of place, he discovered some animal tracks. He followed them from the trailer to the edge of the woods, where they disappeared into the brush.

"Hmm. Seems to be a lot of dogs around here." He scratched his chin and headed back for Jessi.

He entered the trailer to see Jessi attempting to lift the large, very full duffle bag. He moved to her quickly and put one hand on the strap of the bag and the other around her stomach as he leaned over to kiss her cheek.

"Let me get this. I'll be careful."

"Thank you. You know something sad? You are the only good memory I have in this trailer," she said.

"Then let us leave it," he said, and they did. They left the trailer with Jack, as always, opening the door for her. He got in the car and shut his door before she could shut hers, but this time he even had time to toss her bags in the trunk.

Jack slammed the car in reverse, spinning out of the driveway. He pushed the shift to second, skipping over first entirely, and let go of the clutch with full throttle timed perfectly. The tires spun, pouring smoke from behind as they entered the winding road.

The short journey from Jessi's trailer to Jack's room had been silent. They both were lost in their own thoughts about whatever it was they had just witnessed. He sat on the couch with Jessi right up against him. He wrapped his arm around her, and they stared up at a blank TV.

"Are you hungry?" Jack asked.

"Not for the next month, my stomach is still queasy," she replied.

"Hmmm, right," he pursed his lips together flat against his teeth. "Do you want to go to Carla's?" he asked, still looking for something to break the lingering confusion that had latched on to them.

"No, I tried to call her while I was packing and she hung up on me. She's just pissed."

"Should we talk about it?"

"I don't know what I feel like doing," she said still gazing at the blank TV on the wall. "I'm just happy to be here with you, safe." She looked at him. "I'm scared, Jack."

"I'll die before I let anything happen to you, Jessi. You are all the good in me," he said, trying to reassure her.

"I just don't understand what happened, Jack. If we were hallucinating, then why can't I get a hold of Carla? Tell me about how your uncle's body vanished again. If that *was* real, what kind of man could rip a person open, spilling their organs?"

Jack stood up, shaking his head, not knowing how to answer her questions. He offered his hand to her, and she accepted, pulling herself off the couch. Jack turned to the glass doors that led out to the balcony.

"I think some fresh air would do both of us some good," he said.

He leaned up against the railing on his elbows. Jessi approached him from behind and wrapped her hands around him, resting her chin on his back. They stood there quietly, admiring the view of the woods from such a high angle. The feeling of her warm body against him made him happier, but he couldn't free himself from the anguish churning inside.

Chapter IX

The Hellhound

Jack and Jessi stood out on the balcony, not moving for a long time, just gazing out over the back lawn and into the woods. Jessi slid around to his right side so she could look up at his face.

"Are we safe?" she asked, concerned.

"I don't know. I don't know what's happening or who's doing it." Just then, the black dog they had encountered the day before in the study trotted around to the back of the house from the side yard. He kept close to the house and didn't seem to notice Jack and Jessi staring down at him from high up. The dog sniffed the ground here and there, continuing its trot from place to place.

Jack's eyes went wide as he started to piece together the only events in his recent memory. He stood up slowly, placing one hand on Jessi's shoulder, and with his other he signaled for quiet. He backed away from the edge of the railing, moving Jessi with him as quietly as possible. When they were both back inside, he pointed to the couch, and Jessi sat. He then slowly closed the sliding door, inch by inch, making virtually no noise that might draw the dog's attention.

Jack turned to Jessi, extending his hand to her again. He led her up to his bedroom and into the walk-in closet.

"I think there's a connection between that dog and this mess," he said. "Think about it. If it's the same dog we met down the hall, how did he get in that room? How did he get out of that room and even out of the house? We saw him walking down the street toward your place last night, and I noticed dog-sized tracks around your trailer while you were packing your things." He tried explaining the basis of his theory, but that was about as far as he had gotten. He knew one thing, though: he didn't feel safe.

While Jessi stood quietly next to Jack, who was rummaging through the storage in the closet, she thought about what he had just said. After what she witnessed less than an hour prior, anything seemed possible.

Jack found a gym bag big enough to fit clothes for a couple of days. He tied the laces of a few pairs of shoes and draped them through the strap of the bag. He put on a lightweight black coat that hung just below his waist and the black brimmed hat he had bought two days ago. He handed Jessi one of his long-sleeved t-shirts and a baseball hat, which she put on without hesitation or question.

Jack grabbed up the stuffed travel bag with shoes dangling from it and reached for Jessi's hand, looking at her.

"Wow, you're even stunning in my clothes. I can't tell you how sexy that is," he said as he gazed at her amorously.

"Focus, Jack—we were escaping the evil dog, remember?" she said with a flattered smile, the biggest she'd been able to muster since the trailer.

"Sorry, it's hard to focus with you being so beautiful all the time," he said, smiling back at her.

"Is that why you're making me wear your clothes? To help you focus?"

"No, sweetie. That dog was licking me, but when he saw you, he got angry, so I figure if you smell more like me, he might leave you alone if we happen to bump into him."

****

With her hand in his, Jack led her back down to his front door. Before opening the door, Jack pressed his face up against the peak hole for a few moments but did not see any movement. He opened the door, quietly peering around to check the elevator lobby. It was clear, so they moved into it, quickly pressing the button for the elevator. The doors opened immediately. They boarded hastily, and Jack pressed G.

Jogging up the long ramp that led to the cars, Jack grabbed the keys to his favorite car off the hook and unlocked the doors. He opened Jessi's door, got in, and started the engine before Jessi could close her door. She pressed the garage door opener, and the door began opening. He revved the engine a few times, ready to fly out of the garage as soon as the door was high enough, but just as it opened to the height of the hood, the black dog slinked under the opening door, approaching Jessi's side, snarling. Her hand moved to the lock with clumsy speed, and she hurt her fingers when she collided with the door. The dog pounced, his front paws on the side of the car, glaring at Jessi and growling, brandishing his frightening teeth.

Finally, the garage door opened enough, and Jack smashed the gas and popped the clutch with the transmission in second gear. As the car bolted forward, the dog's paws slipped off the door, and it face-planted on the cold cement. The dog sprang to its feet and began to chase them far enough from the garage door that Jessi could close it with the remote without allowing the dog to sneak back in. Jack flew down the driveway and drifted the car into the street, up-shifting to catch traction.

He pushed the car hard and drove it as fast as he could around the winding corners, fearing they may be dealing with some kind of dark magic. Everything was leading his mind to this, his speed, his teeth, and his craving for raw meat. He wondered if he somehow summoned the dog or was somehow tied to it before his memory loss.

"Is there a hotel outside of town we can stay in?" Jack asked.

"Yes, the highway is close to Main Street, and there are hotels off of a few of the exits."

"Okay. We'll spend some time in a hotel, and you can call out of work for a few days. I want to figure out what the hell is going on."

"Call out from work? Do you really think that dog is going to find us twenty miles away from Hollow Wood?"

"Right. You must really like to work," he mumbled under his breath. He thought it would be best not to argue since he was planning on looking around town for some clues to what was happening to him. If she was at the diner, he would be able to keep a close watch on her.

After racing through the rural roads at nauseating speeds, they had covered the distance back to Main Street, where Jack finally slowed the car down close to the legal limit as Jessi gave him the directions. In only a few minutes they were on the highway, passing several exits with signs for hotels, but Jack didn't stop until they had driven forty miles. Finally, he chose an exit with a hotel sign and pulled off the highway just after seven o'clock. The sun had begun its descent, lighting up the sky with radiant colors of pink, red, and orange.

The hotel was directly off the exit. They pulled up to the front door under a large awning. The building was small and old. The siding was faded from sun and battered by wind and storms, the warped wood peeling away from the structure. Jack got out of the car and quickly opened Jessi's door. They entered the hotel together.

Sitting behind the counter was a little old lady who sprang from her rocking chair at the sight of such an adorable young couple.

"Good evening, kids. May I help you?"

"Yes, ma'am, may we have a room for the night, please? On this floor if possible." Jack pulled two hundred-dollar bills out of his wallet, placing them on the counter with a smile. "We're on our honeymoon, and we're traveling the east coast, getting to know our land better as we have with our love," he added, sounding cheesy but intentionally melting the elderly lady's heart.

She stared at the computer for a moment. "I have a room available on the second floor next to the stair access and the elevators that lead to the backdoor." She glanced up at them, noticing the money sitting on the counter. "But I can probably do better for you, sweetie." She began sliding the mouse around, clicking and typing. "Here we go, room 120, last room on the right down this hallway. You will be able to park your car in the back lot, and the back door is right next to your room. Only a hotel key can open that door." She slid the money cautiously from the counter to her lockbox.

"Thank you so much, ma'am, you don't know how much this means to us," Jessi said smiling, clinging to Jack's arm.

Jessi and Jack returned to the car and drove around to the back, where he backed into the spot right next to the door, the remaining lot was just about empty. Jack grabbed all of the bags in one hand, opening Jessi's door with the other, and quickly taking her hand. He locked the car with the remote as they proceeded to the hotel's back door.

After the young couple got to their room, Jack dropped the bags in front of the closet and double-locked the door. Jessi lay down on the queen-size bed in the center of the room. Jack checked the curtains and closed them, eliminating any possibility of prying eyes. He then flopped down on the bed next to Jessi and stared at the ceiling with her.

"What a day," he said blankly.

"What a day indeed."

Jessi rolled herself onto Jack, folding her hands on his chest, staring into his eyes. Her touch made his blood rush through his body as it had before seeing Carla in Jessi's trailer. She dropped her lips to his, kissed him once, and lifted her head away.

"With all that has happened, I thought for a minute I wished it was all just a bad dream," Jessi said with only a brief pause before continuing. "But only for a moment. If it was all just a dream, then the time I've had with you wouldn't be real."

Jack, completely satisfied by her words, moved his hands from behind his head and wrapped his arms around her. She shimmied down a few inches and rested her cheek on his chest, listening to his heartbeat.

"Why is your heart beating so fast?" she asked.

"You seem to have that effect on me," he smiled with his eyes closed, enjoying the moment until Jessi lifted herself off him. Still lying on his back, he opened his eyes at her movement and connected with her gaze. She stood at the end of the bed looking down at him.

"It's just after seven, and I'm feeling hungry now. I bet there's a restaurant somewhere nearby," Jessi said as her stomach grumbled. They hadn't eaten since breakfast.

"You're right. Besides, only old people go to sleep at seven," he said, drawing a giggle from her. He stood up and walked to the door, moving the bags out of the way. He checked the peephole, unlocked the door and looked slowly down the hall both ways. Jack began laughing at himself.

"Nope, no demon dogs," he said, feeling silly for his paranoia. Jessi chuckled.

Jack reached his hand back while he stood in the door ready to move forward. He led Jessi out of the room, walking down the hall shoulder to shoulder with her, hand in hand, flirting. Jessi had her free hand wrapped around Jack's bicep and spent most of the walk staring up at him.

They asked the old lady at the front desk about places to eat in the area. She directed them to a stand full of pamphlets around the corner in a small vending machine lobby.

Jack and Jessi looked through the pamphlets. He, of course, selected the fanciest place on the shelf.

"Jack, I can't afford that," she said shying away from him.

"Please, Jessi just let me take my girl out for a nice dinner. It's what I want, and I wouldn't have it any other way."

"Why do you have to be so perfect?" she asked, still looking away.

Jack pulled her face back to him with one finger on her chin.

She allowed him a small smile. "How is it *me* that gets to be so lucky to have you?"

"I could say the same of you, Jessi. There isn't a woman in the world as beautiful as you, and with your beauty, you are kind, strong, and independent, so the fact that you are here is shocking. Should I recite the situation? You aren't a gullible person, but for me you seem to make an exception and buy into the most insane scenario possible."

"Ugh. You're too perfect, and you don't know it, and if you find out, I hope it doesn't change you." The words seemed to ring in his head. "Now if you will, please shut up and take me to dinner," she demanded with sass through a perfect smile.

"Not until you kiss me," Jack replied. She granted his wish.

It had been a long, strange, emotional day for both of them. Jack felt more comfort then he imagined he would, finally having someone else understand his confusion. Jessi had only ever had one problem with Jack—a worry he might be a little insane. Now that Jessi had seen something the way Jack saw it, she knew it was more than a mental problem or hallucination. Her mystical infatuation with him silenced her intuition that the whole situation surrounding Jack was dangerous.

Their stomachs growled simultaneously, making them pull away and laugh. Holding hands, they walked back down the hotel hallway, past their room, and out through the back door where the car was parked. Jack opened the door for Jessi, but this time he waited for her to get in with his arm leaning on top of the door. He stared down at her, smiling as he shut it. He walked around the car slowly, watching his feet as they took each step, smiling, still thinking about the way Jessi had swept him off his feet entirely. He was in love with her. What Jack didn't know was why he saw people differently from others. He could see the face that was physically there but also the face of the soul. Most people he saw on the streets were distorted, some even scary, but a few, like Jessi, shone with goodness and compassion.

Jack drove them out of the lot, and Jessi navigated from the map on the back of the pamphlet. With only a few turns, about five minutes, they saw the restaurant on the left as they passed. Jack made a U-turn at the next light and drove back the short distance, pulling in to the parking lot of La Cucina.

Jack hopped out. Jessi didn't even attempt to open her own door anymore. He walked around the car, looking through the window at her, smiling. He opened her door for her, held out his hand, and helped her up to her feet. They walked hand in hand through the parking lot to the front door.

"Welcome to La Cucina. Unfortunately, we have a dress code. You must be wearing a collared shirt, and your lovely friend must be in a dress to enter," said a snobby host standing just inside the door.

Jack pulled out his wallet with a smile and handed the man a hundred-dollar bill. "We're from out of town, and our luggage has been lost, but we are eating here tonight as we are, if you please," Jack said in a strong and insistent voice. He slid the money toward the host. Jessi was still wearing Jack's long-sleeve t-shirt over her work clothes. Jack was wearing blue jeans and a black t-shirt with skulls covered by his black collared coat.

"Sir," the host began in an even snottier tone, "it is not about the money, it is about the image."

His words infuriated Jack, so he leaned in to the host and whispered in his ear, "How'd you like a broken nose, and your image blurred?" He clenched his teeth and felt his rage pulse through his veins. Jessi squeezed his arm tightly, reminding him to take deep breaths and relax.

"Dear me, where are my manners? Your table is ready. Right this way," the host said with a hint of shakiness in his voice, accepting the tip from Jack.

Jack and Jessi followed the host to the back of the restaurant, which harbored seven tables and eight booths, all empty. The host gave them a booth next to the window that overlooked a grassy yard that extended down to a lake glowing golden in the sunset.

"What did you say to him to change his mind?" Jessi inquired suspiciously.

"Just a little coercion and bribery together," he said with a smirk.

Jack laid his hands on the table, palms up. She placed her hands in his without breaking eye contact. Just then, a handsome young waiter approached the table with a bottle of expensive wine resting on his folded arm.

"Good evening, folks, and welcome to La Cucina. My name is Brian, and I'll be your server this evening. Allow us to start you off with a complementary bottle of wine, courtesy of the host."

"Thank you. Could we also have a couple glasses of water while we look over the menus please?" Jack asked without looking away from Jessi. She seemed to not even notice the young man speaking, she was so lost in Jack's smile.

"Yes, sir." Brian opened the bottle of wine and filled two glasses. He snapped his fingers at a busboy who quickly brought over two glasses of ice water with a lemon wedge in each.

Jack retracted one of his hands from Jessi's and lifted a glass of wine to toast.

"To love at first sight and fighting the Hellhound," Jack said happily.

"The Hellhound?" Jessi asked.

"In English mythology, an ancient messenger of death is a black dog created by demons, cursing or directly causing a person's death. Seems to fit the description of our new furry friend," he replied, not quite sure how he knew that.

Jessi tapped his glass with a clink and smiled.

"To love at first sight and the other thing, then," she said with a girly giggle.

Brian returned to the table when Jack rested the menu at the edge of the table.

"Would you folks like to place your order?"

Without breaking eye contact with Jessi, Jack began placing an order.

"She will have the steak Alfredo, medium rare, and I will have two filet mignons, rare, with no sides. Ring it up however you need to," Jack said clearly. "When our food is served, we would like to be undisturbed until my plate is clean for at least five minutes."

"Yes, yes sir, whatever you'd like, sir," said Brian, stuttering a bit. Jack smirked, realizing he clearly intimidated the waiter.

After they were alone again, Jessi took another sip of wine and said, "Thank you, Jack. I don't know how you did it, but you ordered exactly what I would have ordered for myself. I have never allowed a date to speak for me like that before." She smiled, completely immersed in all of his magical energy. She could see far beyond his obvious short-tempered rage issues and his odd eating habits to the hero that lay dormant inside of him. The part of her that was reluctant and aware of these relationship warning signs was silenced and stored deep within her as if she were under his spell.

****

Jack and Jessi sat flirting and talking for only fifteen minutes before their food was served, cooked to perfection.

"Thank you for sharing some of your steak with me." Jack grinned as he reached his fork to her plate, stealing a small piece of the cubed steak in her Alfredo pasta.

"What's mine is yours, Jack."

"I might just take advantage of that when we get back to our room tonight," he teased, filling her with sensual emotions that mixed with her wine.

Jack looked down at his plate and the urge of hunger grabbed hold of him. He quickly cut into the plump chunks of filet, trying to avoid picking them up with is fingers and devouring them like his mind screamed for him to do.

He stabbed through several strips of steak, shoveling them into his mouth. His eyes began to roll back in his head with pleasure, and he exhaled a quiet moan mixed with a bit of an animalistic growl. Jessi looked up from her plate to see Jack's teeth stretching down again. This time she smiled, placing her hand on the table for Jack to hold, but Jack was in a feeding frenzy. He ran out of cut strips, dropped his fork, and picked up the rest of the filet, ripping off chucks with his enlarged teeth. Within a few moments, he had cleaned his plate and stolen a few more pieces of steak from Jessi.

"I'm so sorry. I just get blinded by the hunger. I'm so sorry." Jessi was laughing hysterically, and he signaled for her to keep it down.

"It's okay, sweetie. Take a few sips of your wine; it should help calm you down," she said, still catching her breath from laughing and trying to restrain herself at the same time.

Jack lifted the glass to his mouth, smelling the wine as it approached. Instead of being revolted, as he had been by other non-meat products, he was delighted. His hunger felt quenched after eating so much so rapidly.

"How are my teeth?" Jack asked, wondering if the wine was prolonging his unnatural alteration.

"They aren't too noticeable, unless someone who knew you was looking at you, like me. I can't lie though, it's kind of sexy," she said shying away, blushing for a moment.

"Why thank you, so are you, without being a meat-crazed monster," he said jokingly.

"I love you," Jessi said, trembling.

"I love you too. Why are you shaking?"

"You just came into my life, and when I think about what life would be like without you in it again, it scares me."

"That's something I won't let you find out, so stop worrying about it. I love you irrevocably."

Their server, Brian, interrupted the conversation as Jack's plate had been clean for just over five minutes.

"Would you like to try one of our desserts tonight?" Brian asked.

"No, thank you, Brian. Just the check please. Everything was great," Jack replied, still unaware of what the server looked like because his eyes had been permanently fixed on Jessi, aside from his feeding frenzy.

"Yes, sir," Brian said, pulling the check in a black book from a pouch in his apron.

"I think we will occupy this table until the wine runs dry," Jack said to Brian but still smiling at Jessi as he stuck two hundred-dollar bills in the book. "Keep the change, friend. Everything was great," Jack repeated.

"Sir, your meal was under a hundred dollars," Brian protested.

"I said thank you," Jack snipped, sending a glare in the waiter's direction, distracted from Jessi for the first time, forcing Brian to back away from the table with a grin plastered to his face.

The beautiful couple sat at their table until the bottle went dry; each drank three modest glasses. They returned to their hotel room, undressed, and crawled into bed naked. Jack lay on his side as Jessi backed herself against him, feeling her skin against his over the entirety of her backside, his arms wrapped around her.

"I love you, Jack," she whispered, feeling buzzed from the wine and very tired from the emotionally trying day.

"I love you too," Jack replied through the smile her words struck on his face. They allowed their eyes to rest and, in each other's comfort, fell fast asleep.

Chapter X

Snap

For three nights they stayed at the hotel, only leaving to take Jessi to work or to have a meal at a local restaurant. Jessi hid her concern for Carla, who still had not returned to work. She had left so many messages on her phone that her mailbox was now full. Her thoughts constantly drifted back to what had happened in her trailer, but being unable to explain or prove it, she kept her thoughts to herself. They spent the rest of their time tangled together in bed. They had developed such an inseparable bond in the short time they had known each other, it felt as though they could not survive when they were apart. Jack spent most of his days hanging around the diner or down by the ocean while Jessi worked. He could not understand why she continued to do so when he was clearly well-off. He had offered on many occasions to pay her bills, though he found a sense of peace in her pride rather than annoyance at her stubbornness.

On the fourth morning, Jessi woke up first, tangled again in Jack's arms and legs.

"You must be a god," Jessi said. "I am the luckiest girl alive."

"You really like taking advantage of me when I'm sleeping, don't you?" Jack smiled, eyes closed from exhaustion.

"I just really like having you inside me, but I won't wake you up like this anymore if you don't like it."

"I love it," he said with a long, exhaled breath.

Jessi hopped out of the bed. Walking into the bathroom, she started the shower and peeked her head out the door.

"Are you coming?" she asked enticingly.

"Absolutely," he replied, jumping up.

Jack and Jessi washed themselves and each other's backs, kissing passionately in the shower for a short while. Once they dried off and Jessi dressed herself in clean work clothes from her duffle bag, Jack threw on a pair of black slacks to match her black skirt. He also had packed a white button-down to match her work shirt since he was planning to help her on her shift. Had Carla really been so brutally murdered, she wouldn't be showing up for her shift again.

They ran about the room getting ready, Jessi chanting repeatedly, "We're going to be late!"

They jumped into the car, but when Jack pulled out of the parking lot slowly, Jessi looked at him, agitated. "This is the time you pick to drive slow?"

"Jessi, just trust me," he replied with a sinister grin.

He drove off the lot and continued to the entrance ramp next to the hotel. As he merged onto the highway, there were few other cars to contend with so early in the morning. Jack revved the engine in fourth gear, speeding up to a hundred miles per hour, then shifted to fifth and revved it harder. The car purred and begged for more as they climbed to speeds of one-thirty in fifth gear. In just minutes they were pulling off the highway for Main Street. Jack had made such good time; Jessi was more comfortable with him driving the speed limit the rest of the way to the diner.

They pulled into the back lot and got out of the car in the usual manner. Jessi unlocked the diner and immediately began her morning routine. The cook was already in his office processing orders and paperwork, preparing for an inventory of supplies and his morning routine. Jack kept requesting tasks since he was not familiar with the morning procedures, but he did each task faster than anyone possibly could. She laughed aloud in amazement after the fifth task Jack had completed within a few moments.

The diner was sparkling clean; everything was in order for opening twenty minutes early. Jessi and Jack sat down on the stools in the break room. They had only just sat down when the cook came in.

"Hey, kids, you hungry?" the cook offered free food for the first time since Jessi had worked there.

"Are you feeling okay, Cook?" Jessi asked.

"I just wanted to say thank you to you and your boyfriend. The diner hasn't looked this good in a long time. I don't know what you're feeding him, but that boy can clean," Cook said, laughing out the last few words.

"Bacon," she said sharply.

"Bacon?" the cook repeated.

"Yes, lots and lots of bacon," Jack said, grinning.

"Bacon it is then, and eggs over easy with bacon and home fries as usual?" Cook said, rubbing his disgustingly fat gut.

"Yes, thank you," she said politely, then waited for him to retreat to his stove. She turned back to Jack. "Whatever you did to him, he's a better man for it, Jack," she said with a smile, still in disbelief of the severe attitude change in the cook.

Cook had only been gone ten minutes and returned to the break room with two plates, interrupting the young couple kissing by clearing his throat. Jessi dropped from her tip-toes and wiped her lips gently as she accepted the plates from the cook.

"Thank you, Cook." She paused for a moment. "Hey, Cook, what's your name, anyway? I've been calling you Cook since I started here."

"Garry Cook," he replied. "That's why everyone calls me Cook or the cook. It's been my nickname my whole life, seeing as how my dad taught me to cook here when I was just a boy."

"Well, thanks, Garry," she said, trying to be polite.

"It's Cook!" he snapped back over his shoulder as he walked away. Remembering Jack was still there, he added, "And you're welcome."

Jack had nearly devoured the bacon by the time Jessi learned the cook's name, sprouting his enlarged incisors. Sitting quietly while Jessi finished her breakfast, he tried not to expose them, still feeling self-conscious.

Jessi was finished eating just in time for the diner to open. She went out to the front and unlocked the door, not really paying attention to who stood outside. Usually the same three or four tables came in every morning before their shifts. Jessi turned from the door, allowing the customers to enter. As she approached the bar, she heard a familiar, snarky voice.

"Hey, Jessi!"

Jessi spun around in awe. "Carla!" The sight of her brought back the images in Jessi's head as if she were standing in the trailer next to her dangling body again.

"Carla! You're okay?" she said, trembling.

"Yeah, I'm okay, no thanks to you!" she snarled. "And no thanks to this shit diner. I'm just here to resign, and don't bother leaving me any more messages!" She said with a flare of hatred.

"Carla, I'm so—"

"Save it. I'm not interested," she snapped, walking past her to the kitchen window. She leaned her face in, staring at Cook. "Hey, fat ass! I quit your shitty diner!" she screamed through the window.

Jack heard the commotion and moved to the back side of the kitchen door to hear better, but he remained unseen.

Carla turned from the window and stormed out the front door as Cook screamed behind her, "You can't quit. You're fired for being a lazy bitch!"

Jessi went into the kitchen, clearly flustered, to find Jack, but as she passed through the door, his voice made her jump.

"What was that all about?"

She had missed him leaning against the wall as she entered. "That was Carla. She quit and walked out, but that's not like Carla," her voice lowered with concern. "Every day she would talk about how much she needed this job and how she couldn't quit even if she wanted to."

"You should go talk with her, as a friend."

"Come with me," she said as he rested his hand on her lower back and guided her out the front door of the diner.

"Carla, wait! What's going on with you?" Jessi yelled, catching her attention before she rounded the corner.

"Ugh. Jessi, just leave me alone. This has nothing to do with you or your rich douche bag boyfriend," Carla huffed. "I am just leaving town, I have had enough of the coast." She continued walking away.

"So that's it? You weren't even going to say goodbye?"

Carla ignored her pleas and continued to walk down the alley that led toward the back lot.

Jack's brows lowered over his eyes as he was finally feeling like the puzzle pieces fit, no matter how unlikely. He dashed back through the diner into the kitchen, asking Jessi to hold the back door for him so he could get back in. She followed behind him, but he was much faster. The door closed heavily behind him as he crouched behind the dumpster to assess his foe before him.

She popped open the door as quietly as she could. A light fog had settled over the town through the darkness of the early morning. Lit by a nearby street lamp, she saw Jack leaned against the outer wall that concealed the diner dumpsters. His hands were firmly planted on the wall in front of him, peeking around the corner. She looked further past Jack to see the black dog trotting up the alleyway. Jack pushed himself off the wall, walking backward to Jessi, hoping they were unseen by what Jack believed to be a Hellhound, a dog that collects dead souls.

He pushed Jessi into the diner carefully, taking the weight of the door that he closed slowly. He placed his eye over the peek hole in the door and allowed the door to click shut. Though the door was extremely quiet, the dog stopped in its tracks and looked back, snarling. He felt as if the dog was staring directly at him through the tiny peek hole.

Jack went to Cook, full of concern for everyone in the building. "Cook! We have a problem, a real problem—you need to get your customers and yourself out of the diner now, at all costs."

"What the hell are you—"

"Now, Cook!"

The cook's eyes grew wide, then he scrambled to the front of the diner. "Sorry, everyone, you must leave. Your meals are on me, but I need you out!" The few patrons looked up at him confused, unmoving.

"I said out! Now!" The cook bellowed and raised his knife in the air. Everyone dropped their forks and ran for the door. The cook turned back to Jack. "Sorry for arguing, sir, it won't happen again. Just don't let your eyes go black again," he pleaded, shaking, nearly in tears.

"My eyes do what?" Jack asked, astounded.

"When you got mad at me for yelling at Jessi, it was like you were possessed. Dark clouds rolled into your eyes and filled them with black. You aren't here to claim my soul, are you?" Cook pulled the knife back up, pointing it at Jack, his hand trembling from fear.

"If anything, Cook," Jack started, putting emphasis on the name, "I'm here to save your soul. Now do as I say. Leave through the front door, wait on the docks at the bottom of the street for a couple hours, then return to your car and go home. Do you understand?"

"Y-yes, I, I get it."

"Then go!" Jack said, stomping his foot toward the cook. He turned, waddling out the front door with his knife still in his hand.

"Jack, what are we going to do?" Jessi asked, extremely frightened. "Where did the dog come from?"

"Carla. Carla is the dog. I saw her walk into the alley alongside this building, and by the time I made it to the back door, the dog was exiting the alley. I saw my uncle dead then somehow he showed up at home. Shortly after that, we saw the same black dog there."

Jessi believed every word; she had already learned to never disbelieve Jack. If anything, he was a hero, not crazy.

"Jack, that dog was heading to the back lot. What should we do?" she whimpered.

"I don't know yet. Do me a favor and keep an eye on the peephole while I look for a weapon."

She went straight to the back door, leaning her face against the door at the peephole. Jack rummaged through the kitchen, where he grabbed a knife even bigger than the one that the cook had been holding, and tossed it on top of a counter. He checked the storage closet, where he found a mop, broke off the handle, and grabbed duct tape and twine. Jack brought his supplies to the kitchen counter and began taping the knife to the broken side of the mop handle.

After two layers of tape, he spun the rope up and down the handle of the knife, lashing it in place on the large dowel. He began to start another layer of tape when Jessi screamed.

"Jack! Someone's coming, fast!"

He started moving toward her holding his makeshift weapon by the knife handle, worried it wasn't strong enough to use as a spear without a few more layers of tape. He stepped toward Jessi, still standing at least ten feet from her. She stumbled backward and put her arms up to shield herself from the door as it was kicked in, barely missing her. A bearded man stepped in quickly, about to pass Jessi as if he didn't see her. The man stared at Jack with black eyes.

Jack screamed out, "Who are you? Why are you doing this?"

"Tei," the man replied calmly, turning his head toward Jessi, who stood directly beside him, frozen in fear.

Tei grabbed Jessi's neck and snapped it as if it was nothing, tossing her dead body to the floor with such force the corpse slid across the tiles into the wall.

"No! Jessi!" Jack cried as his eyes clouded and blackened, his teeth growing in his mouth. Bones cracked and clashed with a loud, stomach-curdling sound as his arms and legs extended. His muscles began wrapping and generating under his skin. The buttons from his shirt popped off as he charged Tei with his greatest speed.

Tei stood still, his head cocked to one side and his eyebrows raised, impressed by the transformation. Apparently, he had thought he was the only one in this realm who could transfigure. Before Tei could think of what to do, the hulking Jack collided with him, grabbing his throat and blasting him through the wall next to the door. He threw Tei's body against the dumpsters to his left, denting the metal with his body and shoving the spear through Tei's chest.

Desperate, Tei held his hands up. "Wait! Don't you want to know who you are? Why you are like this?"

Jack's each word boomed like thunder from the rage flowing through his veins, but he still had all of his wits and intelligence as long as he kept control.

"I knew who I was, and you took the only thing that mattered to me!"

Tei's body convulsed, echoing the same bone-cracking sounds as Jack. Within moments, Jack was staring down at Uncle Peter.

"Jack, please! What are you doing? Don't hurt me. It's me, my boy, Uncle Peter."

The sight of his uncle toyed with his desire to uncover his memory, the truth. Jack's bones crunched and snapped as he shrunk from his hulking state, now wearing ripped and tattered clothes.

Then, right before Jack's eyes, his uncle began to crumple like paper, his skin folding into itself, his bones seeming to liquefy. The spear dropped to the ground. In only a few seconds, Tei had become a large crow. With one leap, he spread his wings and took off, disappearing into the sky.

Jack ran back into the diner through the hole and slid to his knees, scooping Jessi's limp body. All concept of time and humanity had left Jack completely as he wept. His teeth remained enlarged and his eyes radiantly black. Every scream he loosed echoed through the diner and out into the back alley through the hole in the wall, deep and eerie.

Police sirens whined in the distance, unnoticed by Jack. A hand rested on his shoulder, startling him.

"Jack, you should go. I will deal with the cops, unless you can explain what in the world just happened here," the cook said scratching his head at the enormous hole in his diner.

"I can't leave her, she can't be gone."

"Unless you want to show off your vampire fangs and demon eyes, I am pretty sure the town will have you burned at the stake."

Chapter XI

Nemesis

Jack placed Jessi's body back on the floor gently, as if she would still feel it. Enraged by the murder of his love, he ran out of the building through the back alley. He jumped into his car and tore out of the parking lot with no intention of following any law. He dodged in and out of cars in both directions, crossing over the double yellow lines gracefully as he pushed the car to its limits, sliding through corners at speeds too great for the tires to grip. His senses tingled. Instinct had fully taken over as he navigated the road ahead before his eyes could process the images.

As he approached Hollow Wood, he saw his uncle jump into the road in front of the speeding car a half a mile before the driveway. Jack ripped the wheel to the left to dodge him, putting him in oncoming traffic. He overcorrected, sending the car completely sideways, skidding out of control. The edges of his tires caught too much grip as he slid at speeds nearly a hundred miles per hour; the car began to barrel roll down the street and into the woods at the next corner, only stopping when it slammed into the trunks of two enormous trees.

Jack felt little pain even after discovering blood dripping down his face as the car rested on its side with his door up. He searched his face in the mirror, finding no injury. Infuriated, confused, and suffering heartbreak, he went berserk. He punched his car door, causing it to fly off the hinges as if it was flimsy plastic.

Jack grabbed the doorjamb and launched himself out of the vehicle.

Still hulking in rage, he ran down the street to where his uncle stood. He charged the silhouette, but as he approached, he noticed it was no longer Peter. His shape was now slightly taller, and he smelled of sweat-drenched wool. Tei stood in his place, dressed in a long black trench coat, black cowboy hat, and black boots.

Tei looked up at his charging foe with black eyes, growling with his lips curled back, exposing his dog-like teeth.

Jack pounced at him with his hands out, ready to rip him in half. Tei stepped to the side, pulling a long sword from his coat that glistened as he swung it out of its sheath. In one continuous motion, he slashed the sword across Jack's arm. Blood poured from the gash that cut down to his bone.

Jack saw the attack coming with only enough time to slightly change his trajectory in the air. He grabbed his arm as he crashed to the ground and rolled for cover. He lay for only a moment, the pain ceasing as the injury healed as quickly as his forehead had in the car wreck. He jumped back to his feet, turning to Tei.

Jack bounded at Tei once more, but this time he kept his feet on the ground. As he approached, he raised his huge right hand and came swing down, attempting to squash Tei like a bug under his fist. Tei dodged, rammed his sword through Jack's heart, immediately losing his grip on the haft.

Jack's massive berserker body dropped to the dirt, pushing the sword completely through his chest to protrude from his back. The hilt forced his torso to tilt to the side. Jack's body shrank back to normal size quickly.

Tei, feeling victorious, assumed Jack had simply died, as had any foe he had previously stabbed through the heart. His opponents' deaths allowed him to devour their hearts and take their forms, downloading their memories while he wore their skin. He approached Jack's body with a swagger, then placed his hand on the handle of the sword, pulled it from Jack's chest, and gave his wrist a flick. The blood spattered off the sword all over Jack's tattered white shirt.

Tei raised the sword to the air to sheath it. Jack jumped up from the ground. Grabbing Tei's hand on the sword with both hands, Jack shifted the blade's trajectory and plunged it through Tei's flesh just above his hip. He then kicked him in his chest as hard as he could. Tei's body flew backward through air and crash-landed. The blade, jutting through his body, stuck straight down in the ground. As the rest of Tei's body fell to the dirt, the sword wobbled, almost sliding out. Jack ran to the wounded Tei, ripped the sword from his side, and raised it to cut his head off and avenge Jessi.

Tei kicked Jack back, morphed back into the crow, and flew off, losing only a few feathers as the sword swung down with might and finesse. Jack watched the bird fly off toward town.

Jack flicked the blood off the sword and ran back to the car, still on its side. He climbed into the driver's seat and reached down to the passenger visor, grabbing the garage remote. He then sprinted as fast as he could to his uncle's mansion.

Following the driveway to the garage, he pressed the garage door opener, closing the door behind him as soon as he crossed the threshold. He ran down the ramp to the elevator and rode it to the fifth floor. He crashed through his door, sobbing, dropping the sword against the wall to the right. It wobbled a bit before clattering to the floor. His heart was on fire. He slammed his hands on the wall in front of him, leaving large imprints.

Then he slid his hands up the wall and slammed his forehead against it. As his sobs became tears, he spun himself around and sank to the ground, grabbing his knees and crying uncontrollably. Jessi was dead. He couldn't protect her. The reality ripped through his heart, blasting the image of her lifeless body through his mind. She was gone.

He looked up from his knees and roared, "Why?!" The word came out like thunder. He stretched the vowel for as long as his breath would allow him, rattling the glass windows with his booming voice. He could think of nothing else, not even his own hunger. He wallowed in his misery and confusion until a knock came at his door.

As the midday sun glared through his skylights, Jack wiped the tears from his face and clenched his large teeth, growling; a glance at the hall mirror showed his eyes still black as night. He leaped forward and yanked the door open.

Gavin had propped himself against the doorjamb, appearing battered, his face bruised and a gash on his arm seeping blood. Jack lowered his guard as Gavin fell faint, catching him before Gavin's head could hit the floor.

Jack lifted his body with ease, carrying the unconscious butler to the guest bedroom. After placing him on the bed, he ripped a pillow case apart and wrapped the cloth tightly around the wound. He ran into the bathroom next door, grabbing a roll of gauze, antibacterial ointment, and medical tape. After emptying half of the ointment tube into the laceration, Jack bound the gauze around his arm tightly and wrapped the tape around his arm firmly, creating a cast.

Jack then went to the kitchen and filled a large plastic bag with ice. He returned to Gavin and placed the ice over the worst of his battered face. Gavin began to regain consciousness from the touch of the cold pack. He was moaning and grumbling in an attempt to speak but was still woozy from the massive loss of blood. Jack comforted him, reassuring him that he was there and that he was safe inside the mansion.

"No one is safe. Your uncle is dead," Gavin murmured through the pain.

"I know, I've met the shape-shifter named Tei," Jack said with vengeance flaring in his voice. He remained facing the door with his back to Gavin, who was gently massaging his deformed jaw. "Whatever he is, some of it has gotten inside me, Gavin. You must not fear me. I mean only to destroy him. Jessi will be avenged."

"Why would I fear you? What happened to Jessi?" Gavin asked, confused as he attempted to sit up, allowing curiosity to overcome the excruciating pain. Jack turned around to face him. Gavin's face drained of what little color it held, holding his good arm up in submission.

"Please, no!" he yelped.

"Gavin, I am not going to hurt you. Who do you think wrapped your arm?"

Gavin looked down at his blood-drenched clothes, the bed sheets, and bandaged wounds, wincing in pain. "Thanks, sorry. I just—"

"Can you stand?"

Gavin moved slowly, trying to avoid adding greater pain to his arm and head. He spun himself, allowing his legs to drop from the side of the bed and rocking his body forward.

"Yes, I believe I can."

"I need to drive down to the hotel Jessi and I stayed at the past few nights and collect our belongings. You should ride with me, just in case," Jack said demandingly, but Gavin agreed instantly, not wanting to be left alone. Jack led Gavin back to the garage, checking around every corner.

"Where is your car?" Gavin asked.

"It's in a tree," Jack replied somberly.

"I'm glad to see your memory is coming to," Gavin assumed.

"Unfortunately not. Why do you say that?"

"I'm sorry. I just figured, since you've been driving your own car. Now do us a favor and grab the red key out of the box."

Jack followed his instructions, grabbing a small red rounded box. He pushed a tiny silver button down, and a key flicked out like a switchblade. He pressed the unlock button to locate the vehicle.

The car was in the corner of the garage. Jack hadn't even noticed it yet because it hid behind a truck. He found it now only because its blinking lights reflected off the wall. The car was black with a sleek, sexy design. Each side of the rear had two small circular lights, one slightly bigger than the other, with a chrome emblem of a horse rearing in the center of the trunk. Jack opened the passenger door to assist his wounded butler; he was already seated in the driver's seat, revving the engine by the time Gavin reached the car. Jack looked behind the visor over the passenger seat to reveal another garage remote.

He waited to press the button until Gavin was seated. The garage door made it halfway open just as Gavin's car door had finally closed. Jack dropped his foot on the gas and was once again weaving in and out of traffic with ease.

"I must say, this is quite a bit more exciting than any of the business trips I accompanied Peter on, for the past couple years anyway," he said as he gripped the seat with his uninjured arm.

Jack responded only with a grin, proud of his quick reflexes.

As they drove, Jack asked Gavin question after question, trying to discover more about his life while explaining a bit of his own adventures in the process. Gavin obliged happily since Jack had saved him. When they pulled up to the hotel, Jack parked in the same spot he had parked with Jessi, but didn't move from the car right away. Instead he sat there fighting back tears, dreading entering the room where he had made love to the woman of his dreams that morning, only hours ago. Now she was dead.

Gavin looked at him remorsefully. He fumbled through his jacket pockets taking a swig from a small glass bottle.

"I have something for you. Your uncle seemed bothered several days ago and said that if anything should happen to him, I was to give you this." He pulled out an envelope and handed it to Jack, who took it reluctantly. He was unready to read since his eyes were fogged with the tears he was barely holding back. He stuffed the letter in his pocket to read later.

Jack finally got out, moving quickly into the room, leaving Gavin in the car with locked doors. He grabbed all the clothes from the floor and put them into the bags where they would fit, careful not to ruin any of Jessi's pictures in the duffle bag. Jack returned to the car with the bags, noticing the engine in the back where the trunk had been in his car. Gavin reached across the seat, pulling the lever that popped the front latch. The duffle bag barely fit in the narrow hatch, but the other two bags fit in nicely in front of it. Jack closed the storage and mounted his seat, speeding off back toward Hollow Wood Manor.

The sun had just begun to set as they parked. The light fog was still looming, creating the most vibrant pink and amber sky. When Jack and Gavin returned to the fifth floor, Gavin retreated to the guestroom bed. Jack plopped himself on the couch with Jessi's duffle back between his legs, open. He sifted through the pictures, tears invading his eyes again, but he gritted his teeth so tightly that a sob would not escape. He lifted the most recent picture of Jessi and stared at it while grieving. Finally, he tucked it into a hidden jacket pocket and stood up, feeling the full torment of his heartbreak and failure. He moved toward the front door with his eyes fixated on the blade resting against the wall.

He took up the sword with one hand; the blade was shimmering in the last drop of sunlight coming through the balcony door. The blade had been forged to perfection, a flawless double-edged blade without a knick or scratch in its highly reflective beauty, and not a drop of blood had contested the small whip taken earlier to clean the blade.

The blade was long; the hilt likewise to offset the weight of the blade. The hilt was ebony, and silver bands had be inlaid to create dips for the fingers. Separating the blade from the hilt was the golden head of a bear seeming to eat the blade. Jack wielded the sword in his right hand as if it were weightless, admiring its beauty. At the bottom of the blade, nearest the hilt, intricate markings were carved into the seemingly invincible blade.

Jack carried the sword into the guest room, still admiring the blade.

"Gavin, would you happen to be gifted in many languages?" Jack asked, hoping his uncle had had need of a translator.

"In fact, I am. What have you got there?" Gavin replied, giving Jack hope.

"I took this sword from the man who calls himself Tei. There is some kind of writing here, but I don't know what it is." Jack gestured to the blade as he handed it to Gavin for further inspection.

"Hmm, I should have known if you couldn't read it, I wouldn't be able to, young master. I have been your teacher since you were merely eleven. You should have most of my knowledge of languages," Gavin said, as he admired the blade's craftsmanship, studying every detail.

"You mean you raised me?" Jack said, compelled and confused.

"Your memory has truly failed you. Your uncle felt it was best to protect your identity, and his, so he preferred you did not attend normal schools. Since he was always working, for many years, you accompanied him on each trip as I drove him and waited on his needs. While he worked, I schooled you in the many languages, histories, and cultures of the world. You were extremely adept at mathematics but slept through American history. Now, it is time for me to be your teacher once more."

"What do you mean?" Jack asked impatiently, with a hint of arrogance.

"If you are to wield this blade properly, you will need a refresher in self-defense and fencing, should you be faced by an armed Tei again."

Jack thought this wouldn't be fair to Gavin as he had an extraordinary strength and quickness that even Tei was unable to best, but Jack complied and followed Gavin to the elevator.

Once inside the elevator, Gavin reached into his pocket and pulled out a key. He stuck it into a lock embedded in the elevator's panel under the floor-select buttons. He twisted the key with one hand and pressed B with the other.

"We're going to the basement?"

"No, we are going to the Base," Gavin said through a crooked smile, his eyes narrowed.

The Base? Jack thought to himself, allowing the confusion to fill his face.

The elevator descended quickly as usual, but when it stopped, the doors didn't open. Gavin grasped the railing in the elevator and said, "You might want to hold on, young master."

The elevator took off backward, horizontally, with great speed. Jack stumbled forward, bouncing against the door. When he finally caught his balance, he pushed himself off the door against the elevator's inertia. He reached for the railing, pulling himself along it to the back wall next to Gavin.

"You weren't joking," Jack said, dazed as the elevator continued rushing. It began to slow, coming to a complete stop. The doors opened.

Chapter XII

Not Your Ordinary Butler

Jack peered out and stepped forward into a large open room. The floors were a dark hardwood with a thick glossy varnish. Along the walls of the vast room hung suits of armor and weapons of ancient samurai, medieval knights, modern soldiers, and many that seemed of another world. Gavin stepped out of the elevator behind Jack, smiling as he gazed around the room.

"I can't tell you how many hours your uncle and I have spent crossing swords in this room," Gavin said as he walked past Jack, still looking around.

Gavin walked across the entire room until he stood facing the only empty space on the wall, directly opposite the elevator. He placed his hand on the hilt of a sword hanging on the wall to the left of the empty section and pulled it down, then placed both hands on the wall, pushing it in with all his might. The wall gave way, moving forward only an inch. Gavin stepped back as the door slid itself into the framework of the wall to the right, revealing a hidden room, much smaller than the first.

Jack followed Gavin, watching as he lifted a blade from a small wooden rack. The floor in this room was padded, and the walls were mirrors. Gavin turned and handed Jack the sword he had acquired from Tei in battle. He gestured for him to stay put while he exited the small room and hung the sword he had just removed from the rack out on the wall in the massive room.

"To begin your training, Jack, you must first place the sword on this rack. You will meditate on the blade and make yourself its master."

Jack obeyed without understanding. He placed the sword on the rack next to Gavin's and knelt on the padded floor. Gavin knelt next to him, bowing to the sword propped up in front of him. Jack did likewise.

"You must forget all of your pain. Find calm within your heart. You must allow the sword to see that you are worthy and faithful," Gavin said softly with his hands pressed together flat in front of his heart and his eyes closed. "You must feel the sword's presence and allow it to fill you with its history, with its power, with its soul."

"My sword has a soul?" Jack asked, slightly tilting his head to the side with confusion.

"Every sword made by a passionate blacksmith has a soul of its own. The samurai believed men were not born with souls but earned them. When a man had earned his soul as part of the tribe, he was given a sword. They believed this sword was their very soul, and they were right, partially," Gavin explained. "Every living being is born with a soul, as is every great weapon forged from the sweat and work of a man's hand. No warrior can become stronger than when he melds his soul with the soul of a weapon earned. You won this sword in battle, making it rightfully yours, and now you must become one with it. Now stop talking and be still. Try to listen for the sword's voice." Gavin turned back to his sword, which he greeted as an old friend.

Jack sat on his feet, kneeling before his sword with his eyes closed, his hands placed firmly together. He tried to calm his mind, but images of the early morning flooded him with pain. The sword lay silent. Gavin began to hum and chant syllables on a low, steady tone, intending to help Jack's mind relax. Jack unknowingly grunting in pain from the visions his mind cast.

The chant began taking over Jack's mind, making his head swim. His mind slowly darkened as the images began to fade. Soon Jack's mind sat in complete darkness as he focused on the mesmerizing chant. Without meaning to, he had sorted the rhythm and pattern to the chant and was humming in with perfect unison with Gavin.

They sat lost in their chanting trance for what felt like only minutes to Jack, but hours had passed on the clock above the door. Jack stopped the chant. Though his eyes remained closed, he could no longer hear Gavin chanting either. A woman's delicate voice entered Jack's mind. It was the sword, speaking in a language he didn't understand. The only thing that stuck in his mind was the first chant of the woman's voice in his head saying *Sireth Jessoteth* repeatedly.

Jack opened his eyes and looked directly at the sword that lay before him. He whispered, "*Sireth Jessoteth.*" The sword began to emit light from within; blue canvassed the room, startling Gavin. He opened his eyes to look at Jack, who slowly moved his hands to the blade lying on the rack.

Jack's hand wrapped around the hilt as the light dimmed in the room, though the sword still glowed. The light traveled into his hand and up his arm. Jack's eyes became black again as the light traveled to his chest, spreading throughout his body in all directions. As the light covered his heart and neck, Jack began chanting, "*Sireth Jessoteth.*" He placed his other hand on the hilt, lifting the blade vertically before him with outstretched arms. The air began to spin around his body as the blue light spread to his neck and up his chin. When it reached his mouth he roared, and his body levitated beside Gavin. Then the light passed over Jack's blackened eyes, forcing the black to retreat, and his eyes began emitting blue light, causing excruciating pain. He roared, exposing his enlarged teeth once more.

The light then imploded to Jack's heart as he collapsed to the ground from the few feet in the air. Jack looked down to the sword in his hands and felt the bond. "*Sireth Jessoteth,*" he whispered again as he caressed the blade that emitted the blue rays in response to his fingertips. Gavin placed his hand on Jack's shoulder, capturing his attention. When Jack turned his head, Gavin was visibly startled. The blue light still cloaked Jack's eyes completely.

"I can see your fear, Gavin," Jack said smiling, feeling the power of the sword coarse through him like electricity. "Do not fear me, my dear friend," he said kindly.

"Your eyes went black again, and now they are a blue light. Of all the magic I have seen, I have never seen such a bond with a human," Gavin said.

"With a human?"

"In a place that cannot be reached by any vehicle made by man, where magic was born, there are man-like beings that created all magic, called the Álfar. Only the Álfar have ever been so connected with elements of their world," Gavin said, staring at the sword in Jack's hand. "The writing on the blade is that of the Álfar, a language unknown to me, as I have only spent days with the Elvin culture far from their homeland. The few I met spoke in our tongue as they are far superior to us."

"You mean to tell me there are uncharted places on Earth?"

"Theirs is a land not of Earth, but of Farion. Your uncle had found a way to travel between dimensions, and with his will to do good, a great fortune was thrust upon him by those whom he helped. Master Jack, I believe it is time for you to read your uncle's letter."

Jack reached into the inner pocket of his jacket and pulled the sealed envelope from within. Upon doing so, a picture of Jessi fell out. He watched as the photo fluttered to the floor before him. It filled him with sadness. He quickly placed the picture back in the same pocket, fighting back his emotions. Jack carefully tore the envelope open. He pulled the letter out and unfolded it to begin reading:

Dear Jack,
Throughout my long life, I have helped thousands of people and creatures who stood for greatness and peace in our lands and others. I truly hope you read this with the utmost intention to believe and understand.

You have been living with me since you were only an infant, and my faithful friend Gavin and I watched over you with great pride as you grew into a strong man. Now it is time for you to know the truth of who you are. I wish I could be telling you this in person, but in a few short hours I believe an assassin to be coming for me as my most coveted creation has been stolen by our greatest foe, Teiwaz.

You come from deep within the Farion woods, the son of a spirit guide, the majestic bear, and an ancient Álfar woman. Teiwaz has since slain them both. He has stolen your father's blade, Sireth Jessoteth, *crafted by magic with metals unknown to Earth. It is of the utmost importance that you recover this blade as your own, as it is your destiny to wield your true father's blade.*

Before your parents were murdered by Teiwaz, they used their magic to make you mortal and human, with no power or magic, so you could grow as a humble man. I vowed to the bear spirit who guided me to victory for centuries of their time, and to your mother, who granted me eternal life from sickness and age, that I would care for you and love you as my own kin, and so I have.

Please, confide in Gavin, as he is the only family I have left aside from you. I raised him from a boy and employed him from the age of eighteen to be my butler, but in truth, he has been my greatest ally and my dearest friend through the course of his life. Now he will be your greatest ally in the battles to come.

You must be strong. You must be cautious. And please know that my love will be with you always.

Sincerely,
Peter

As Jack read the letter, he wished his memory served him better so he could know the man who wrote such words of passion and wisdom for him. His eyes swelled as he turned to Gavin. "Have you read this?" he handed the letter to Gavin for his review.

"No, Master Jack, Peter gave it to me week before last and told me to give it to you should the worst happen, and so I have," Gavin replied with only honesty and devotion in his eyes as he began to read the last thoughts of his beloved master.

"Will you teach me how to fight?" Jack asked humbly.

"I thought you'd never ask, young master."

Jack and Gavin reentered the large museum-like room and stood within ten feet of each other. Gavin stood strong and sturdy, grasping the hilt of his sword with both hands and with the tip of his blade pointing to the ground just behind him.

"Come, attack me," Gavin said confidently.

Jack closed his eyes for a moment. The energy of his sword surged through his body. His eyes opened as he obeyed the order, lifting the sword above his head as he began to charge. Gavin ripped his sword up underhand and knocked Jack's sword away from him, slapping his sword on Jack's head with the side of his blade.

"You just died, young master." Jack charged back at him in a similar manner, and he easily repeated the same move a second time.

"You're dead again," Gavin said, chuckling at Jack's novice approach. "You must let go of your rage until you have the mind to use it. Use your mind to feel the area around you. Let your sword speak through your swing. Stop trying to be strong and start trying to be water."

"Be like water, right," Jack said, trying to be mindful, imagining how water would fight. He stepped back from Gavin as he readied his sword once more and closed his eyes. The image of Jessi walking in her high heels with such grace entered his mind. Suddenly she was walking across stones through a river, watching each step she took. She looked up directly at Jack, and his heart nearly stopped as it melted.

"I love you, Jack. You must love *Sireth* as you loved me," Jessi said in her sweet voice that Jack missed intensely.

"I let you die. I wasn't strong enough to protect you, Jessi," he spoke back to her in his daydream, the words echoing in his head and out loud for Gavin to hear his inner turmoil.

"It's not your fault, Jack," she said softly. "Tei is strong, and you did not know your foe or your strength. You must let me be at peace, and you will become the greatest hero of all of Earth's history. I have seen it."

"He's too strong, and I feel weak without you," Jack protested.

"You and Tei have much in common, but you have two things he will never know. He is merely a copy of the man he truly is, so he lacks humanity. He is corrupt and evil and does not know compassion or love. You loved me, Jack. Now let the river take you. Follow the current, Jack," she said as she walked across the stones of the river in his mind, slowly fading away.

"Wait, Jessi! I don't understand! Merely a copy? Please don't go, I have so many questions," he exclaimed.

Her voice echoed one last whisper through the vision. "Follow the current. Let yourself fall in love with her. *Sireth Jessoteth. Sireth Jessoteth.*" The words vanished.

Jack stood at the edge of the river watching the water roll through the rocks, unstoppable and smooth. He stepped into the stream, becoming one with it as his mind kicked him back to reality, standing before Gavin.

Jack drew a deep breath through his nose. He exhaled, moving the sword, which seemed weightless. The power of the sword directed the blade with momentum. Gavin raised his sword, blocking blow after blow with no time to take the offensive. Gavin folded, panting heavily and staring at the clock as Jack still bounced in his ready stance.

Jack's face was as calm as if he were sitting on the dock watching the water while Jessi worked. His motion became fluid. His strikes each came with great power, knocking Gavin back, an expert swordsman, forcing him to retreat. His back hit the wall, and Jack lifted his sword, preparing for a kill strike.

"My lord! You're a fast learner!" Gavin screeched, waking Jack from the trance he had fallen into as he danced with his sword. He held the sword up with one hand, admiring it as it radiated the blue light that reminded him of Jessi's eyes. He smiled, remembering the vision.

"That Jessi of yours seems to give you great power, young master Jack. I could hear your words as you spoke to her, and whatever she said seems to have been sound advice."

"Tei murdered her this very morning, but the vision felt so real, like I could reach out and touch her. I miss her, Gavin," Jack said, beginning to whimper. Just then Gavin pushed him away and drew his sword and took a swing at Jack's exposed neck. In a flash, Jack's blade came up, blocking the attack and deflecting it to the side.

"Gavin, I've had enough! Allow me to grieve!"

"Do you think Tei will wait for your sobbing?" Gavin yelled back at him, taking a jab for his heart.

Jack lifted his hand high with the blade pointing to the ground and spun himself fully around, knocking Gavin's blade back.

"Do you think your opponent cares for anything other than power and control?" Gavin continued, advancing another attack blocked by Jack. "Tei does not fight for love." Gavin now struck out every few words, with Jack blocking. "He does not fight for freedom or peace!" The swords clashed. "He fights for dominion, to conquer all, and devour all." This time Gavin brought his sword straight down. Jack caught it with a horizontal blade, forcing him to one knee.

Jack's mind filled with the words Gavin spoke, analyzing and absorbing as much information as he could. He allowed enough rage into his heart to gain his strength. His eyes darkened but remained solid blue. He jolted his hands up, tossing Gavin's sword upward. Jack sprung up, his feet leaving the ground as he swung the sword straight down, mirroring Gavin's last attack. Gavin got his sword up for the block in time, but Jack's force was too great. Gavin's sword ripped from his hands and the tip dug into the floor half of the length of the blade.

Gavin simply stared up at him, "This is astonishing," he said as he fought to catch his breath again "We have been dueling for eight hours, nonstop, and you have already made such great improvements. Your connection with that sword is deep. You were never a fast learner," he teased.

The passage of time seemed much less to Jack in his extreme focus and connection to the soul of his sword through the vision that helped teach him the meaning of serenity.

Chapter XIII

History with a Side of Spaghetti

Gavin attempted to pull his sword from the ground where it stuck but lacked the strength. Though he had just proven his strength, it wasn't enough to dislodge the sword. Jack rested his hand on his shoulder. Gavin stepped away, looking at him wearily. Jack, with his sword in his left hand, placed his right hand on the hilt of Gavin's sword, lifting it from the floor with ease. Jack let the blade dangle as he handed it back to him. Gavin knelt before Jack, bowing his head as he reached up to receive his sword. "I'm afraid there is little else I can teach you about swordplay, Jack. Your muscles have clearly not been affected by your memory loss, and they picked up a few tricks along the way, as you have in many of your lessons in life," Gavin said in an apologetic tone, regretting his resentment toward Jack for being so naturally gifted. As usual, Gavin had begun the lesson and Jack had finished it, eventually becoming the master of every topic Gavin taught him. "You will truly become the greatest hero of our realm if you choose to fight for love and not for personal gain, young master."

"Of our realm?" Jack asked eagerly.

"Yes, you were born of a different realm, which is full of magic and wondrous creatures beyond Earth's capacity for understanding, and you have somehow reversed the magic your parents' cast to make you mortal. You fight with their power inside you. You are ready to help this realm, but your home realm is another story, and you won't be ready to see your home until Tei is defeated here," Gavin explained, carefully to not overwhelm him. "We should retire to the main floor. In Peter's study you will find journals and artifacts that tell the epic tale of your uncle's life."

Jack and Gavin went back to the secret room, placing their weapons on the rack, closing the hidden door after them. Once they were on the elevator, Gavin twisted his key and pressed the number one. The elevator took off horizontally, but Jack had readied his stance for the abrupt departure. When the doors opened, they were at the end of the first-floor hall beneath Jack's living quarters. They proceeded down the hallway toward the entryway, turning to their left through a door.

They walked through a series of hallways with numbered doors. Jack mumbled under his breath, repeating the numbers in the order they entered through them so he would be able to find his way back. Finally, after several minutes of walking through many hallways, they entered a door into an immense library with a large oak desk at the back, submerged in papers and maps.

Jack stood in awe as he looked up and around the entire study. Towering shelves filled with books of all languages lined every wall from floor to ceiling. Two ladders were attached to the shelves on either wall. Gavin pointed Jack in the direction of the desk as he began to adjust and climb a ladder for specific books strewn throughout the library to conceal their true worth. In a few minutes he brought a dozen volumes to the desk and began unfolding Jack's past with him. Jack sat down at the desk and began perusing maps of the land of Farion and those of Earth with small triangle markings here and there on each map.

"You see," Gavin said, pointing to a map in front of Jack, "The triangles were the best places to use Peter's teleporting device, though it has been a few years since Peter and I had traveled by such means. Peter's device had broken upon on our last reentry to Earth, and Teiwaz stole the remaining functional device."

"Wait, so that's how Tei got here? He stole one of my uncle's teleport devices?" Jack said, intrigued to hear the rest of this story.

"Ah yes," he sighed. "On our final visit to Farion, Tei tricked us, gaining important maps we were creating while exploring the region and the teleport device we had traveled there with. Luckily, Peter had hidden a spare, in case the worst should happen."

"No one ever tried to take it back?"

"Unfortunately, we were unprepared for battle, thinking it was best to retreat and return physically and mentally prepared for the fight. But we were forced to teleport from a weaker spot, and the teleport device was destroyed once we returned. Peter was hopeful that he would find a way back to Farion to get the device back before Tei figured out how to use them and the maps together," Gavin said as he picked up some books and walked off, somberly.

"And we've seen how that ended," Jack said as he began to flip through more and more papers on the desk.

It wasn't until his stomach began to rumble audibly that he looked around again. Gavin offered to make him dinner as it was late. They had been dueling well into the night and had already spent a few hours exploring the study. Jack declined his offer, suggesting they take materials and retire to the kitchen together. He smiled, happy to see Jack had turned out to be as kindhearted as Peter had always been to him throughout his life of servitude.

Gavin suggested some useful material that wasn't too sensitive to remove from the well-hidden study. They gathered two books and a map of Earth with secret markings. The key to understanding the secrets of the map resided in Gavin's mind only, as Peter had died never trusting another soul on Earth. Gavin recited the key to the map as they walked through the maze of hallways. Jack never took his eyes off the map, completely unaware of the doors they passed through, unlike his previous venture to the study. He navigated from the mere sound of Gavin's footsteps and voice.

Jack felt confident he had the map's key memorized as they approached the kitchen on the opposite side of the first floor's main hallway. Gavin stepped through the door as Jack paused for a moment, reviewing something on the map. Then he folded the map, concealing it in his inner jacket pocket opposite Jessi's photograph. Gavin stood by the sink washing tomatoes when he looked back at Jack in the doorway.

"Do you like spaghetti?" he asked, smiling.

"Actually, I can't stomach anything but meat," Jack confessed, hoping not to frighten Gavin the way he had Jessi.

"Okay, well I like spaghetti with chunks of beef, and we have plenty of beef to go around. How much do you suppose you'd eat?"

"At least a pound," Jack answered, recalling his past few meals.

"Okay, two pounds it is!" Gavin pulled meat out of the freezer and placed it in the microwave to defrost. Gavin continued peeling the skin from tomatoes and mashing them into a sauce, adding spices as he went. When the microwave beeped, signaling the food had finished thawing, he pulled the packs of meat out and opened them. He dumped all the meat out on a large cutting board. As he turned to get a knife from the drawer behind him, Jack approached his side.

The smell of the raw meat seized Jack's nostrils. Snarling, he picked up a slab of uncooked beef. Biting into it, his incisors grew once again, tearing through it easily. His bones cracked and crunched as they expanded in his mouth.

Gavin spun around with the knife in his hand; the sound triggered Gavin's most faithful instinct, that which had kept him alive for his years traveling with Peter—slay the monster quick. Without conscious thought, Gavin stabbed his knife through the back of Jack's shoulder.

Jack roared like a ferocious beast, glaring with agony at Gavin as he caught his breath from the pain. "How many times do I have to ask you not to fear me?" he asked, releasing his chunk of meat with one hand to remove the knife from his shoulder and toss it in the sink to his left, returning to eat as if nothing had happened.

"I'm sorry, so sorry, Master Jack!" Gavin said in shock. "I thought you were Tei! The sound your bones resonates is so—familiar," he trailed off as he tried to gather first aid throughout the kitchen, mumbling, "And it's been a long week."

Gavin watched as the wound closed, leaving behind only the blood that had already dripped.

"You're immortal, Master Jack!" he exclaimed. "Only immortals can heal in such a manner."

"Please, Gavin, just call me Jack," he replied, ignoring the comment as he picked up another piece of raw beef, growling in satisfaction.

"Jack, when did this happen? I mean, when was the last time you were injured and it didn't heal?"

"I don't know," Jack said between bites. "I was hoping you could tell me. I still don't remember beyond a week ago."

"As a boy you would come inside with scrapes and bruises; you even broke your arm once falling out of a tree." Gavin knitted his brows, clearly deep in thought. "About a week or so ago, Peter showed up here, ringing the doorbell. I had thought he was still in bed. He was acting strange and then made me take him all the way down to Main Street. He said he was looking for someone, but he didn't say who. I don't believe he ever found the person he was looking for because he had me bring him home eventually." Gavin paused a moment, piecing the rest of that day together. "When we arrived you were outside waiting for us with Jessi, and Peter went back to bed in the middle of the afternoon, which is also unlike him. Was it Tei I had been driving for days? We drove from town to town in search of something. He was very vague on details. We stopped inside small diners and shops, unusual for Peter, but I didn't question." Gavin began to gasp for breath in disbelief that he hadn't recognized that his own friend, father figure, employer hadn't been himself until the imposter attacked him.

"Gavin, it was Tei who put the gash in your arm, wasn't it?" Jack asked, concerned, as Gavin got back to creating spaghetti sauce.

Gavin retraced the morning's events somberly. "Yes, I saw him change from the Hellhound to Peter. I attempted to retreat to the car, but he transformed into the dog as he charged me, taking a bite of my arm as I struggled to close the door. It closed on the beast's head, knocking it back enough for me to get away."

"How is it your arm healed so quickly?" Jack asked, beginning to wonder if Gavin was still Gavin. He had just realized that he had left Gavin alone in the car back at the hotel. What if Tei had transformed into Gavin and had been following him around all day to learn more about him?

"Health potions, my boy. One thing your uncle always brought back from Farion. Plenty of ingredients only found there," Gavin answered quickly. He sounded truthful and natural as he spoke. Jack began to relax, realizing his paranoia.

Gavin continued cooking his sauce and took the second pound of beef away from Jack so he didn't devour that too. As the sauce simmered, he chopped the beef into smaller, bite-size chunks, tossing them in the frying pan. The room had gone quiet for a few minutes as Gavin focused on his sauce and Jack stressed his mind for more questions for Gavin.

"Gavin, how does he do it? Are there a lot of shape-shifters in Farion?"

"Shape-shifters, yes, but they can only turn themselves into an animal using concentrated magic after years of practice and study with the Álfar. Tei is the only one I know of in the past hundred years who has become a spirit walker," Gavin answered, forgetting his food for a moment to stare at the ceiling. It seemed as though he was reminiscing, anticipating more questions from his inquisitive student.

"Spirit walker?"

"Listen, Jack. In Farion, two massive dimensions coexist. There is the living realm and the spirit realm. There have been a few who could walk in both and communicate on both sides. They called themselves realm seekers. Your father was the keeper of the dead, so to speak, or the guardian of the spirit realm. The spirit realm is a peaceful place, mostly. If a spirit was troubled, your father would restore balance, knowing that if one realm fell, they both would fall. Your mother was an enlightened elder who was able to walk in both realms. Although she had no obligation to the spirits, as did your father, she was a kind soul, and they would speak to her, show her things to which the living are not granted access. Since the Álfar could not die of natural causes or old age, she used her gift to help her people and many others throughout her long life."

Jack listened intently, absorbing every detail Gavin revealed, trying to bridge the gaps between everything he had experienced during this chaotic day.

"So Tei is one of these realm seekers?"

"Not exactly. One must be born with the gift or take it from one so born. Tei took it from two. First, your mother; Tei had slain her to lure your father into his trap. Once he had acquired your mother's abilities, your father attempted to avenge her only to die also. Your parents sensed that Tei would be coming since he had slaughtered many innocent people who crossed over to your father's domain in distress.

"Peter explained to me that Teiwaz had found a rare black magic that allowed him to control the bodies of those he killed, and after decades of conjuring he mastered it. He quickly became power hungry. When souls began arriving with no bodies, just clouds of light, your parents, in their wisdom, made you mortal and sent you home with Peter to be raised by one of their most trusted friends, far away from Teiwaz and your magical destiny. Unfortunately, they were unable to defeat him. After their deaths, Teiwaz perfected and practiced his new abilities. He eventually discovered that if he ate the hearts of his victims, he could rip a hole in the spirit realm, keeping the souls to himself so he could conjure their bodies to live again with his mind while absorbing the spirits' memories. Dark times befell Farion from the imbalance left in the wake of your parents' murder, but you must save Earth from Tei before you can even think about a day in Farion."

"Is it possible to make a double of yourself? Earlier when I saw Jessi in my dream, she told me he and I would always be different because he was only a copy of the man he truly is and because he will never know love."

"She said that?" Gavin asked surprised.

"Yes. She also said I would be the greatest hero in all of Earth's history. That she had seen it."

"You are full of surprises, aren't you?" Gavin said with a grin. "I should have you try reading a few scrolls during tomorrow's training. It sounds like you might have been realm seeking within Earth's spirit world. You are lucky to have someone who loves you on the other side as your mother did. But I must warn you, it's very dangerous on Earth, and, yes, there are spells to create a double, but you need to steal someone's body to do so, meaning you must commit murder," Gavin warned.

"What do you mean it's dangerous here?"

"Earth is also made of two realms, but the spirit guardian here is much more fickle. Some spirits he burns for all eternity and others he allows into his kingdom, where he rules with an iron fist. If he catches you in the spirit realm, you may end up stuck there until you defeat him, and he is nearly the oldest of all spirits known in both Earth and Farion."

"You mean the devil?" Jack asked with a sarcastic chuckle.

"That is his most common title, and, if we are lucky, he may destroy Tei for robbing him of souls. But even if he does, I believe your Jessi was right—we would only be free of a double, a clone, and you would lack the experience of defeating him yourself."

Jack had it settled in his mind; he would carry out his quest, his destiny. He would spend as much time as Tei allowed him to prepare for his battle. For now he and Gavin needed rest. He wrestled with the influx of knowledge bombarding his mind, and for the first time in the past several days he was grateful he had no other memories adding to his thoughts.

Once Gavin sat down, the meal finally prepared, Jack stood up from the table. "I think I should try to get some sleep, Gavin. Thank you for everything today."

"Jack." Gavin twisted the spaghetti noodles on his fork. "Perhaps we would be safest to sleep in the sparring hall tonight. It's nearly impossible to infiltrate, and there are a couple cots down there, if it's all the same to you."

"As you wish, Gavin, you are the one with experience in such times as these. Would you consider bringing your dinner? I am extremely tired." Jack yawned. It had been an emotionally draining day, losing Jessi. She had been his best and only friend until Gavin, who at first seemed to loathe him but now was coming around.

Gavin stood up from his seat, turning toward the cabinets to find a bowl with a lid. He dumped the spaghetti into the bowl and sealed it shut with his fork inside. He stacked a few napkins and signaled for Jack to assist him in carrying his meal. He poured a glass of milk, offering one to Jack, who declined as he wasn't sure if he could stomach even milk. Instead, Jack requested a bottle of wine, though the alcohol did not affect him as it did most men. Gavin obliged the request, handing him a bottle of merlot and a corkscrew.

Gavin picked up his meal while Jack quickly scooped up the papers and the map. Gavin led the way back to the elevator with only light-hearted chatting for the duration. Jack truly appreciated the company of the man. In the elevator, Jack held on to the back railing tightly while Gavin braced his back against the door so he could prevent the glass of milk from spilling.

"Thank goodness for lids!" Gavin said as the spaghetti rose up the side of the bowl when the elevator took off horizontally. They both smiled at each other, their friendship blossoming.

When they reached the large training room, Gavin directed Jack to the cots, then sat on the floor with his legs crossed, erect with perfect posture, and began to eat his meal. Jack brought the cots to the secret door, pulling the sword hilt to the left of the door and pushing the wall with his elbow to avoid setting down his bottle or the two cots in his other hand. The door slid with ease, unlike when Gavin struggled with all his might to open it. Jack entered the secret room and rested the bottle of wine on the floor out of the way so he could set up the two cots, each in front of their respective swords.

Jack sat on the side of the cot, lifting the bottle and pulling the corkscrew from his pocket. As he uncorked the bottle, he hollered into the large room, "Gavin, the cots are set, would you be keen to share a glass of wine before bed?"

"Ah, that sounds splendid, actually," Gavin replied, chugging the rest of the milk from his glass. He then picked up his bowl and joined Jack, closing the secret door behind him.

"Just in case," he said as the door shut.

Jack and Gavin shared the bottle and a few good laughs before they fell asleep in their cots. Jack was happy to have someone to talk to, especially to have someone who knew about his past and could understand the changes he was experiencing. Gavin was happy to finally see the young boy he had helped raise on the path to returning home.

Chapter XIV

Testament of Will

The next morning a loud scratching sound and violent banging woke Jack with a start. He sat up in the cot, struggling to make sense of the sound. Then he looked over at the other cot to realize it was empty. Jack sprung to his feet, pulled the lever on the back of the secret door, and waited impatiently as it opened.

Gavin was standing with his ear pressed against the elevator door, his sword in hand. He looked back to see Jack and whispered, "Jack, get your blade and close the door."

Clearly Gavin was alarmed. Jack complied without hesitation. Within a few seconds, Jack had the magnificent glowing sword in his hand, and he stood beside Gavin while the door was still sliding to a close. Now with his own ear to the elevator door, Jack could hear the scurrying sound and scratching much clearer. The pounding sounds had ceased for the moment, although a faint audible ruckus, that of thousands of nails pinging and clamoring against the elevator shaft, drew closer and closer.

"What is it?" Jack whispered quietly.

"Scout soldiers of Tei's, I think," Gavin whispered, turning back toward the door with a scared but focused look. "I hope I'm wrong."

The sound came to the other side of the door before suddenly becoming silent. After a moment of stillness, the sound of many growls and snarls sounded off in unison just beyond the threshold, spreading for what seemed to be a long distance behind the door as well. A sudden slam came upon the elevator. Jack and Gavin both leaped back, readying their swords. The doors shuddered as whatever was behind them slammed against them. Jack looked at Gavin, feeling the moment of battle approach.

"Jack, you must settle your heart and let your sword be light. If I'm correct, what's about to come through those doors looks frightening enough to freeze anyone in fear. You must keep your wits and take their heads, or they will not die."

"Could we not hide in the secret room?" Jack inquired in a trembling whisper.

"They can already smell us. Our flesh to them is like the beef you smelled last night. There is a chance they may retreat if you hide and I stand and fight," Gavin said gesturing for Jack to flee back to the room.

"I will not hide and cower while you die for me." Jack raised his sword as the rage filled him. He whispered *Sireth Jessoteth* repeatedly with his eyes closed. The sword's blue light brightened, illuminating the entire room. The atmosphere in the room was flowing with energy; he could sense the surge of magic that would be battling with them.

Jack's eyes opened in time to see long, discolored fingers prying open the sliding doors by inches. Both men stood watching the creatures attempt to rip through the doors, their mouths snapping and gnawing as they drooled over each other to the smell of living flesh they craved.

Gavin stepped back to establish his footing as the door opened enough for the torso of one of the creatures to push through. Jack lifted his sword, swinging it down through the crack of the door straight to the ground. The blue light exploded through the elevator shaft, knocking hundreds of slim, undead bodies back and cutting the first to emerge in half. The two halves crumpled in their gore, propping the door open six inches.

Blood-curdling screams filled the shaft as the creatures got back on their feet, some walking upright and some on all fours. They rushed the door, sticking their arms through the large crack, trying to grab at Jack. He swung his sword up under their arms, lopping them clean off.

Gavin, still behind Jack's frontline position, called to Jack over the screams, "Hold your hand out! Imagine emitting lightning, or punch the ground and see your foes repulsed!"

Jack drew in a breath and grasped the sword with both hands. He held it straight above his head before slamming it to the ground with all his force. The blade sliced through multiple creatures with a single swing, and when his sword struck the floor, wind escaped through his chest at an unearthly speed, focused through the opening of the door. The body parts piled in front of the door, along with all the creatures against it, flew backward and much further down the shaft than from the first explosion from his sword, allowing the doors to shut completely.

"Whoa!" Jack exclaimed as he stroked back his hair, which stood in all directions from the wind.

"Yeah!" Gavin screamed, delighted. "I knew your father wouldn't leave you completely unprotected!"

"That was a new one," Jack replied, exhilarated.

"Given the traits of your sword, I'd say your father asked it to awaken your true power as an Álfar."

"Anything else I should try?" Jack asked as the sound of the creatures returned to the door rapidly.

"Whatever you do, do not think of using fire. Your uncle learned the undead are immune, but this house is not! Magic may be of little use. Removing the head is all that comes to mind."

"Okay, good to know. Any more tips?"

"Yes, don't die!" Gavin yelled with a smile, preparing his sword again as undead fingers protruded through the crack between the sliding elevator doors once again.

Jack looked back toward Gavin as he pointed his illuminated sword to the elevator button that would open the doors. Gavin gripped his sword and nodded. Jack allowed the tip of his blade to push the button, and the doors opened. The elevator had been mostly destroyed since the disgusting beasts had ripped open the back wall in pursuit of their fresh flesh. Jack began swinging his sword from left to right, cutting his foes in half. Legs toppled to the ground while undead innards oozed from torsos crawling on the ground, still hoping for one bite of fresh meat. Gavin followed Jack closely, quickly decapitating the crawling bodies. Jack's eyes began to emit blue light, his sword moving so fast a visible blue streak lingered with each swing.

Jack entered his place of tranquility, meditating on the fluid motion of water as he fought. His sword swung all around him with perfection. Gavin continued cutting the heads off any bodies that remained moving.

Hundreds of undead began scaling the walls and ceiling, entering from all possible angles relentlessly. Jack retreated under them, holding the palm of his hand out toward their distorted bodies. He pulled his rage from his heart, pushing it vehemently through his fingertips. Lightning ripped out of his hand, striking one of the creatures down. Electricity pulsated through its body as it seized on the ground. The current was so strong it jumped to the surrounding undead creatures, causing them to drop to the ground in electric shock. While his enemies were stunned, Jack dragged his blade across the floor, separating the heads from bodies, rendering them motionless.

As he was feeling a sense of accomplishment, Gavin yelped from behind. Jack glanced back to see an undead creature latched to Gavin, who was using all of his might to keep it from eating through his neck.

"Gavin!" Jack ran toward him.

Jack's sword swung clean through the creature's neck, and its body fell limp on top of Gavin. Blood spewed from the bite on his neck as Gavin attempted to keep it pressurized.

"Jack, you must keep fighting!" he tried to shout, but the blood gurgled in his throat.

The rage became stronger in Jack's heart. His eyes darkened, emitting a black light with a blue hue still radiating around it. His teeth grew as his bones began cracking and jolting from within his body and his legs and arms grew longer. The muscle generated around the extended bones and burst through his clothes.

One of the creatures jumped at Jack as he morphed into his berserker form. In defense he kicked forward. His foot mashed the creature's skull, descending through its body well into its torso. Jack stood up straight, releasing a thunderous roar that shook the walls. He kicked again, flipping the body from his foot at several approaching creatures, causing them to stumble. Jack stared at Gavin, who lay motionless on the ground. He lunged for Gavin's sword and charged the oncoming army of agile, flesh-craving creatures, stomping the heads of any that fell, crushing them under his enormous feet. He easily swung both swords side to side with incomparable speed. He ran into the elevator cart and jumped out of the backside that had been forcibly removed into the shaft, clearing dozens and dozens of creatures in fury as they mindlessly attacked him.

Jack was becoming weary, losing the focus of his rage. A few undead scampered along the ceiling and dropped down behind him. They charged his unprotected back in an attempt to knock him over but were unsuccessful. Jack swung a sword over his shoulder through one of the creatures with such force he pierced his own back. He roared again in agony as he removed the blade, spinning his body while swinging the sword in a circle around him to knock the creatures down. He punched the ground as hard as he could, causing the floor of the shaft to crack open. The force wave blasted the creatures back vigorously, splattering them against the walls. It seemed he had finally won the battle.

The walls were painted with the fluids and parts of the undead creatures he had so powerfully destroyed. Once he determined no more viable enemy threats remained, he sprinted back to

Gavin's side. He slid on his knees as he approached him, scooping him up into his arms. Gavin's hand fell limp from his neck, revealing the bite marks. Jack began weeping as he attempted to keep his composure. He had to hold back his aggression so he didn't mistakenly bring the whole house down.

But then something happened, a miracle it seemed. The wounds in Gavin's neck began to slowly heal. First the swollen redness around the puncture disappeared, and then the markings vanished without even a scar. All that remained was the dried blood staining Gavin's skin and clothing. Jack stood up with ease, still cradling his friend. Just as he began to walk toward the secret room, glass dropped from Gavin's other hand, shattering on the floor.

Puzzled, Jack looked down at the broken glass but continued to get to safety so he could better assess the butler's condition. He carefully lifted his elbow to the height of the hilt that unlatched the door, grunting as he moved to push in and slide the door. Once inside, the door fully secure behind him, Jack laid Gavin on the cot, still seemingly dead, though his body was somehow healing. Jack put his ear to Gavin's mouth; he heard nothing, felt nothing. He put his ear to his chest hoping for a heartbeat, but found silence.

Suddenly Jack remembered Gavin mentioning something about healing potions, which must be why his neck had begun to heal. He looked around the room frantically until his eyes came across a satchel on a bookshelf against the far wall. He quickly began rummaging through it, pulling several glass containers full of a red liquid from the bag. He squeezed Gavin's cheeks, forcing his cold lips apart and emptying the red potion from one glass container into his mouth.

Nothing happened.

Jack could not accept losing the only other person he cared for. "Gavin! Wake up!" Jack slapped Gavin's face gently, hoping to wake him, but Gavin remained still on the cot. Jack stood and began pacing back and forth, thinking of what to do. As far as he knew, there was no coming back from dead, as Gavin had explained. He stopped pacing and returned to his tutor's lifeless side. "I need you, Gavin. I can't do this alone." His words were pure sincerity as he grasped one of Gavin's hands.

"Sure you can," Gavin whispered in pain, "It just wouldn't be as fun."

"Gavin! You're alive!" Jack leapt to his feet.

"Just barely," Gavin muttered. "Give us a couple more vials, would you? My health is still very low. Two should do."

Jack obliged quickly, feeling excitement he was sure only moments before he would never feel again.

"You were dead, Gavin."

Gavin explained after he finished the second vial. "No, Jack, once I'm dead, no amount of potion will bring me back, but one potion can save you from dying if taken in time. Luckily for me, I drank the one from my pocket just in time." He slowly sat up on the cot as if he were severely hung over. He held his face in his hands as he braced his elbows on his knees while the potions took effect. Within a couple minutes, Gavin was back on his feet. "Now how do you suppose we get back upstairs?" Gavin asked, full of vibrant life once again.

"That's simple," Jack said with a big smile, feeling proud. "I really am quite strong. I could climb the walls of the elevator shaft with you on my back." Jack held his arms up and flexed them in a heroic pose.

"I guess it's worth a try. Anything would be better than sitting down here starving to death." Gavin looked around for supplies they may need, refilling the front pocket of his satchel with potions from the cupboard. Then he moved to the opposite side of the room to pull four scrolls from a dusty shelf, stuffing them in the main compartment of the satchel.

"What are those?" Jack asked.

"They have the wisdom of magic used by those who stand uncorrupted by evil. Though many spells other than those contained here may be used for good, these are some of the strongest battle spells. Should you make it to Farion, you could seek out the Álfar to learn spells that can make a seed grow into a tree in minutes or allow you to take control of the vines that hang in the forest, but for now these will have to do. Your uncle was entrusted with them at the same time he adopted you. Now that responsibility falls to you," Gavin said, handing the satchel to Jack.

They gathered their swords to sheath them as they returned to the large sparring room. Gavin walked to a pair of black cloaks that hung on the wall, one bigger than the other. He removed them from their hooks, handing the larger to Jack.

"What are these for? Heroes don't really need capes, you know."

"Show some respect, young master!" Gavin snarled. "Our Peter designed and made these cloaks himself. They will block any attack but a straight stab. Though you will still feel the strike, the cloak will keep your skin from splitting. Also, they are made from a rare Farion material given to him by the Álfar, so they will be able to absorb magic attacks as well. The cloth will not burn or fray under a fire or lightening spell. I believe if you use the berserk spell, this cape will not rip, it will grow with you. Then you will not end up looking like the tattered mess you are now."

"Truly, I didn't know. I apologize for any disrespect, Gavin," Jack said, feeling stupid.

"It's fine. Go grab those karate gi and try them on," Gavin said, obviously annoyed with Jack's attitude. Without another word, Jack plucked the outfit from the wall. He draped the clothing over his arm as he turned back toward the secret room.

"I will be back in just in moment."

"Don't be ridiculous. It was I who bathed you as a child and changed your diapers. Just be quick about it. I am starving! I'll turn my back if it comforts you, you silly boy," Gavin said, degrading the young man who still lacked his memories.

The clothes were clearly too small, the pants failed to extend past his ankles, and the sleeves didn't quite reach his wrists. He turned to Gavin, feeling ridiculous. "I don't think they fit," he said with a chuckle, imagining what he must look like.

Gavin didn't even give him the satisfaction of a glance. "Use a spell, young master."

Jack held his hands together flat in front of his chest as he closed his eyes to feel the energy coursing through him. He readied his hands then opened his eyes while punching the floor, sending a pulsating shockwave of air all around him. Gavin fell over on the floor as everything within twenty feet fell off its mounting on the wall.

"Damn it, Jack! You couldn't pick something a little less destructive?" Gavin exclaimed as he scurried to his feet only to begin rehanging armor pieces and weapons on their original mountings. Jack held his arms out and looked down at his feet.

The clothing had fit itself perfectly to his form. He strapped his sheathed sword to his back and other gear securely around his waist and chest.

Once Gavin had finished cleaning up Jack's mess, they each swung a cloak over their shoulders, buttoning them under the neck. A big black hood hung off the back of the cloaks that could easily conceal the hilts of their swords. The button that kept the cloak secure under the neck was a similar black stone to that of the hilt of Jack's sword. He imagined the small smooth stone would allow the cloak to unfasten with ease. In a test to defy his new magical clothing, he began kicking the air, jumping and spinning, fighting the empty space in front of him only to realize the cloak was extremely sturdy yet ultra-light.

Gavin had wrapped a few more weapons in a large square of rawhide that he strapped over his shoulder. He nodded to Jack once he was ready, and the two headed for the broken elevator. Jack followed behind him at first, but as they approached the ripped-up elevator cart, he placed his hand on Gavin's shoulder, stopping him and taking the lead. Gavin gasped when he saw the disgusting mess of undead flesh and parts plastered to the wall.

"How did you ever?" Gavin said under his breath, almost inaudibly.

"I punched the floor while I was berserk, and they all splattered on the walls," Jack said plainly, as if he expected Gavin to already know the answer to his own question.

Ignoring his childish attitude, Gavin pushed on Jack's back and they began to jog down the extremely long horizontal shaft. The light from the room no longer reached them, so Jack decided to improvise. Holding his hands out in front of him, he closed his eyes and focused on creating a ball of light.

"Illuminate!" he yelled, but nothing happened. He tried a few more times before conceding he had yet to learn the appropriate spell. He smirked at Gavin in the remaining dim light from the constant glow of his sword.

"Perhaps we could make it if my sword were shining brighter," he mumbled, hoping Gavin would be able to tell him the spell he required. Gavin just nodded with a smile. Jack reached back, grabbing the sword's handle and spoke its name, "*Sireth Jessoteth*." The sword glowed brightly under his cloak and lit the tunnel.

"Ah, that's a bit better," Jack said as he started to jog again. Gavin was not following.

"I do believe when your uncle built Hollow Wood Manor there was no electricity for an elevator," Gavin said, staring up on the walls. "Interestingly enough, this elevator shaft was originally a labyrinth of tunnels intended to confuse any intruder attempting to reach his secret lair. This was long before my time at his side, but I remember he told me stories to that effect."

"What are you looking for, Gavin? Is there a quicker way out? Another secret wall with a ladder and escape hatch or something?" Jack began staring at the walls.

"That I cannot be sure of. However, I do believe these torches may light the way, perhaps," Gavin said smugly, gesturing to the wall.

"Hmm, I think I can handle that one," Jack said, relieved his magic could aide them. "Get behind me and wrap yourself in that cloak. This will be hot." He closed his eyes, raised his hands, and took a deep breath. Grunting, a powerful ball of fire pushed off his hands and travelled with speed throughout the entire tunnel, lighting every torch along the walls.

"Well that did the trick!" Gavin exclaimed with a chuckle.

They continued jogging for several minutes until Gavin gasped, out of breath.

"Are you all right, Gavin?" Jack asked. If they were attacked again, Gavin would be of little help. He worried for him.

"Maybe I could climb on your back now." Gavin laughed as he keeled over, holding his knees and panting.

Jack, without hesitation, grabbed Gavin's arm and slung him over his shoulder. Gavin yelped in surprise then continued laughing as Jack went to full sprint carrying him. The laughter turned to a nauseous moan as Jack approached the vertical shaft.

"Uncle Peter could have left in a ladder or two," he grumbled as Gavin let out another moan. "Don't you throw up on me, Gavin," Jack said as he jumped up on the wall, grabbing support beams that ran the length of the shaft.

He jumped from support to support with Gavin dangling over his shoulder, looking straight down at the long drop. The mangled door to the first floor hung open where the creatures had entered the shaft. Jack jumped for the opening. As he leaped, Gavin slid from his shoulder and began to fall. Jack swung one hand free from the ledge he'd caught, grabbing Gavin's ankle just before it was beyond his reach. Gavin's body stopped with a jolt, and he swung into the side of the shaft, smashing his shoulder on the wall. He screamed in agony. Jack reacted as fast as he could and followed through on the original plan; he swung

Gavin up and over him, to land outside the first-
floor door.

Jack stabilized his footing before making one
last great leap. He grabbed the ledge of the door,
slowly pulling himself up only to see Gavin on the
floor propped up on his good arm, clutching the
other across his chest. His face was pale as a
ghost, and he was shaking, staring across the
space at something.

"Gavin?" he said as he glanced away from the
butler to look around for the cause of his terror. At
the other side of the elevator lobby, the black dog
stood with its head down, snarling as it prepared to
pounce on Gavin. Jack ripped the sword from its
sheath while lunging for the dog. It jumped clear
over him, landing at Gavin's feet. It turned
immediately back to Jack as he was the true
threat. Jack spun around as the dog lunged at him
this time, catching him by his throat. He shoved
his blade through the dog's stomach, tossing the
lifeless beast out into the hallway, and rushed to
Gavin's side.

****

A mist had settled in the woods, as the beast
ran with great speed. Once he had finally lost sight
of the mansion grounds he transformed once again
to his human form. Tei paced back and forth near a
large boulder under the early morning sky.

"How were they able to defeat my army? The
sword must have given him powers. This will not
happen to me again! Not in this realm. I must find
it. I said I would find it! I will defeat him, there
must be a way!"

He continued to contemplate his next attack
while walking through the peaceful forest.

Mumbling to himself about his crushed pride, he kicked rocks and branches in frustration and pulled at the hair on his scalp.

"I will not be well received when I return home, to me," he said cocking his head to the side. "Where has this boy gained his power from? I told myself there was no magic in this realm. Electricity sparked from his fingertips as he waved his hands in frustration, leaving burn marks and scars on the encircling trees.

"Why! Why is this happening again!" his booming voice echoed throughout the woods, sending birds and wildlife running. He watched with a grin as his surroundings reacted to his anger.

"I do believe I have identified my next move. What better way to discover my enemy's potential than to spy on him," he let out a sinister cackle before transforming into a crow. He flew off back toward the mansion to learn what skills the boy possessed.

Chapter XV

Calm before the Storm

"No, you imbecile! Cut his head off! It's Tei!" Gavin screamed in disbelief.

Jack scrambled to his feet, running to the hallway. It was empty; no dog, no Tei, only a small puddle of blood that had smeared as the dog slid to a stop.

"Is he gone?" Gavin asked from the floor, rummaging for potions in his satchel.

"Yes, he's gone. I'm sorry I let you down," Jack said. He could have ended this whole nightmare, and he'd missed his chance.

"Do you know how he makes his undead army?" Gavin asked.

Jack shook his head in ignorance.

"He murdered each of those poor people and enslaved their spirits before they could move on to the afterlife. He forces them to do his bidding in death, to die again, so to speak. It is the darkest sort of magic I have ever heard of."

"There were hundreds of them, maybe more than a thousand." Jack looked at the ground, shaking his head in sorrow.

"Right. Each one was from this realm. They had families, peaceful lives until he came and slaughtered them," Gavin said sharply, feeding the pain swelling in Jack's heart. "You didn't know, Jack, but next time you have a chance like that, damn it, take his head, please!"

"Yes, sir."

He helped Gavin to his feet; Gavin was already recovering quickly with the help of the potions he'd consumed. Once he was standing and stable, he patted his pockets until he found his pocket watch. He held it tightly in his hand before returning it, securely.

"Now, how about some breakfast," Gavin said as his breathing stabilized. "Then I suggest we remain in the study to decipher our next move."

They returned to the first-level kitchen where Gavin sat at the table. The jacket Jack had been wearing the night before was draped over a chair. He picked it up, searching through the pockets for the picture of Jessi. Once he found it, he plopped down in the chair opposite Gavin, gazing at the photo. His heart ached as if it had knives thrust through it at every angle. The pain was excruciating to him, the most pain he could remember. It was unbearable. Even though his physical pain had been dulled by magic, bleeding his rage to cover his pain, Jessi's death could not be dulled in his heart by anything.

After Jack and Gavin got something to eat, they returned to Peter's study. Jack began reading his uncle's journals, learning about the Álfar and the magic of Farion. Even after experiencing magic at his own fingertips, it sounded like a fairytale. He learned more of how he could channel his power through meditation and bring his imagination into reality. He began to understand how he moved so fast around Jessi. His will alone to put himself beside her was strong enough to accidentally trigger the magic within him. His magic had started awakening from the moment he found himself in the alleyway over his uncle.

Jack studied for hours, looking for an answer to the most confusing question: How had he reversed the magic of his parents' mortality spell before having the chance to touch his father's sword? The search began to frustrate Jack as he flipped through journal after journal labeled *Magic Abilities and Traits* and found nothing that helped answer the question. He began wondering if he had been corrupted or possessed by Tei; the thought drove him mad.

After gaining a wealth of knowledge, he eventually gave up searching. His next question to answer was: How could he fix Peter's broken portal device, and what did it look like? He sifted through stacks of journals until he came across one labeled *Secret Doors and Dimensions* under an original title that had been scratched out and worn down to illegibility over time. The journal appeared to be ancient, but the writing was Peter's. Jack opened the cover to the first page, dated 1757. He began reading as Peter explained what seemed to be an irrelevant project meant to discover a means of energy that could power lights without flame over a hundred years before Edison would invent the light bulb. He flipped page after page of sketches that resembled a car that drove on three wheels and was mostly constructed from wood with metal straps similar to the hoops of a wooden barrel. It was theoretically to be powered with the same source as the flameless lights.

17 October 1757

While out for an afternoon walk today, I found the oddest thing on the forest floor. It was sitting slightly hidden in a bush just before the grassy meadow at Look Out Point. The strangest thing was that I felt it as I walked past. Something was pulling me, drawing me closer. What I found was simply fascinating!

A small rounded stone with only a few roughed edges. Grey in color and it was nearly weightless. I can only assume that the stone was a completely smooth sphere before it was abandoned and left to the elements. When I hold it in the palm of my hand, I can feel its energy pulse through my body!

I will begin testing tomorrow to see if the energy can be harnessed or magnified. This would by quite the addition to my horseless wagon!

Jack continued reading, mesmerized by the inventions and creations Peter had imagined could be powered by this pure energy source. Many of the experiment notes indicated that the inventions had worked for a while, but the output of the power element was too great for the materials available.

He read several pages, spanning a few chapters of this extremely fascinating journal. Peter's discoveries would have pushed forward so many inventions throughout history, perhaps without the need for nuclear energy or crude oil. The journal was filled with all of Peter's failed attempts to choke back the power of his innovation until finally he discovered something astonishing.

20 April 1758

There must be a way to create light without a flame transferred from a single energy source. If I am to be remembered for anything, it should be for my many years of research for flameless lighting. There have been far too many causalities among friends and colleagues from oil lamps and candles that could have been prevented.

With two small rods and a thin wire pulled from steel wool, strung between the posts, covered by a glass milk jug I have created light without flame, but only for moments. The glass jug ultimately explodes from the electromagnetic pulse released upon power overload from the small stone of pure energy. I have been experimenting on containing the power source to limit and evenly distribute its raw energy for months now, with no success. I have destroyed countless engines but I know with the proper exterior, it can be controlled. I will perform more tests on the reactions to different metallic materials in an effort to stabilize the source energy emitting from the stone.

The next pages were filled with more drawings, designs of boxes and other containment compartments, detailing months of trial and error failures.

18 July 1758

Iron seems to have the most stabilizing effect on the stone I have encountered so far. I have created a small, iron box to fit the power source. The two piece box fits together with an equal proportioned top and bottom. I have melted the inside of each, sculpting a smooth concave space to closely fit the stone sphere. Once I placed the power source into the box, it began to react immediately, trembling as if the iron was gathering a magnetic charge and the source was spinning at high speeds inside. It was magnificent! The sound it generated was just like the day I found the stone in the forest, only intensified.

I placed the new power unit into a makeshift fitting in the three-wheeled wagon, wrapping a strap over it to secure it in place. Then, I pulled the lever to initiate the engine's starting sequence. The parts of the engine began moving with such power and torque, the mere idle of the engine twisted and strained the wooden frame. It began to crack and the iron straps of the wagon shimmied toward the engine. The contraption roared louder and louder. Just when I felt like it would be another failed experiment, something extraordinary happened to the power unit's outer iron case. A blue light shone through small cracks that followed a small design, burning its way through the iron. The engine seized again when the power source reached its peak, but this time, it pushed energy out from its core with such force that I was knocked to the ground with a violent shove. There is something about the design of cracks in the iron box that allowed the radiant blue light to escape! I will further study this and attempt to replicate its meaning.

Later, Peter inspected the power cell closely, examining the cracks and semi-designs created by the power source as its energy climaxed. The iron box had cracks and imperfections that did not emit any light. Other cracks curved and swooped like some kind of unknown writing, still glowing with blue light.

Peter began creating box after iron box. He added curves on the cube's sides that protruded from the edges where the two pieces met, and carefully carved markings along the outer sides of each plane of the cube, attempting to emulate the markings that emitted the blue rays from the first box. Each box he tried failed, resulting in gashes in the metal that destroyed Peter's excellent and difficult craftsmanship. After months of attempts, Peter had logged in the journal only short notes explaining each small but significant change to the box's design. At last he found the combination the power source seemed to be trying to show him.

Excited but nervous that he may have failed yet again, Peter placed the power source into the iron cell and closed it securely. The box hummed with power, and the symbols all around the box began emitting the strong blue light from every side of the iron cube. Peter smiled as he stared down at his power cell glowing back up on his face, convinced he had finally gotten it right.

The next entry noted he was going to try the power source in the vehicle as he was sure he had completed a proper cell that accepted the power source with grace. The words reached the bottom of the page. Anxiously, Jack flipped the brittle page. Instead of small rough sketches or descriptions, he found a note from Peter:

5 September 1759

The most amazing thing has happened! After so long, studying this strange power source that had been lying simply on the forest's floor for me to find, I have discovered something beyond my wildest dreams. This power source is not of this world, or this realm, as my new friends refer to the existence of our two very different realities. After creating what was supposed to be a power regulator to fuel my inventions, upon sealing my perfected iron casing with its engraved symbols, it activated to my touch, and it seems I have instead created a gateway to either a parallel dimension or a rip in space to travel to another realm, called Farion. The details are still scarce, and my confusion is great, though the creatures I have met and walked with are real and not a mere hallucination.

A spirit of this realm recognized me as an outsider immediately. Luckily for me, he saw honor and strength within me that even I don't see. He bestowed upon me another stone identical to my first power source. Since my return, I have already fitted it to its new iron shell. He made mention of another gift he said would grant me power I would recognize when I needed it most. I am still confused, but I can say I have never felt so alive!

After Peter's note, the journal went back to the usual sketches and descriptions, but now the notes were about creatures he had met on his journey and began to look much like all of his other journals Jack had been studying prior to finding the oldest of them. Had Jack read this before the past few days, he would have been sure his uncle was insane, but after all he had witnessed, the words captivated him. Jack read page after page, learning about a culture called the Álfar, described by Peter as magical elf creatures with pointed ears, greenish skin, and the ability to manipulate elements in the form of magic. Apparently they were extremely intelligent, able to learn Peter's language very quickly and communicate with him within only days. He'd made sketches of each significant being he encountered and noted its role in society. Drawings of plants and herbs were categorized by their abilities when added to potions or other alchemic purposes.

Jack also read a great deal of an Álfar woman who could walk in the spirit realm of Farion, consult with the spirits of the past, and simply return to walk with the living. Her age was great, granted by magic, and kept by her sweet, innocent love for all life. He traced her image with his fingers slowly, memorizing every detail. There was something about her that felt so familiar to Jack. As he continued to read deeper into her story, he recognized this to be his mother. The tale of the Álfar who fell in love with a spirit guide; though forbidden, their love was too strong to be stifled by the restraints between realms.

Jack continued flipping through journal after journal of Peter's visits to Farion. The knowledge intake was like a drug to him; nothing else mattered other than consuming all the information he could. He caught bits and pieces of his past life and the story of his parents, how it was foretold they would mate to create a being of two realms, a godly being who would be capable of great or terrible things.

The story continued unraveling before him, covering the course of hundreds of years and gaps between Peter's leaps from Farion to Earth's realms, each time with stories of heroic adventures with glorious rewards. He read about the methods of keeping his immortality on Earth concealed with cheap parlor tricks all the way to the information he had learned from Gavin. Not much was written on Teiwaz, except that the Álfar feared his great hunger for power. The Álfar council decided they would make the child born of two separate realms human. They would send him far from the grasp of Teiwaz and his evil to be raised by the kind-hearted warrior they had befriended, Peter.

Jack sat back in his chair, overwhelmed by the plethora of knowledge he had absorbed though Peter's journals. Bewildered, he struggled to wrap his young memory around the history he had read.

His mind buzzed as images began flickering in his thoughts. Jack closed his eyes to gain more focus on what his intellect was attempting to comprehend. The magic inside him seemed to be extracting his memories from whatever hiding spot they lay dormant in. The past few days he hadn't been able to recollect anything of the past, but now, after reading so much of the magic Peter had encountered and experiencing some of his own, Jack began believing, allowing his inner soul to take control.

Chapter XVI

Memory Lane

Images of Jack's past flashed through his mind. Being a small child came first. He remembered Peter's loving, tender heart, caring for him when he returned home with scraped knees or came to his bedroom frightened by the dark. He also began remembering his arrogance toward Gavin. The back of his neck began to sweat; his face flushed from embarrassment for the way he had treated Gavin throughout his teenage years. Suddenly he understood the attitude he had endured from Gavin until the past day.

Then the images changed. They no longer seemed his own. Instead, the figure of a bear sculpted from blue light approached in his mind, walking with great might. The bear growled with a boom as he walked toward Jack's consciousness. Jack stared at the luminous bear before him, now extremely vivid. The bear's growl became words in Jack's soul.

"Son, I am Tragen, the spirit guide, known as Rauha Opas. I have been destroyed by your new foe. You have come so far as a man, and I am so proud of you, son, but be wary of the vengeance I can see burning in your heart. Fight not for anger, but for love. The magic within you came from your mother and me, both of us from separate realms of Farion and elders of our realms."

As the bear revealed himself and spoke to Jack, he simultaneously injected visions of his own memories into his son. Jack saw flashes of the forbidden but unstoppable love his parents shared along with the visions of immense love that had been displayed throughout the history of Peter's life. Tragen showed the pain throughout the histories, to show what it meant to fight for love, not for vengeance.

The flashes were quick but he was able to capture their meaning. He saw Peter and a much younger Gavin, rallying troops for war against a monstrous invasion of Norog where they were significantly out numbered. Then, a young man, no older than himself, watched his village burn to the ground by a vengeful dragon. The man and his wolf companion embarked on a lifelong journey to eradicate evil and protect the innocence of the quant villages they travelled too. He saw the Álfar village, where his mother resided, sacrifice their freedom to protect and contain a dark and unrestrained evil.

Jack understood clearly that if he were to continue living in his regret for not saving Jessi, if he allowed the hate he had for Tei to fill him, he would become the very thing he had come to despise.

"How are you here, Father? Have you truly not been destroyed?" Jack inquired, feeling hope rise.

"I am no more. When you were born, you came into dark times," Tragen said. "Teiwaz had tasted the hunger for power that had begun as vengeance against the people in his town whom he felt had betrayed him. Your mother and I knew our time was coming. We knew our love was only a weakness in Teiwaz's eyes and that he would use it against us. In preparation for our departure, we called upon Peter, our dearest friend and the most courageous warrior we had encountered. We entrusted him with you.

"Using our combined magic, your mother and I concealed your identity while also creating vessels of enlightenment within you to activate once you were ready. What you see of me now is merely an apparition embedded within you, galvanized by the awakened magic inside you and the presence of our most terrible adversary, Teiwaz. Another vessel I left behind was my sword, *Sireth Jessoteth*, which I carried from before my time as Rauha Opas. I used its power, combined with my strength and will as one of the Álfar, to keep our home safe from predators and trespassers such as trolls, goblins, and banshees. The sword's true power never revealed itself in the hands of Teiwaz because we made it so. The sword can only be in its true state in the hands of my kin, in the hands of my only son. When love is strong within your heart, *Sireth Jessoteth* will reveal its strongest power, emitting a blue light that will course through you."

Face hot with shame, Jack looked away from the apparition of his father. "Father, I fear Teiwaz has corrupted my very soul. I cannot consume anything but raw meat. When I get angry, my eyes turn as black as coal, and when I am enraged, I transform, growing in size as my muscles seem to double. I feel as though I am tainted by his evil."

"When Teiwaz opened the portal to Earth, he aimed to kill Peter with it. He missed, opening it on you and rendering you unconscious. The gateway's energy merged with yours as it happened, and that is what caused your memory loss and your premature magic use. This I can see in your memories. Perhaps as Teiwaz entered through the portal into this realm part of his life force was sewn into your soul, giving you access to some of his traits."

Jack breathed easier but still had questions. He looked up at the bear again. "I had a vision after my true love was murdered by Tei. She came to me the first time I used your sword. She told me Tei was 'merely a copy of the man he truly is, so he lacks the full knowledge of life.' What did she mean by that? How do I defeat him?"

Tragen stomped his front paws, stepping backward as he expelled a massive roar.

"What is it, Father?" Jack asked, frightened by the vision, the bear's anger echoing within Jack's mind.

"That scoundrel! It is not Teiwaz himself that walks this realm hunting you," Tragen explained furiously, stomping his paws once more. "He has used a forbidden magic, replicating himself, giving him the ability to be in two places at one time. That is the only explanation for his powers passing to you without taking them from him. The soul is the most intricate part of the universe, perfect in design, pure in every aspect of creation and evolution. To tamper with the soul is forbidden. By replicating himself, the memories of his own and of his abomination will begin to merge, and he will slowly go mad. You must stop him before he destroys the natural order of all realms."

Tragen calmed his voice and stepped toward Jack's consciousness, lowering his massive head under Jack's arm. He embraced the bear as Tragen began speaking again. "Jack, your journey ahead will be long and treacherous. *Sireth Jessoteth* will show you what you need to see; that is why she became Jessi. *Sireth Jessoteth* discovered what your heart values most. As long as you hold love for her in your heart, *Sireth Jessoteth* will reciprocate your desire to be with your love. You must not do this alone. Do not fear to love. Use the powers you have gained from Teiwaz as your own, and let them be his bane. I must leave you now to your task, but you must know your mother and I love you very much. It almost destroyed us to give you away. What we did was for your protection. It has been foretold you will become the most powerful being in all realms known to me; the path you choose to walk is your decision alone." Tragen's voice reverberated as the vision began to shimmer away.

Jack's eyes opened, and a tear rolled down his cheek. Gavin stood in front of Peter's desk where Jack had been sitting in silence, conversing with his father. Gavin stared down at him with sympathetic eyes.

"Are you alright, young master?"

"I saw my father."

"Your father was a magnificent soul, and what he left of himself in you was for you."

"I saw images of you and Peter battling deformed human-like beasts, what were they?" Jack asked curiously.

"Ahh yes, the Norog invasion. They brought a plague of fire and destruction upon Farion. The dark álfar bred with goblins to create an unstoppable army. Luckily, we were able to send them back to the land which they came from in an epic battle. We were outnumbered by thousands. Let the memory of this encounter fill you, and meditate on it for a while. You will need to understand his advice before you can reach your potential."

"He told me not to fear but to love. But if I love as he did, Tei will use it against me again, as he already has with Jessi, and I am sure it will lead only to my destruction." Jack looked away as his thoughts ran rampant.

"Jack, my life is forfeit. I will follow you until the end."

"You would die for me after all of the misery I caused you throughout my younger years?"

"I see your memories are truly coming back, then. Peter was my master, my employer, my father, as he was yours. He is gone now and has left me with you. You have the heart of your parents, and you were raised by the love of Peter and myself. All children resent those who beg to teach them, to keep them safe, but you must not be a child any longer."

"Gavin, you truly are a dear friend, and yes, my memory is serving me again." After a pause, Jack added, "Please Gavin, I am not your master. I am your friend and apprentice. It is I who should call you master."

"Ah, dear boy, Peter has left everything to you, including my service."

"Then if it is all mine, I hereby give half of everything to you and release you of your duty as a servant. Spend the remainder of your life as you choose to, with great fortune," Jack said adamantly as he wrote the agreement down on paper and signed it.

Gavin's jaw dropped, his chin trembled as if he were fighting back tears. "Jack, your kindness is unmatched, but my choice is to continue my service and my loyalty to you, as always."

"If that is your decision, I must insist you refer to me as Jack. I am no one's master." Jack paused for a moment. "In fact, you are my master. You must once more be my teacher. Help me learn all I can to prepare me to face Tei. We will need more than just sword training. I will need your assistance researching magical spells and their effectiveness."

"I am your equal, Jack," Gavin protested.

"You are not. Your knowledge is immensely greater than mine. Though my strength is great, I must learn to use my mind as you would have wished of me in my youth."

"So be it. I will be your teacher once more," Gavin agreed with a smile as he placed his palms flat on the desk, leaning his face down closer to Jack. "So when shall we begin, my young *friend*?"

****

Over the course of the next few months, Gavin and Jack did not leave the grounds of the estate. Instead, they sparred daily, utilizing a different room in the mansion every day, keeping the battles new. Retreating to the library most afternoons to study old books and journals for endless hours. Jack discovered he was now able to read most of the journals and books that had not been translated from their original Álfar language, providing him a wealth of knowledge of his origins. Gavin, not being immortal, slept five to six hours a night, usually on a couch in the study, while Jack did not allow himself a moment's rest, though Gavin did on occasion find Jack snoozing in a pile of books. They tried to remain focused on preparation and not think about the damage that Tei was doing to the quaint town of Braxton and beyond until Jack was ready for the battle.

After the first week or so, Gavin had taught Jack how to use his basic magic skills by simply strengthening his imagination. He could turn his hand to solid stone to stop a blade's attack; he could create and hold fire in the palm of his hand then manipulate it into objects. Once mastering control, he enjoyed transforming a simple fireball into a small dragon that chased Gavin around the library.

The bond between the two men strengthened. Jack had never seen Gavin so relaxed before; he had always been at work. Gavin had never seen Jack so eager to learn and listen, and neither of them had laughed in front of the other so freely.

Since access to the training grounds had been destroyed during Tei's attack on the manor and would require a lengthy renovation, they did most of their sparring within the walls of the estate. Gavin would hide around corners and try to attack Jack with a wooden blade to test his pupil's intuition and reaction. After being hit by the heavy wooden blade several times at the crest of his skull, Jack became adept at protecting himself even when he least expected danger. Soon Gavin upgraded to his real sword, and Jack would stop the blade promptly without causing injury to himself, Gavin, or the sword.

They had just over three months without any interruptions from Tei, though the thought of his attack was always forward in both their minds. Gavin had expressed his concerns over Jack's readiness to battle Tei on numerous occasions, despite the unknown of his whereabouts or what treachery he was casting upon this realm. But finally, Jack had acquired all the knowledge of magic and battle Peter had left in his library. With nothing left to teach his young apprentice, Gavin agreed it was time to attack.

"Do you believe Tei is simply staying away to better his own strengths in hopes of destroying me quickly upon our next encounter?" Jack inquired.

"Perhaps your powers have already surpassed any powers a replicated Tei can muster. Regardless of Tei's reasons for disappearing, you have learned all you can from me, Jack. Your sword fighting skills are flawlessly fluid and natural, and your magic is unstoppable as long as you remain calm and focused."

Jack had gained much more strength in swordplay through Gavin's guidance. He felt assured of his abilities and hoped Tei would send more creatures of less power than his own so he would have true practice against foes that wanted to kill him. Gavin was a skilled opponent but was wary about pushing his sword through Jack's body, even knowing he would heal.

"Jack, you have grown so much in a short period of time. I am truly proud to have you as my friend. Please, though, do us a favor and keep your head on your shoulders and your heart in your chest. These are the only two things that won't ever grow back if they are taken from your body," Gavin said, lacing his fears with humor.

Jack nodded. He heard the words clearly and envisioned the terrible consequences. The thought of losing his head or being torn open like Carla sent a shiver up his spine.

"I will do my best not to let you down in that respect, Gavin. I will do my best indeed." Jack rubbed his neck with one hand while holding the other over his chest.

Gavin let out a chuckle at the young man's anxiety. He was sitting on the floor in an oversized living room with vaulted ceilings they had converted to their new sparring room. He tucked his feet under himself and began meditating while Jack conjured stone golems with his magic then repeatedly dispersed them with attack spells. Stone golems were a great opponent to practice spells on, for they were quite resistant to the elements, forcing Jack to focus on their chemistry. Fire seemed to bounce off the rocky surface but heated it to the point of glowing red. Casting ice-cold water behind the fire cooled the stone rapidly, causing it to become frail, and a blast of lightning helped expand the cracks and even dismantle limbs, stunning the golems. Finally, conjuring magic stones from his palms and blasting them forth as rapid as bullets, he smashed the stone golems into dust.

Jack was filled with determination and strength. He didn't fully understand his life or the foretold destiny Peter and his father had suggested, though his memories had been slowly returning. The shroud of confusion still surrounded his head and stifled his breath. He closed his eyes and thought about Jessi. He missed her face, recalling the permanent dismissal from this realm that had been thrust upon her, and it tore into his heart. The pain overwhelmed him as he forgot his surroundings. When he opened his eyes again, the room seemed different somehow. He felt even stronger. He realized he wasn't breathing; he didn't need to. The magic in his blood was more powerful than air and pulsed through his veins like a raging river.

Chapter XVII

A Friend in Need

Gavin had trained Jack, an incredibly fast learner, in all the abilities he could. Jack was prepared to bring the battle to Tei. They had not heard from him since the attack on the mansion diverted by Jack's rookie efforts. Even though neither had left the grounds of Hollow Wood Manor since the attack, Gavin hoped Tei was so frightened by Jack's display of raw power that he would crawl back into whatever dark hole he came from. Jack hoped the opposite; vengeance still burned inside his heart, living in the memory of Jessi and recovering memories of Peter and the person he had been. He was not the same person now; he was better.

Jack suited up in the cloak and outfit bestowed on him by Gavin then strapped his sword to his back under the hood to conceal his weapon perfectly. Gavin prepared likewise, only with daggers on his sides and a slim crossbow on his back. Jack was ready first and began planning out loud while Gavin finished preparing himself.

"First we need to get back to Main Street. It seems he is around that area most," Jack suggested.

"Where exactly do you think those monsters in the elevator shaft came from, Jack?" Gavin replied, looking up at him from the sack he was tying shut.

A lump of guilt sat on his chest as he remembered the undead attack. "All those people were from town? I probably knew some of them as acquaintances, maybe even friends."

"Precisely, but you must not dwell on such things. The monsters you killed were no longer human. The murder of each of them was already committed by Tei himself. Feel as though you freed their spirits from any further treachery or enslavement. He has been treading on a path that ought not be tread by any soul." Gavin shook his head. He fumbled with his pocket watch, turning it over in his hand before returning it to his pocket. "Teiwaz devastated Farion with unthinkable destruction. He will use any magic that will allow him victory, even if it condemns him in the afterlife. Many spells of dark magic can mark your soul, and some are so malevolent they will leave you disfigured by an evil look or stench to match your blackened soul."

Jack listened intently, thinking about how most people appeared to him. Jessi was the first beautiful person he had seen since the alleyway, and Gavin was one of the few others who seemed untouched by the dark taint that blurred his vision when he looked at people. Connecting that with Gavin's speech about souls, he realized he had been seeing the truth of the soul itself rather than the physical body since his magic awakened.

The two men retreated to the garage. As they made their way through the house, Jack began dwelling on souls, wondering what his looked like after years of treating people terribly. As his memories returned, he could only feel grateful he was allowed that time with amnesia and Jessi to show him the meaning of love and true happiness. He could remember how he felt before all this started; he seemed to everyone else to be the one who had everything, befriending only the super-rich and bullying all others. His actions had been foolishly shallow while Peter and Gavin frequently travelled during his teenage years. His soul, he felt for certain, must be tarnished greatly.

Gavin selected a set of keys out of the box, and they walked to the end of the garage to a sleek, black car. Gavin stored their excess supplies in the trunk. Jack stood by the passenger-side door waiting for it to be unlocked.

"I will drive you as I drove your uncle, and together we shall not be defeated!" Gavin boasted over the insecurity in his voice.

"And I shall do my best not to let you down," Jack replied with a grin.

They got in and buckled their seatbelts. With a twist of the key, the engine whined a high-pitched but powerful scream. The car tore out of the garage and with great ease; it seemed to eat every corner in front of them as if they were simply driving straight. As they approached the densely-populated town near Main Street, they saw no other cars driving on the road, though abandoned cars stood on the curbs with some in the woods, damaged or charred.

Both men understood what they were driving into; this was the work of Tei. They weren't sure how far Tei had traveled over the past three months Jack had been training, but so far the destruction covered the miles between their home and Main Street.

Gavin did not bother to look for a parking lot off the usually busy street. Instead, he pulled down Main Street itself, allowing the car to glide quietly, still emitting a dull rumbling sound as they rolled along the cobblestone streets. All the businesses seemed closed; no one walked the streets.

"You don't suppose we could have been here earlier? We could have saved these people?" Jack wondered out loud.

"We would have perished had we tried," Gavin replied. "Although it is you he seeks to destroy, his actions brought silence to these streets."

"I should have returned for Jessi. We could have buried her on the grounds of the estate," he sighed with deep remorse. "Her bones have probably been picked clean by the birds."

"Don't torture yourself boy. What's done is done, and there is no changing the past. You must take what you have learned to move forward. He murdered Jessi and countless others in his lust for power. He sees your love and compassion as weakness; you must show him it is your strength!"

They continued down the length of Main Street to the docks, passing an abandoned diner along the way. Gavin turned the car and began back up the hill. He slowed to a stop as he tried to focus on something up the street, off to the side of a building. He thought he saw movement, but as he strained his eyes, nothing was visible. Before he could turn to Jack to explain his anticipation, Jack was out of the car, raising his hood over his head. Gavin put the car in park, but as he reached for the door handle, Jack signaled to him to remain in the car. He obeyed, locking the doors and cautiously observing his surroundings.

Jack walked up the middle of the street, looking from side to side down each alleyway he passed. Everywhere he looked, he felt as if someone had just been there watching him, but still he saw nothing except the silent buildings around him. His heart rate grew stronger, the magic coursing through his veins. He closed his eyes and went to one knee as he reached out with his mind, feeling the disturbance that devoured this peaceful town.

His thoughts became more uneasy as each second passed. A low rumble started in the distance, snarls and howls approached as the ground began to tremble beneath his feet. Jack stood up, opening his eyes as the noise intensified. He brushed the hood off his head slowly, wrapping his hand around the hilt of his sword behind his neck as he watched the street.

Suddenly, eyes peered around a building close by. It was a creature like those he had slain in Hollow Wood Manor's training room. He stepped toward it slowly, but it disappeared quickly, retreating to the shadows. The rumbling sound grew louder and closer. Jack pulled his father's sword from its sheath and held it in front of him, grasping it firmly in both hands.

A black cloud rolled off the sea, bringing a thick fog from behind him with unnatural speed and choking out the sun. Looking up the street, Jack thought at first he saw the buildings move, a wave pushing the very rubble of the road down the hill to him. As the wave drew closer, he could see it was an army of charging undead. Jack met the massing horde head on while the black cloud settled overhead and dense fog surrounded them. As he approached the colossal mob of undead, blood-craving creatures, he swung his sword around full circle without missing a step that would slow his sprint. Bodies went flying as blood rained down on the street. He punched the ground, and a wave of pure electricity shot forward, throwing more of the creatures back. He did his best to keep them from passing him to reach Gavin, who still sat safely in the car.

Jack continued to swing the sword, emitting blue light that cut through the creatures as easily as the blade. He cast spell after spell, lighting the creatures up with lightning and freezing them solid so he could smash them to tiny pieces. He shot stone spikes through their heads and shocked them with lightning long enough to stun the creatures in a group so he could cut them down with unrelenting ease. His blood-lusting rage satisfied him as he tore easily through the creatures with little resistance. Just as he felt close to victory, he glanced to the top of the hill and saw two giant silhouettes approaching through the fog.

They had the shape of enormous men with large lumps sticking off the shoulders, wielding massive clubs and swatting the undead off to the sides to reach their target. The undead rolled off the street and scaled the buildings.

Jack persistently dispersed the small feeble monsters as they flooded out of every alley and building while he awaited this new foe's arrival. The horde finally began to thin, and those that remained slowly retreated, snarling and snapping their jaws at Jack, making way for the giants. The monsters were close enough for him to assess their threat. They towered above the three story buildings that lined the street, jagged chunks of rock sprouting through their skin. The rocky earth protruded from their humped backs and bulging muscles.

As the giants approached, Gavin's voice cracked behind him from the car window, "Trolls!"

Nodding to acknowledge Gavin's warning, he watched the trolls bound toward him.

"I would be angry too if I had lived my whole life in agony from stones ripping through my skin," he chuckled to himself. He sheathed his sword and bent down, placing both hands on the ground. He closed his eyes. Just as the trolls raised their clubs to pulverize him, Jack stood up quickly. Blue light shot from his eyes, and the cobblestone road rose with his hands as he stood. He let out a scream and slammed the ground back down in its place, sending an eight-foot wave of cobblestone and mangled undead at the trolls. Both trolls wobbled on the unsteady pavement. One stumbled backward, tripping on its own club, and fell through a tall brick building, sending shockwaves as he crashed to the ground. The other stayed on its feet, but just barely.

Jack charged the troll that still stood. He jumped as high as he could, pulling the sword from his back and stabbing the troll through its knees. The troll bellowed, shaking its leg in an attempt to get rid of the pain. Jack held onto his sword as the giant flailed and kicked. His body was tossed around like a rag doll as he held on for his life. The troll finally stomped his foot down, dislodging the sword from his knee as Jack fell back to the ground with sword in hand. It peered down at the tiny man who offended it as it raised its foot over Jack's head, stomping the ground. Jack punched the pavement again just as the troll's foot reached him. The shockwave propelled the foot back up in the air, causing the troll to stagger long enough for Jack to hop back a few paces.

He readied himself while the troll steadied again and lunged forward for revenge. A bright flash exploded on the troll's face. Jack looked back over his shoulder to see Gavin with his crossbow braced on the open car door. Jack smiled and charged the troll. Another explosion lit the troll's face as it swatted the air around its head.

Jack leaped into the air with his sword over his head. He cleared the troll's foot as it stumbled, landing on its wounded knee. Jack thrust the sword down, cutting through the knee with great ease. He scaled along the massive leg, clinging to the unnatural earth that swelled from its skin, gashing open any flesh he passed over. Sparks flew from his sword when he stabbed or scraped any stone parts of the troll. Climbing up over the fat gut, he mounted its chest. Jack raised the sword, stabbing it straight into its thick calloused skin, piercing its heart. Its arms jumped up in reflex as if it were reaching for the sky, exhaling one last mumbled roar. He rode the monster as it crashed to the ground. Its arms fell limp, and Jack felt victorious for only a moment.

As he stood on top of the dead troll, the other that had smashed into the brick building lifted itself back up, preparing for attack. Hundreds of the undead creatures scattered from the remains of the building, launching another attack. Jack cast spells left and right, swinging his sword back and forth in exhausting repetition. Arrows from Gavin's crossbow flew by his head as he dispersed the undead just as before, but this time they were unrelenting in their attack even when the second troll climbed back out of the building to its feet. It swung its giant club as Jack dove, rolling out of the destruction path. The club tossed several of the small creatures through the air. Most of them splattered on the buildings surrounding both sides of the street. The troll tried to swing its club straight down on Jack, but he was able to dodge again. Instead, it burst through the cobblestone sidewalk, leaving a crater.

Jack sheathed his sword and closed his eyes for a moment to gather his thoughts. He held his hands palm up in front of him, slowly curling his fingertips and flexing his arms. All of the debris from the pavement and destroyed buildings levitated, gathering in front of Jack. He concentrated on the floating debris in his magical grasp. Some of the pieces combusted into flaming stones while others froze over into ice blocks. Jack raised his hands slowly over his head. The suspended debris followed his command, rising far above his head. The troll began to charge. When Jack stepped forward, throwing his hands out toward the troll, the debris ripped through its body, knocking it back. Blood poured from gaping wounds all over. Pieces of the debris tore its skin from its ribs, exposing them completely on one side with the smell of burnt flesh filling the air. The troll teetered on one leg before finally falling on its back, landing at the feet of the first dead troll.

Jack was immediately flooded by the undead monsters again as he fought his way to the neck of the second troll. Kicking, punching, and slicing his sword through the small creatures, Jack made time for one fatal strike through the troll's neck. He pushed his magic into the severing neck wound and kicked the head away from its body. The enormous, rocky head rolled off to the side of the road, bouncing past Gavin at the car, all the way down into the ocean.

Jack still hadn't had a moment's rest from the hordes of undead. He laughed sinisterly as he cut them down, light shone from his eyes as his anger swung his sword. Jack began running up the hill through the fog, cutting down all before him in search of a bigger challenge, in search of Tei.

Expecting to find his nemesis, he instead found nothing. He looked back down the hill, covered in the dark shadow of the clouds. Thousands of bodies riddled the streets. A building that was once white now dripped red, and large chunks of debris were strewn along the once busy street. Jack stood at the top of the battlefield he had almost single-handedly conquered. The feeling of victory seeped back into his heart as his ears perked to an elegant tune, the most beautiful song he had ever heard. It was coming from the waterfront at the bottom of the street.

As Jack made his way down the hill toward the music, he saw Gavin was already approaching the courtyard before the docks. Both men were smiling in a stupor as they enjoyed the harmonious melody, making their way to the water's edge. Gavin reached the water first, where three gorgeous women stood in the water wearing all white, their perfect breasts peeking through wet gowns and luscious blonde curls. Without interrupting the beautiful song, the women signaled Gavin to join them in the water. He ripped off his cloak, tossing it to the ground as he dove to join the young women. The women circled around him, running their hands all over his body and through his hair, slowly removing the remainder of his clothes. One of the women started kissing his neck, embracing him by the top of his head. She pushed his face down into her bosom, pushing harder until he was submerged.

Gavin followed with ease, but as his head went underwater, he could no longer hear the song, and he began to panic and struggle. Instead, he heard the wretched screeches of old hags. He jolted around, fighting to bring his head above the surface just long enough to gasp for air. He kicked his legs and swung his arms, but the three women overpowered him in the water.

Jack cleared his head as he watched his friend being attacked, realizing the song was a spell. He unsheathed his sword and rushed to the shoreline, pointing his blade at the seductive women.

"Release my friend or lose your heads!"

"Won't you join us, love?" one of the women asked, her back turned to him.

"I will say it one more time," Jack shouted, but his words failed when the woman who had spoken to him turned. "Jessi. You're—but you died." Jack fell to his knees, the blade resting on the ground under his hand.

"Join us for a swim, won't you?" the woman moaned seductively.

He slid himself into the water, leaving his sword at the edge with the hilt touching the waves rolling in. He waded through the water to Jessi, wrapping his arms around her. The song was once again audible, and Jack felt completely at ease until Gavin burst out of the water.

"Jack, no!" he gasped before disappearing under the water again. "It's a siren!" he choked and gargled, just barely breaching the water with his mouth.

Jack shook off the enchantment as he watched Jessi wilt into a haggard old woman. Her skin sagged, hardly staying attached to her skull, with gray, matted hair tufted in all directions.

"What are you?" Jack exclaimed as he jumped back to the shoreline to grasp his sword. The decrepit old woman lunged at him as he attempted to lift himself out of the water on the seawall. She grabbed his ankle and ripped him back into the water. As he slipped from the wall, his right hand grasped the sword. He stood tall in the shallow water, bringing the sword above his head. With all the aggression and emotion the siren had stirred from within him, he bore his sword down on the top of her head, splitting it in two all the way to her chin.

The remaining two hags screeched and wailed, releasing Gavin. He jumped out of the water, pulling the daggers from his side, attacking the old women who held him under, shoving each of his blades through their wrinkled, decaying faces.

Jack grabbed Gavin, dragging his weakened body back up to the seawall, resting him in the grass next to the docks. Gavin lay on his back staring at the blackened sky.

"If it seems too good to be true—" Gavin started with a smile on his face. Jack plopped down next to him.

"Then it probably is, my good friend," Jack finished for him. They shared a nervous laugh, knowing they had both been tricked and almost taken by mere sirens after defeating an army. Jack held his hand out to help Gavin to his feet. As he accepted and pulled himself up on Jack's arm, his face turned grim.

"What is to come next? I haven't seen the likes of these creatures since I met them in Farion. Until now, I had always believed us safe from them in this realm."

"Whatever comes, let them come. We will cut them down just the same!" Jack screamed out to anyone listening, feeling too powerful to fail, too strong to fall.

He walked toward Main Street again, squinting through the fog as he looked up the hill he had conquered with a dull smirk of self-assurance. His senses were heightened from the battles he had endured. The water stirred behind him, but when he turned to look, he only saw the waves rising and falling. He continued on his path. Suddenly, he heard a loud splash with a growl that curdled his insides. He spun around to see Gavin still gathering his effects at the water's edge.

A giant kraken rose from the water, its scaly tentacles whirling through the air past its dragon-like head as it raged. The beast's neck towered out of the water. It came down with the swiftness of a rattlesnake. The kraken snatched Gavin off the ground and lifted its gaping jaws. Gavin could not hold on long. He dropped into the belly of the beast.

Chapter XVIII

Belly of the Beast

Jack felt ashamed for egging on the conjuring warlock he was battling. He stood astonished by the size of the great sea dragon that had so easily devoured his last and only friend. He was merely an insect in comparison to its immense neck and head, and the body remained submerged in the deeper water.

Jack allowed his emotions to fill him, visualizing all the pain Tei had brought upon him. He had watched his friend be consumed. He had seen Jessi's neck snap before him. The man who had raised him as his own kin was murdered and his soul stolen.

Jack sprinted at the kraken, screaming. The monstrous dragon-like head sprung down at the ground, permitting Jack to jump up into its mouth, tucking his feet to dodge its razor-sharp teeth.

The kraken retreated into the water and began swimming off to sea. Jack slid down the tongue carefully so he would not lose his footing. He slowed himself on the ribbed surface of the kraken's throat. Losing his grip as the monster dove into the water, he fell for a few moments, smashing from side to side within the beast's elongated neck. Finally, the kraken was horizontal, retreating to the depths of the sea; Jack was able to stand upright as he sprinted down the throat to the stomach. The smell inside the beast was almost unbearable, but he thought he heard the quiet echo of a voice.

The voice was Gavin, griping, "This is disgusting. Ugh, it's dreadful!"

"Gavin!" Jack shouted down the dark tunnel.

"Jack? No! You didn't get eaten too! I hope this is a hallucination from the blood loss and these nauseating stomach gases," Gavin grumbled.

"Gavin! Where are you?" Jack yelled again as he pushed his way through undigested whale parts and other unimaginable pieces. "*Sireth Jessoteth*," he said, and the tunnel glowed a radiant blue, allowing him to see. When he finally reached the stomach, he spotted a severely wounded Gavin.

"No, Jack. You are supposed to save us, not die in the belly of a kraken!" he snapped in disbelief as if Jack hadn't listened to his lessons.

"Gavin, we will get out of here together, and we will fight another day," Jack tried to reassure Gavin, but his left leg had been bitten off at the knee when the kraken grabbed him. He rushed to Gavin's side to inspect the leg and the makeshift tourniquet Gavin had constructed from his clothes.

"Gavin, roll your shirt to bite down on it as hard as you can. This is going to hurt a lot," Jack instructed, holding his hand behind his back as he conjured a flame that engulfed his palm. Gavin did as he was told.

He pulled his hand from behind his back, and swiftly grabbed the wound with the fire in his palm, searing the raw incision shut. Gavin thrashed and winced in pain, growling through the bundled-up shirt in his mouth. Jack quickly cooled the fire with ice. The extreme temperature changes along with the agony put Gavin into deeper shock, numbing the throbbing pain.

"Jack, I feel cold everywhere," Gavin said, concerned.

"You're just in shock. Stay with me, friend; it will pass. When it does, you are going to feel some serious pain, but for now, we need a plan to get out of here."

As the words fell from his lips, they felt a rumble and heard a sound like geysers warming to erupt.

"What do you suppose that was?" Jack asked.

"We are in a stomach, unfortunately. I'm betting we are about to be digested," Gavin replied with fear in his eyes.

Jack pulled out his luminous sword and stabbed down through the stomach with all his might, but the skin of the stomach stretched. Instead of cutting, the tissue just bounced the sword back up. He returned to Gavin and pulled his arm over his shoulder and lifted him to his remaining foot.

"So, do you have any ideas?"

"Well, we could try to go back the way we came." Gavin pointed toward the entrance of the throat. Jack helped him hobble across the stomach through all the sinew and slop of Earth-realm sea creatures that were new to the kraken's tastes. As they approached the throat, the esophageal sphincter closed, propelling them back across the stomach into the disgusting mess.

"That's okay. That end has teeth anyway," Jack mocked, but without a smile.

"Well, there's always the other way out of a digestion system, but it could get messy," Gavin replied with a half-smile but mostly with disgust at the thought of it.

"That seems to be our last choice out of the only two we had," Jack agreed.

The companions moved to the back of the stomach in time to hear the nerve-wracking sound of the geysers again. Steam began pouring up through the sinew closest to the throat, then off to the sides. The steam was discharging everywhere, hemming them in. The temperature was rising rapidly.

"Jack, we can't survive much longer. We will boil to death!" Gavin gasped.

Jack inspected the back wall opposite the throat and found a small place that appeared to be a scar. He pushed on it with his hand. The soft tissue allowed his hand to squeeze through. Retracting his hand, he found it dripping with clear ooze. He pushed through again with both hands, trying to stretch the small hole he had discovered. He pulled on it with his mighty strength, but it only snapped shut. In a final attempt, he knelt, pushing his hands and arms into the unknown, opening them with his inhuman strength to fit his head. After a few minutes of squirming, he was able to get his body through, where he landed with a thud on a stiffer surface.

****

Gavin stared at the wall where his friend had struggled; he attempted to push on the wall but the muscle was too strong for him to budge. He would need Jack's strength to get through. Then he noticed he was sitting over the last geyser to burst. Everything in the stomach began to simmer. In a panic, Gavin pushed on the wall again to no avail.

Then a hand ripped through the hole, grabbing him hard. Jack pulled Gavin through the hole just as the last geyser exploded, sending hot steam through the hole as it slapped shut.

"That was close," Gavin said breathlessly as the blue light illuminated the new chamber they had stumbled into.

"Well, we don't have much time. Where do you think all of that boiling hot muck is going once it's all just a simmering juice?"

"Maybe it will take a few hours to dissolve and move on," Gavin hoped.

They began moving through the tunnel they had discovered within the kraken, assuming it was part of its intestines. They tried to move quickly, but Gavin was wounded and could only hobble on his remaining leg as he hung on Jack's shoulder. After gaining several yards of the tunnel, they suddenly heard a new sound of shriveling leather. The tunnel started constricting, getting tighter and tighter. Eventually it had become so tight the men were forced to lie down, crawling.

"We must be going deeper!" Gavin squealed as the tunnel caved in around him. "The water pressure is going to crush us!"

Jack attempted to reach his sword, but the tunnel had bound too much, his arms were stuck in place. The kraken was swimming deeper to help its digestion. It was born at the depths of Farion's most treacherous sea before Tei summoned it to Earth. It only surfaced to feast on shipwrecks and smaller sea creatures before returning to the seafloor. The more water pressure, the less work its body would have to do to push the contents from the stomach into the intestines. As the tunnel tightened around them, Jack pushed Gavin forward. Jack squirmed and wriggled to see behind him but only saw an orange glow. It appeared to be lava pouring from the stomach through the hole they had used.

"Oh no, Gavin, oh no!" Jack said, panicking.

"What? What's happening?"

"It's digesting already!" he yelped.

Just then, the tunnel began expanding rapidly. The more it stretched, the faster the steamy fluid poured from the stomach behind them. Jack began crawling as soon as he was free to move again, pushing Gavin along quickly. Within moments, they were able to stand, as the tunnel continued to widen past its original size.

"We must be nearing the surface, Jack!" Gavin exclaimed with excitement that dulled as soon as he looked back to see the sweltering fluids splashing toward them.

Jack began pounding his fists on the walls surrounding them; they felt stiffer compared to the rubbery stomach. He unsheathed his sword and sliced the wall open with ease. The beast was muffled as it rumbled and screamed under the water. Jack swung the sword again, cutting a vertical line from the intestinal walls down to the floor. After grabbing Gavin, they moved further down the enlarged tunnel, pausing only for a moment to watch the stomach fluid divert from the digestive system into the beast's body as planned.

"Jack, cut us out here," Gavin demanded, after they made a few more yards of progress down the dark tunnel, lit only by Jack's glowing sword and a dim orange light emitted by the smoldering stomach fluid far behind them.

He obliged, carving down through the intestines. The men tumbled from the safety of the tunnel, plunging into darkness. As they dropped, Jack never lost Gavin's hand, grasping his sword tightly in the other. He stabbed the sword into the nearest intestinal wall he could find while they were still falling. It ripped through the soft tissue, allowing sunlight into the beast's body. Blood spewed with intense pressure, but they managed to hold on. The kraken had surfaced for only a moment, quickly submerging again. The hole Jack created in the kraken's side began to rapidly fill with water.

He pulled Gavin up higher to clutch the edge of the wound then tucked his blade back into its sheath to get a stable grip. As the blood and water discharged over them, the ocean finally filled the inside of the body enough to let them swim out of the dying kraken.

Jack kicked hard for the surface, guided by basic survival instincts at first but not feeling faint from the lack of air. He looked back down to see Gavin struggling with only one foot. He darted back down, the weight of his gear helping the descent. Gavin's body began jolting, and his eyes widened as Jack neared. Jack grabbed him under his arms, kicking his legs with all his might to surface his drowning friend.

The sea was restless as the men breached the surface, struggling to stay afloat. Gavin was unconscious. Jack looked in all directions for land or something to rest on, but they were in the middle of the ocean; he saw nothing but horizon. He held his arm around Gavin's chest, embracing his back to his own torso. Holding out his other hand over the water, he closed his eyes and focused his magical energy. Icicles slowly formed around them as the water under their feet froze. Soon they were buoyant enough to float. As the salt separated from the freezing water, it pushed to the surface of the block, making it rough and easy to stand on. The ice structure spread under the water. Within only a few moments it began to emerge, lifting the two stranded men on the deck of a seaworthy vessel of ice.

Chapter XIX

Sailing Home

Jack pulled off his cloak to shake it out; its magic permitted it to dry almost instantly. He watched with a grin as the droplets squeezed from the fabric without a touch. He promptly laid the cloak next to his friend, carefully sliding the cold, limp body onto it in hopes the cloth would shield his friend from the freeze of the ice and the rough layer of salt. He placed both hands together on Gavin's chest and began CPR. There remained no sign of life, no dispelling the water from his lungs. Jack kept pushing harder, but still no effect. After minutes of constant compressions on Gavin's chest, he began to cry.

"No! Not you too! No!" As he said the words, he raised his fists in the air, pounding them both down on Gavin's chest, choking as he bellowed with sorrow.

Just as his fists struck Gavin's chest, an electric charge from Jack's hands flowed visibly throughout the lifeless body, flung unknowingly from his grief. Blue light rushed through Gavin's veins as Jack watched, astonished. When it reached Gavin's face, his eyes and mouth opened,

J.J. Dice

emitting a light so bright that Jack fell back to cover his eyes.

As the light faded, Jack peered around the arm he used to shield himself from the brightness to see Gavin staring up at the sky, still comatose, but with his eyes and mouth open. His chest was moving ever so slightly. Jack rushed to his side and began compressions again. Finally, Gavin started coughing. Jack pushed a few more times. Gavin jolted up from the uncomfortable salty deck and spewed the rest of the water from his lungs. Jack jumped to his feet with laughter.

"Ah-ha I did it! I can't believe I did it!"

Gavin looked around with a dazed and disoriented expression, remembering the traumatic experience he and Jack had just endured, then flopped back down to rest.

Relieved he had not lost the last person he cared for in life, Jack shifted focus to the fact that they were stranded in the middle of the ocean with only a raft constructed of magic ice. He knelt and closed his eyes. The ice began to expand, extending the platform they were resting on in all directions. A clearly constructed ship was taking form with a bow, stern, and two masts. He took a deep breath and opened his eyes, admiring the ship they now sat upon. It wasn't of modern shape, much more like a brigantine, complete with even the sails and crow's nest.

"A pirate ship, Jack? Do you suppose the ice sails will work?" Gavin smiled, marveling at the magic.

"I'm not sure, really. I just focused on the first thing that came to mind for something that could float and that just happened to be a pirate ship. I am certain it is not made to scale, just fragments of my memory from books or movies. Though the sails are made of ice, I am sure more magic could help us get moving back home."

"Yes, good idea," Gavin agreed. "I've left my bundle in the trunk of the car, and it's rather important we retrieve that."

"What's in the trunk?"

"A device Peter invented for trapping an immortal, seeing as how they are so hard to kill," he replied.

"I thought you needed to cut off the head?"

"Quite right. There were many stories told to Peter and me on our travels, immortals having their body parts hidden in different corners of the world. Some were so powerful that they had the extraordinary ability to summon their hidden pieces by using the power of the heart alone. When the head is severed from the body or the heart has been pierced permanently the immortal will be dead, temporarily anyway. An immortal's soul is forever tethered to its body. If one were to place the head back to the shoulders and wait a while, the body would eventually heal itself. If the head was just cut off, it would heal quickly, but a skeleton could take over a week to fully reanimate. Peter must have been creating a way to stop Tei from summoning his own extremities with an invention. The immortal will feel the spikes through his eyes but won't be able to see, feel the spikes in his heart but won't be able to act. The immortal will be lost in pain," Gavin explained. "If you lose your head, I would imagine Tei would keep it in a similar device on his mantelpiece to ensure your everlasting departure."

"Sailing west to the coast then, and thanks a lot for that lovely thought," Jack said with dignity as if he were truly captaining a ship. He looked back at Gavin, who was awkwardly balancing on his remaining foot. "And for my first mate, a peg should be fitted," he joked, reaching out to Gavin's leg. With a wave of magic, he stood on a peg-leg made of ice. They both laughed, Gavin feeling a little humiliated at first, until he walked on it successfully.

Jack climbed the stairs behind him to the helm of his ice ship. He grasped the wheel while raising the other hand straight toward the sky. The ocean began to rise under the ship, higher and higher, until it seemed as if they were flying. Then the water flushed forward in a massive wave, carrying the ship at the top. The wave slimmed at the front from under the hull, and the ship leaned forward down the massive wave, surfing down with great speed. As it reached the bottom, it had amassed tremendous speed in addition to more magic. Standing at the helm, Jack cast wind at the back of the sails.

At the speed Jack held the ship traveling west, the shore came in view within the hour. Both men rejoiced, praising the land after their terrible ordeal with the kraken. Jack was becoming weary from concentrating tremendously hard to keep all of his magical creations from melting or slowing.

The ship neared the land. Jack collapsed, exhausted, onto the ice, releasing the magic that propelled the ship. Immediately, the vessel slowed; the ice began melting, leaving a film of water over the deck, making it extremely slippery even with the salt layer that was now only contributing to the melting process. He braced himself on the deck with both hands. Gavin stumbled and slid to Jack, trying to help him up. Both men, exceedingly fatigued, made their way from the helm slowly down the slippery steps back to the main deck.

As they cleared the deck and headed for the bow of the ship, Jack's strength slowly returned enough to support himself and to help Gavin, who was now even more exhausted after nearly drowning then carrying Jack halfway across the ship with only one leg. The two men stopped twenty feet from the bow, and Gavin leaned against the rail, pulling his cloak around him to separate his skin from the salty ice. Jack stood tall, looking forward over the hull, expecting a collision with the seawall. The ship was becoming less stable and frailer every second it floated through the water. When Jack was sure the ship was about thirty seconds away from its collision, he grabbed Gavin, and they secured themselves in anticipation. The ship crashed to a halt. It cracked across the middle, weakening even more.

"Did we make it?" Gavin asked, a note of relief in his voice.

"I don't know. We hit much sooner than I expected." Jack looked over the edge. They were over twenty feet from the seawall. He walked to the bow and cautiously peered over the front of the ship.

"Gavin, hold on!" Jack screamed as he watched the kraken moving slowly in front of the vessel. It started rubbing its scales across the ship under the water. Chunks of ice broke from the bow and sails. The center of the ship had already been weakened from the impact with the kraken, so each block that fell from the sails to the deck knocked out large chunks into the water.

The sound stopped, and Jack lost sight of the slow-moving beast. He had already been sure they had killed it once when they cut their way out, and now Jack was hoping it had used the last of its life to scare them once more before dying.

Just to be sure they were safe, Jack patrolled the perimeter of the deck, cautious of the broken sides and giant cracks throughout the ice. Gavin peered off the opposite side and gasped. Before he could speak, the kraken leapt from the water toward the ship.

Jack spun around at Gavin's gasp and beheld the kraken. It looked most like a dragon, but its wings were short and thick, used as fins to cut water instead of air, and its neck was extremely long. Its front arms stretched forth with long webbed fingers and giant claws sprouting from their tips. The legs were large and extremely muscular with giant webbed feet. A dozen long tail-like tentacles extended from its backside, pulled forward around its body, reaching, wiggling, and squirming in search of its prey.

The kraken missed landing on the deck, its head running into the side of the ship near Gavin. He slid on his only foot and ice peg to the side and was propelled off the vessel. Jack lunged after Gavin and plucked him from midair. He tossed Gavin back to the deck, but lost his footing, leaving himself to be the one to fall.

Jack plummeted from the ship and splashed hard in the water onto the stunned but rising kraken's back, just under its neck. The giant monster seemed dazed from its collision with the ship. Jack was likewise dazed, but kept his wits. He unsheathed his sword and ran up the slight incline of neck for the head, taking advantage of the disoriented beast as its head bowed low. Holding his sword in one hand, he sliced and dodged as the tentacles tried to swat and grab him. They fell limp into the water as he sliced them clean off. He continued charging the head of the beast. His blade pointed behind him when he dove.

Raising it over his head with both hands, he plunged the long brilliant blade downward into the sea dragon's skull.

The kraken jolted from the water, lifting Jack with it. He held onto the sword, attempting to straddle the beast's neck, but it was much too large to get his legs around. The kraken shook its head violently, trying to dislodge the blade. Just as his grip began to loosen, the kraken dropped its head and dove. Jack was able to get a new hold on the hilt of his sword during the fall, but now the kraken was dragging him underwater. The beast splashed back out again, thrashing in all directions, submerging Jack repeatedly. Eventually, as the kraken snapped its head back, Jack's body weight swung from the hilt, ripping the sword form the beast's skull and sending Jack flailing through the air with sword in hand.

Jack splashed into the water from a great height. The impact felt like landing on concrete, stunning him. The sound of Jack's body splashing into the water caught the attention of the wounded monster, and it dove into the ocean to search for its prey. Jack, still dazed from the impact, was sinking but clutching his sword tightly. He looked up in the water as he sank and saw the kraken charging down at him. He kept his body limp, allowing his course to continue deeper as the monster approached.

The kraken opened its mouth, thrusting forward to swallow him a second time, but as it approached Jack snapped into action. He spun, kicking hard to divert the kraken's path. Then he spun again, allowing his rage and frustration to fill him as he swung the sword upward with all his might through the water. The blade caught the corner of the kraken's mouth, slicing a gaping gash through its face to its neck. Blood tainted the water around him. The beast screeched so loud, even under water, Jack envisioned his head exploding as he watched the kraken struggle.

His battle was not over yet. Having thought they were rid of the beast before, Jack wanted to be certain this fight would be its last. He swam deeper toward the plummeting kraken, relying on his immortality rather than his breath. He grabbed hold of the beast's tail, sheathing his sword so he could begin to climb down the falling beast's body. The kraken was still alive despite the horrific wound. It was stunned, focusing only on the pain of the attack, not paying any attention to Jack as he climbed down the tail, past the legs, and finally over the stomach to the giant chest.

The kraken's scales were large and thick, making it easy for Jack to maneuver himself along the sinking monster. He held himself to the chest, pressing his ear against it, to find the heartbeat. Its pulse was rapid, making it easy for Jack to get a fix on the heart's location. He withdrew his sword with one hand, still gripping a scale with the other, and plunged the sword through the chest as deep as he could until the hilt met the serpent's scale. The kraken emitted a final agonizing screech, but the sound faded quickly. The beast was finally dead.

Jack released the scale. Holding tightly to his sword, he kicked off from the kraken, launching himself from the body to propel back to the surface once more. His vision began to flicker and fade from lack of oxygen and strained magic. Determination forced him to kick harder.

Just when thoughts of giving up entered his mind, feeling weak and exhausted, he looked up and saw Gavin peering over the side of a large ice block, the last remnant of the ship.

He swam as hard as he could, rejuvenated by the sight of his friend, and his body breached the water. Gavin extended a hand to pull Jack aboard the block so he could rest.

"You all right, Jack?" Gavin asked with wide eyes. The young child he had raised was the man who had spent the day battling evil and defeating a kraken.

"I think so. It's dead. I'm tired of killing it, so it better be dead," Jack chuckled.

"You truly are remarkable. You just fought a giant monster beyond my worst nightmares, you nearly drowned, and yet here you sit laughing."

The two men began paddling with their hands toward the docks so they could use the height of the ice block to get out of the water. Once on stable ground, they staggered off the docks and collapsed exhausted in the soft grass. Gavin turned over to kiss the ground.

"I never understood why people kissed the ground in the movies after being at sea for a while, but I can understand it now," he laughed.

Jack simply smiled as he stared up at the sky. The black clouds had rolled off while they were out at sea. The sight was both comforting and concerning to Jack. If the eerie black clouds were gone, that must mean Tei had left the area before Jack could even lay eyes on him. This was a relief because he was physically exhausted and did not want to fight any more battles today. But he worried Tei may be murdering more innocent people and turning them to flesh-craving monsters. The unsettling feeling took over all else when Gavin jumped up and put his hands on his head.

"No! This can't be!" Gavin shouted with true fear in his voice. Jack jumped to his feet to see what Gavin was yelling about.

"Gavin, what's—" Jack started, but then his eyes caught what was upsetting Gavin. The trunk to the car was open, and they hadn't left it that way.

Jack sprinted to the car. He grabbed hold of the trunk, looking down into emptiness.

"Damn it all! How would he know we had the device with us?" Jack exclaimed in disbelief.

"He must have spies, or telepathy, or maybe just dumb luck, but no matter how he knew, he now has the power to imprison you for all eternity," Gavin said grimly.

Jack slammed the trunk shut and kept his hands on the back of the car firmly, leaning his body weight upon them. He stood there for a few moments deep in thought. His eyes began clouding over, and the fear turned to rage inside him. He didn't know how to find Tei, and Tei now had a way to ruin him.

The pair got into the car. Gavin drove despite his missing leg, replaced by an ice peg sufficient to work the clutch. Jack stared out the window dazed, swimming in thoughts of his battle. Neither of the two men knew what to do at this point, so they began to travel back home. They had only come to Main Street on a hunch in the first place and were lucky enough to find Tei's minions, though not lucky enough to fight him directly.

Every road they drove down was abandoned. No other cars, no pedestrians walking or shopping. Once they returned to the mansion and parked in the garage, Jack and Gavin scavenged pieces to fashion a better leg so Jack didn't need to draw focus to keep the ice peg frozen. Even though Gavin enjoyed the ice because it kept the wound numb, he looked forward to having better grip with the leg from an old wooden chair.

After constructing a new peg from the chair leg and fastening hardware they scavenged in the garage, Jack was feeling starved and made his way to the kitchen. Gavin followed behind. Neither of the men had anything to say after their excruciating day.

Jack took off his cloak and sword and set them on a table before continuing to the fridge for a pound of raw beef. He smelled it and smiled for the first time since retreating from Main Street. His teeth grew at the scent, and his eyes clouded over again as he devoured the meat in a few quick gulps. Gavin watched in disgust as the man he had once tried to teach manners ate like an untamed animal.

"Are you not hungry, Gavin?" Jack snarled through his fangs, slightly covering his mouth with his hand to block any of the food that he was chewing from escaping.

"I was, but I've lost my appetite," Gavin huffed.

"Sorry, I still don't have control over this whole thing yet," Jack replied through a grin, exposing his frighteningly large incisors. Gavin smiled, but a shiver crawled up his spine as he stared at Jack's teeth.

After Jack finished a second pound of beef, his strength became fully replenished.

"Why do you think Tei is hiding? If he has such treacherous monsters to command, why does he not just come here and crush us?" Jack asked, trying to start a brainstorm more than expecting a direct answer.

"I'm not quite sure, but I'd say he's intimidated by you. You have decimated thousands of undead, two trolls, and even conquered a kraken, the largest sea creature I can think of. We gave him over three months to prepare while you trained and studied. I'm actually quite surprised he hadn't brought a bigger battle to you." Gavin clenched his pocket watch in his fist.

Chapter XX

Dark Strategist

Tei was truly petrified of Jack. He paced back and forth in a dark room, contemplating his next move. His mind raced with thoughts and encounters that had led him to this realm. It was foretold by the Álfar that a pair of warriors would end his reign. Tei was able to trace one of the two back to Earth's realm through Peter. In an attempt to destroy him, he had opened the portal to Earth too close to Jack and accidentally transferred some of his own powers to him upon entry. Though he had been lucky enough to take Peter's life as he came through the portal, he believed at that point he had just killed the threat. Considering his mission complete, he had let his guard down. He'd shown up at Hollow Wood Manor transfigured to appear as Peter, living his memories and attempting to intrude on the wealth of knowledge kept by Peter both within himself and within the mansion. When he had met Jack and Jessi, though, he only recognized Jack as distant, human kin. For some reason he had not had access to Peter's full memory of who Jack was. But he had still felt the presence of magic more powerful than his own. He'd begun to follow the young couple around, trying to discern which was of importance and whether he would be able to persuade them to work for him.

Tei had roamed the mansion in his dog form, searching for Peter's library. In one of the several libraries in the house, Jack and Jessi had intruded on him. He had licked Jack's face, which allowed him to absorb several memories. Though Jack's memory was damaged, Tei had sensed the magical bond with Jessi.

Though Jack was the one who held the magic, he had unknowingly been casting a love enchantment on Jessi from his emotions. The enchantment was so powerful her aura had glowed with magic. At first, Tei had mistaken her for the one with magic and growled and snarled when she approached him. He had learned little from Carla but realized his mistake when he finally got his fingers on Jessi. Tei had not known that Jack would be able to wield the powerful weapon he had stolen from Farion before entering this realm. He regretted losing it so easily, knowing the powers it holds.

He had then believed Jack to be alone, without friends, love, or guidance. He had sensed the butler's annoyance with Jack, never imagining him to be any threat. He hadn't thought Gavin would become the teacher to train Jack so well.

Tei had watched over Main Street as Jack and Gavin conquered everything he threw at them. His plan of summoning some of the fiercest creatures and beings of Farion, the sirens, kraken, and rock trolls, should have destroyed Jack as planned. But Tei still had reason to fear his own doom as the pair of warriors left the Main Street battle victorious.

Tei was still on Main Street in the tallest building, festering in his paranoia, examining the device he had stolen from the trunk of Gavin's car.

"I finally have it back! I will be so pleased. Now if only I can trap that pestering boy, I will surely not be rid of me when I return," he ranted as he admired the device structure.

The mechanism was made up of three parts. A hollowed mask of metal folded open from the side. Inside the mask, two spikes protruded inward from the eyes. At the neck of the mask, two blades slid over one another when the device closed, like a pair of extremely sharp scissors. A dip in each blade would avoid severing the spine completely to allow the immortal wearer to feel the constant pain with a conscience mind. Thin ingot arms sprouted from the back of the mask and from the chin with a metal latch at the bottom of each.

The second part was a chest plate. He flipped it over to view the side that would press against Jack's body. A curious mechanical wheel was tracked with thin but sturdy spikes that arched out to the side before straightening out. He flipped the chest piece back over, and examined slots that would cover over the collarbone.

The third and final piece was a back plate without any significance other than latches on the sides to connect the three parts securely with a lock.

Tei set the equipment down and sat in an oversized chair in the luxury suite he had acquired. He stared at the luminous plated gadget on the table, pondering its importance. The only way to stop an immortal was to permanently pierce the heart or separate the head from the body for all eternity. A smile, crooked and foul, swept over Tei's face.

Tei deliberated, tearing through his twisted mind, conjuring a way to stop Jack, kill Gavin, and take over this realm as its all-powerful ruler. He rose from his chair, leaving the safety of his secret lair to stroll down the deserted Main Street. He arrived at a hunting store full of camouflage gear and guns hung on racks behind the counter. As far as he was concerned, he had conquered the town, slaughtering all of its citizens and consuming their souls with his dark magic. He could claim everything else as plunder.

After examining a few pistols and firing one at a wall to test its effectiveness, he proceeded to murmur an incantation while throwing his hand forward. Fire ripped from his fingers and blew a huge hole around the small bullet hole. He tossed the pistol on the floor, rolling his eyes and huffing.

He walked to the far right behind the counter where a door labeled *Employees Only* led into a back room. There he discovered a plethora of firearms and swords hung on the walls.

Tei paced around the room, plucking swords from their racks and striking them on the ground, testing their strength. The first few swords bent at the sheer force of his swing, and one even snapped completely off. Tei was quite disappointed with this realm's quality of metallurgy, but he persisted in finding a blade to his standards.

Finally, he swung a sword at the floor that caused fiery sparks as it connected with the concrete, but the blade remained intact. He struck it as hard as he could on the metal shelf, causing the shelf to split, and the blade survived.

He strung a belt under his jacket, sliding the sheath onto the belt so it hung down his right leg, then tucked away the sword. With his new weapon he was ready to make an attempt at his revised plan to defeat Jack.

****

Jack and Gavin had eaten and now lay in a common room on the first floor with two couches big enough for a grown man to lie on comfortably. Both men needed the rest, for their entire day had been filled with fright and battle. As slumber embraced Jack, he slipped into a dream wherein he stood in a green forest with trees taller than any building and beauty beyond anything on Earth. Around him on the forest floor were flowers unknown to him, yet familiar, with radiant colors. As he slowly looked around, admiring the beautiful scenery, he heard a voice carried on the wind. Soft and loving, sweet and innocent, Jessi's voice filled his heart. The words were inaudible, even when a light appeared to sway between the trees, approaching him. As it drew nearer, the light grew taller, eventually assuming the shape of Jessi's beautiful body.

She continued toward him with her hand outstretched as if asking for him to take it. He stepped forward, extending his hand as he walked. His heart was full of the undying happiness he had felt for the few short days he had had Jessi in his life. His eyes softened with tears as he smiled in perpetual joy. His knees weakened, but he forced himself to continue to meet Jessi's hand with his.

When he was only feet away from her, the ground began to rumble. The forest floor cracked open between Jack and Jessi, creating a canyon between them. Jack dropped to his knees and yelled her name across the gaping chasm only to hear his voice echo in reply. He sat there on his knees, gazing across at Jessi as she stood staring back. Her determination to reach him was unstoppable. The light illuminating her presence lifted her from the ground as she proceeded across, walking on air.

Jack stood and stepped to the edge of the cliff, watching her walk to him, anticipating her arrival with great pleasure. It had been months since he had seen her last in a vision he'd had as he meditated. He missed her so intensely he ignored the unreal character he so eagerly awaited.

She came near again and once more reached her hand out to Jack. He still stood at the edge of the canyon wall and held out his hand to receive hers. Finally, their fingertips touched, but as she slid her hand into his she fell from the invisible floor she had been walking on, almost tugging Jack off the cliff. She glanced up at him with a smile as he looked down frantically, petrified of losing her again. He extended his other hand, grabbing her wrist, attempting to pull her up. As he was getting her to safety, she snarled, exposing dog-like teeth. She planted her feet on the cliff wall and attempted to tug Jack off the ledge. Startled, he quickly let go, lifting his hands away from her. He calmly watched as Jessi's face became her own again as she plummeted down the crevasse.

Jack sat up panting, drenched in sweat.

"Jessi!" he shouted, rousing Gavin from his slumber.

Gavin asked Jack about his dream, but Jack lied and told him he couldn't remember any details, except for Jessi falling. He remembered everything: the image of her face transforming was imprinted in his head like the haunting dreams he had had the first few days after his memory loss.

For a while, Jack sat on the couch, reliving his nightmare over and over in his head, trying to make sense of it. As the initial intensity diminished, he eventually discarded the vision as another meaningless dream he was torturing himself with in the guilt he owed Jessi.

Gavin stood up from his couch and stretched his arms in the air, yawning. As his arms fell back to his side, he glanced over at the clock. "Wow, it's already after midnight." He yawned a second time. "We slept for at least six hours. How are you feeling, Jack?"

"I'm feeling well rested. Not hungry again yet." Jack smiled and rubbed his hand over his stomach. "I still have all my parts, too. How's your leg feeling?"

"It twinges and burns, but I can manage with a few pain pills I have stashed in the kitchen," Gavin replied with a grunt as he took a step on the uncomfortable peg.

"Shall we find you an eye patch and a big hat and call you captain?" Jack mocked lightly. Gavin smirked at him but didn't satisfy Jack with a response. Instead, he motioned for action.

"I'm headed to the kitchen for the pills. Then I think we should have another look around downtown." Gavin limped past Jack and patted his shoulder.

Jack turned and followed him to the kitchen, making more peg-leg jokes, trying to make humor out of the kraken's treachery. Finally, Gavin spun around and grabbed Jack by the collar of his shirt and growled.

"One more joke about my leg, and I'll cut both of yours off while you sleep and burn them so it takes you weeks to grow them back, you snot-nosed little brat!"

"Whoa, Gavin. I was only joking," Jack said with his hands up in a sign of surrender.

"It hurts. A lot. Unlike you, my pain is not dulled, and my limbs don't regrow! My leg is gone forever. I think you could be a bit more sensitive," Gavin cracked like a whip.

"Yes, sir. It won't happen again," Jack said sincerely then muttered, "Grouch." Gavin looked at him once more with disgust, and Jack raised his hands again, surrendering.

"Don't fall asleep around me again, Jack," Gavin said through an evil smile.

Gavin took his pain pills, and the two men left the house in the same car Gavin always chose.

"So what's the plan?" Jack asked.

"We need to explore Main Street up and down. Tei must be hiding there somewhere. We must retrieve Peter's device and somehow fasten it on Tei. The downtown area has been all but abandoned or killed off, however you prefer to think of it. Perhaps Tei is hiding out somewhere visible to us at night, unless he has the ability to see in the dark and does not require the use of electricity," Gavin replied.

"Seems easy enough. Do what we couldn't earlier: sneak past someone who could be anyone and then get him or her to wear something he or she surely knows is an eternal prison for immortals," Jack said sarcastically, diluting the seriousness of their task.

"It would be easier if you would grow up and stop acting like a child," Gavin grimaced.

Back on the empty road again, driving through the curves and bends, the headlights cast eerie shadows on the abundant trees that lined the roadway. Jack stared out his window in a trance, repeating his vivid dream over and over. Witnessing

Jessi's face turn doglike, watching her fall into the darkness of the canyon. The thought was driving Jack mad—if he had only been faster that morning in the diner, he could have stopped Tei from snapping her neck like a twig. But the honest truth was that Tei was too fast and close to Jessi as it happened. Jack could not have stopped her death no matter what he did that morning. Still he dwelled on it. The car was silent while Gavin drove; Jack remained preoccupied in his guilt.

"I understand why you are so rude and crass. I'm sorry for not being more understanding with you. You have been through a lot over the past few months, and I do truly feel sorry for you," Gavin said sincerely. "But you need to remember Peter was like a father to me also. I, too, have lost loved ones throughout this war that you are just discovering, and now I've lost a leg."

"I'm sorry, Gavin, it's a coping mechanism. I was aware of your adventures and your loss, that's why I assumed you could take my cheeky humor. I didn't ask for any of this, but I haven't complained much about it either."

"No, you didn't ask for this, nor did I. I simply vowed to serve Peter for all he had done for me. He took me to places I could never have imagined, and I am nothing but thankful for that. If not for him, I would have been left for dead. If not for him, I would not have met her," Gavin choked on the last word.

Jack looked at him with sorrowful eyes, perceiving Gavin was a heartbroken man too. He recognized the pain, acknowledging Gavin would choose not to speak of her for the same reason Jack chose not to reveal the details of his dream.

"I am sorry, Gavin. I did not intend to hurt you. I care very much for you. I'm just scared, and I'm hurting."

"It's okay. I understand, and I'm sorry for being so sensitive about my peg leg." Gavin glanced at Jack with a small grin.

"Argh, matey!" Jack hollered. They both howled with laughter after a strenuous day.

"I'll have to accept my peg leg eventually. I suppose sooner would be better than later," Gavin said between boisterous laughs. He closed one eye and growled at Jack like a pirate.

Gavin returned his attention to the road ahead, where a man was standing. Jack remembered how Tei caused him to crash before with the same trick, but there was not enough time to explain why Gavin should ram the person. Even though they had not seen a living person in months, instinct guided Gavin to swerve to miss the man in the road, losing control. Thick smoke billowed from the squealing tires, spinning the car in circles.

As they spun, both driver-side tires gripped the pavement, causing the car to roll. Glass shattered as the car tumbled off the road into the dark woods. They flipped over a dozen times before finally slamming into a tree upside-down. Jack frantically removed his seatbelt, releasing him to fall to the roof riddled with shards of glass. He looked over at Gavin to notice he was bleeding from a head laceration and his skin was pale. Blood pooled below as his head dangled just above the dangerously sharp debris. Jack ripped the shirt from his back and spread it beneath his companion to soften his drop. The belt was unmovable, locked in the violent crash.

Chapter XXI

Betrayal of the Heart

"Gavin," Jack whispered before shouting, "Gavin!" He grabbed his shoulder, shaking him, but there was no response.

Jack was infuriated. His anger was uncontrollable, and he morphed into his berserk form. The protective cloak stretched with ease to his new massive size. He kicked his door twice, feeling it come loose. The third kick ripped the door from its hinges, sending it flying into a tree where it bent like a piece of paper curling around the trunk. He climbed from the upended vehicle on his hands and knees, leaning back in to grab his sword from the back seat. He then stood, grasping the car with both hands, and gently flipped it back on its wheels. Looking through what was once a window, he assessed the extent of Gavin's injuries. He had shards of glass and twisted steel sticking from his face, shoulders, and chest. Jack grabbed the loose shirt to apply pressure to his unresponsive friend's oozing abrasions.

Jack's attention turned back toward the street where Tei stood with a sword drawn. Still hulking, Jack drew his sword, sprinting at Tei with inhuman speed. As he neared, Tei thrust forward with his sword. Jack swiped the strike to the side and punched Tei in the face with all his might. The warlock was thrown backward through the air by the brute force of the blow.

Tei jumped to his feet. Ripping his jacket off and throwing it to the ground, he roared as his face began to alter, curling and snarling as Jessi's face had in Jack's dream. Jagged teeth lined his mouth, which stretched into a snout. He charged back at Jack, who awaited him. Jack slid the tip of his sword across the ground, bringing it straight up in an attempt to cut the dog in half, but Tei deflected the strike.

The swords clashed rapidly and repeatedly. Tei's attacks were constant but careless against his opponent's impenetrable defense. Jack finally saw an opening after what seemed like an eternity of swordplay. Tei raised his sword over his head to bring a devastating blow down on Jack. With a flash of blue light, Jack plunged his sword into Tei's chest. Tei's attack froze as the blade tore through his skin. He leaned forward into Jack, bringing them face to face. Tei snapped his deformed jaw at Jack's chin as he pushed back from the snarling teeth.

Jack kicked Tei off his blade. He spun through the air, landing on his fists and knees, sliding on the pavement from the power of the kick. Tei roared as he squirmed, transforming into the Hellhound. Snapping bones were visible as they rearranged under the skin before the fur sprouted all over. Within moments, Jack was no longer witnessing Tei's alteration, he was glaring into the dark eyes of a large black dog.

The dog turned to the woods to flee. Jack sheathed his sword, tracking the dog as fast as he could. Even with his unnatural speed, he could only track Tei audibly, seeing him in the moonlight bounding around trees off in the distance. Jack started screaming as he tailed the Hellhound.

"You took my parents! You took my friends! You took the woman of my dreams! Stand and fight me, you cowardly dog!"

He had lost sight of the dog and could no longer hear it racing through the dry leaves that canvassed the forest floor. Jack slowed to a walk before halting, attempting to hear anything. Then a sound caught his ear from the side. He turned just in time as the dog lunged for his neck. Jack got his hands up to push the attack away from him, slipping back on the leaves. While he was off balance, the dog began to run through the woods. Jack sprung forward in pursuit of his foe once more.

Jack burst out of the woods miles from the scene of the car wreck, miles he covered quickly at the speed he was running. He looked both ways down the road on which he emerged, recognizing it immediately. He was at the end of a dead-end side street leading to Main Street.

"Oh, this isn't good," Jack said softly, as if here were accompanied by a friend. A growl came from down the street, and he advanced toward it. After passing a few of the small apartment buildings that lined the street, another growl came from behind. He spun around, but could see nothing. Then he heard more growling in front of and behind him. In the dark of night, with only a few flickering street lamps, people stumbled from every alley, growling, moaning, and snarling at him. Jack pulled his sword out, gripping it tightly.

He closed his eyes as his emotions rose, but instead of focusing on missing those people he lost, he fixated on the love he felt for them. The sword radiated a brighter blue light. The light infused his hands, traveled through his arms, and eventually covered his body, pulsating from his head and shoulders.

As Jack expected, it was not people emerging from the shadows but undead, whom he could see clearly now with blue lighting the entire street. He stood there with his sword in his hands, waiting for the creatures to surround him. He glanced around, trying to estimate how many, but their numbers were overwhelming.

The ugly, decrepit beings encircled Jack, stepping closer and closer. He raised his sword and smashed the blade to the ground, sending out a pulsating wave that threw everything around him back with immense force. Then he spun in place with his sword extended, cutting through the necks of every undead creature within reach. Jack swung elegantly and quickly, cutting down the attackers as they continuously charged him. As he looked over the frontline, there seemed to be an endless supply of demons coming for his life. He raised a hand to focus his energy as a ball of fire formed hovering above his palm. He cast it forth across several of the undead, combusting their clothes but unable to slow their pace. He swirled his hand in front of him, projecting a gust of wind at the closest creatures, but they stood back up and persisted.

Jack fought off constant attacks with fierce aggression for over an hour. Anger and frustration ultimately won his attention as he twisted around, pivoting the sword, punching and kicking his way through the horde. To his disadvantage, he brought his stride too close to the side of the road. Creatures scaled the walls with ease, the slower monsters shoved off as dominant creatures scurried past.

As Jack neared the building blanketed with agile undead, several of them leapt from a third-floor balcony. The first landed on his back, knocking him off balance. Jack reached over his shoulder to grab its neck as if it were the hilt of his sword, but all that followed was a head and the first few vertebrae as the body collapsed from his back. The second landed with its feet on his shoulders, shoving Jack to his knees. Its balance was magnificent, teetering only slightly on Jack's shoulders as he dropped forward. It reached its rancid hands past his cheeks, curled its pungent fingertips under his jaw, and gripped the soft of his neck.

While Jack fumbled with the demon latched to his head, a third dropped on top, knocking it loose and sending the trio tumbling to the pavement. By the time Jack got to his feet to face the two demons, the horde wrapped their arms around his neck and legs around his waist, grabbing his clothes, holding him still as they scratched at him unsuccessfully through his protective cloak. The two creatures that had hurled themselves on top of him were crouched and ready to lunge again.

As the two undead gracelessly flew through the air, Jack closed his eyes, time seemingly at a halt. Acknowledging the great peril, he attempted to focus on the memory of Jessi's face, her laugh and all the things that made him love her instantaneously. Jack's blue glow grew strong once more. Drawing in a deep breath, he smiled as he opened his radiant sapphire eyes. The horde surrounded him grabbing and pulling from all directions. He relaxed his arms to his side, dropping to the ground. He knelt for a moment as he focused his energy, ignoring the pesky beasts attempting to rip him to shreds before pounding the pavement with his mighty fist. The earth shifted under his feet, dividing the road and sidewalk with its shockwave. All the creatures within a ten-foot radius were hit with a force so great it launched their bodies hurling through the air. They splattered on the crumbling walls of the buildings to either side.

The buildings were devastated by the blast. The walls were blown apart two floors high and fifteen feet inward. The foundation was shattered by the shockwave, triggering the walls to collapse like a landslide, pulling down each floor as the building fell. Jack proceeded forward, swinging the sword in circular motions, flipping through the air. The building debris rushed to the ground behind him, pouring over the sidewalk and into the street, slaughtering every creature in its path.

Jack continued concentrating his emotions on every moment of happiness he could remember and the time he'd spent with people who loved him, fueling his aptitude. *Sireth Jessoteth* channeled his power, funneling magical energy from the blade, extending its cutting reach. The smoother he swung the sword, the further the deadly light expelled its physical attribute. He watched as the defeated foes floated away weightlessly as if time had truly slowed. His body felt as if he were not exerting, simply moving leisurely, cutting through the undead as if their bodies were made of air.

The lights surrounding his body became increasingly brighter. Creatures he had dispatched repeatedly were still getting up. Jack took in all his might as his inner light shined a blinding beam and pulled his sword up in front of him. He spun his body, swinging the sword around with both hands and dropping to one knee as he finished the second full turn. The light exploded outward from Jack, and the sword slash reached out, blasting all the creatures through walls and each other. Creatures within a thirty-foot radius were simply vaporized.

Jack had exhausted himself with his magic after hours of straining his abilities. While he felt time had slowed, he was actually moving faster, and he felt as though he was hardly moving because the spell he was channeling made it so. But now the blue light faded from him and only glimmered in the sword.

Listening to the last of the creatures scurrying off up the walls and down the allies, he stayed down on one knee in complete darkness, unable to find the strength to stand. Jack's spells that blasted the creatures to bits and even knocked down a building, also knocked out the power. Jack could only see a few feet in front of him from the dull glow of the blade. His mind swirled, his body trembled, and he struggled not to lie down. Jack's blood ran cold as he realized this is when he would come—this was what Tei had been waiting for.

Footsteps approached, but Jack was paralyzed, stuck waiting for his imminent demise. Waiting for the sting of cold steel on the back of his neck, Jack closed his eyes, not scared, only sorry. He felt remorse for all the people of this town who had been tortured and turned into Tei's slaves; he was sorry he had disappointed his uncle Peter, who had raised him from a boy; he was sorry he was unable to avenge his friend, who lay dead in a car miles away. He was ashamed he could not justify the murder of Jessi, the woman with whom he discovered love at first sight. As he wallowed in self-loathing, a familiar voice spoke.

"Jack."

Jack spun around at the sound of Jessi's voice. Though his vision was blurred from exhaustion, he could see it was Jessi in the flesh, not a dream, not a spirit. Her face was covered in dirt, her hair separated in clumps, sticking out in all directions, and her clothes were torn and tattered. A fond memory of Jessi crawling out of bed in the morning wearing nothing but a sheet flashed through his mind. A smile crept across his face as his eyes lit with disbelief.

"You can't be here," Jack demanded.

"Jack, it's okay. I'm okay," she said sweetly.

"It's too dangerous, the creatures—" Jack struggled to get the words out. His body began to ache from the extreme battle it had endured.

"They all ran from you. You are—amazing."

"I watched you die. I held your lifeless body." He recalled the painful memory, trying to keep his wits through his exhaustion.

"That creep cracked my neck. He thought he'd snapped it." She pulled her head down with her hand, making an awful sound as her cervical spine popped and cracked. "I was unconscious for a while. When I woke up you were gone."

"I'm so sorry, Jessi." He thought about what she was saying and couldn't believe he hadn't even gone back to look for her, but he'd been sure she was dead. He'd held her body; it was cold with no pulse.

"I figured you had gone to save the day, but when you didn't come back, I hid in the diner. There is an attic and plenty of food. Those creatures would come out every night, sniffing around the diner and climbing on the roof, pounding." She began strong but fell weak at the end as she told him about her fear. She knelt, pulling Jack's arm over her shoulder, attempting to stand, but she was unable to lift him.

"I'm going to need a little help here," she insisted as she prepared to stand again. As she pushed up, Jack thrust his feet under him, barely stabilizing his weary legs. Most of his weight was leaning on Jessi as she began slowly pulling him forward, forcing him to walk. "We need to get you off the street quick. The diner isn't far."

"I can't believe you're here," he murmured.

"Believe it. Now move your ass so we both don't get killed," she said kindly but with obvious ambition.

The pair hobbled through an alleyway, past the collapsed building, out onto Main Street, and across the road. They went down the alley that ran parallel to the diner and entered through the back door. Jack leaned up against the wall while Jessi secured the entrance by sliding a shelf in front of the giant hole in the wall Jack had made with Tei's body months prior. As she began to fasten the door, she peered out, looking both directions down the narrow alleyway as though someone were watching them. She thought she saw something move behind a corner, but brushed it off as paranoia, finally shutting the door and locking it.

Jessi helped Jack to a booth she had pulled back into the kitchen, out of view from the windows. He sat down with a thump, still weakened from the blast he had conjured.

"Meat," Jack said. "I need to eat."

"Sorry, Jack, there isn't much of anything left. I've been here for months," she said with an undertone of sadness that tore into Jack's heart, adding to his guilt.

"It's okay, it's not your fault," he said, comfortingly as he extended his hand to caress her shoulder, but she pulled away in disgust. Jack noticed her face was no longer glowing with purity. It was distorted and tainted like most people's.

"I know it's not my fault. Actually, if it were anyone's fault, it would be yours!"

Jack winced at her sharp words. He wanted to cry from the pain of his heart crushing. The woman he loved had to live in this diner for over three months, hiding from flesh-eating demons, alone and scared. Tears forced their way from his eyes.

"I'm so sorry, Jessi. I'm so sorry I didn't come back," he said through the flowing tears.

"You should be! You screwed me, and when you were done with me, you left me for dead. You said you loved me!" She screeched in his face. "If it wasn't for you, Carla would still be here, this town would still be here! You killed them, Jack! You killed them all, just by being here."

"No! I would never hurt an innocent person."

"What about me? You hurt me! You ripped my heart out and abandoned me!"

"I'm sorry. I thought you were dead," his words fell from his lips with pure honesty through his sobs. "I've been lost without you. I hallucinate your presence. I search for you every night in my dreams!"

"You've been lost without me? How do you think I felt here alone without you after you promised to protect me, Jack? You're a coward and hardly even a man. I don't even know why I just saved you from the street—maybe just so I could kill you myself." She continued ranting, smothering him in guilt, exploiting his dazed and exhausted mind.

"Jessi, you don't have to kill me. If you wish me dead, I will take my own life. I said I loved you, and I meant it. I thought you were dead. If I had known you were alive I would have fought the entire world for you," he confessed sincerely, still trying to pull himself together.

"Well, you didn't fight the world for me. You ran away like a scared little boy, leaving me here to be monster fodder. So go ahead and kill yourself!" she demanded. "I watched you the first time you came back into town. I watched you battle those giant creatures in the street. I watched you get eaten by a dragon that jumped out of the water. When you were gone I checked your friend's car to find anything I could use to help you—"

"Did you check the trunk?" Jack exclaimed, interrupting her story.

"Yes. I found some kind of sick and twisted armor that appears to kill whoever wears it," she raised her eyebrows inquisitively, waiting for a response.

"Ah, then Tei doesn't have it!" Jack sighed with relief, slightly grinning, but still too weak to move.

"Well, now I see how easy it is for you to forget about my problems," she said, scowling. "You are a womanizing jerk and you ripped my heart out. If you really want to take your life for me, the only way I will ever be happy is to see you in that armor."

"You want me to be lost in pain?" Jack questioned, as he looked up at her, perplexed but understanding how hurt she was. "You know if I wear that, I will be able to feel pain for as long as I wear it and hear everything around me. But once it is on, I will be as useless as a paperweight, unable to speak or move. I will appear truly dead."

"Then I can see what you saw the last time you looked at me," she snarled as she pulled a tablecloth off the armor.

"Tei might as well win. He's taken everything from me. He took my parents, he took my uncle who raised me, he took my mentor, and made me think he took you, so now you rightly hate me." Jack pulled the armor across the table so it sat in front of him. He opened the chest plate. Seeing the spikes that were to pierce his heart caused a shudder to flow down his spine. He struggled to get to his feet and stood over the device, looking down at the open chest piece.

Jessi shoved him from behind, causing him to fall forward into the chest piece. The spikes jabbed through his heart. They dug so deep they pricked against the inside of his back.

"You got what you deserved, Jack," she cackled in his ear.

His eyes stayed wide open while his mouth dropped, gasping for air. She placed the back of the armor over his shoulders, latching it tight. Jack squealed and gasped one last time before succumbing to the contraption.

She picked up the helmet, placing the back of the device over Jack's soft, silky hair. Smiling with great pleasure, she secured the metal prongs to the shoulders of the chest armor so the helmet was tightly in place.

With one hand, Jessi grabbed the back of the armor, yanking Jack from the table where he lay face down, and threw him to the floor on his back. The blade at the back of his neck lodged his spine into the crevice of the blade. She took the facemask from the table and squatted on his stomach. The mask was the last piece of the armor. It would send a blade through the front of his neck, severing his throat, and send spikes through his eyes to his brain, shutting down everything but his pain receptors and hearing.

She rested the mask on his face gently with both hands. Then she dropped her body weight down hard, causing the mask to crush into Jack's face and snap shut. She latched it quickly as Jack's blood spewed from the cracks of the armor.

"Ah, Jack. How easy it was to defeat you. So young, so immature, so stupid around women," Tei's voice hissed from Jessi's lips as her bones began snapping and jarring under her skin. Her body grew as the bones stretched the flesh, returning Tei to his true shape.

"You'll be glad to know I killed Jessi when I snapped her neck. I squeezed her throat so hard I felt my fingertips touch all the way through her pretty little neck. You probably won't be so happy to hear that I ripped her heart out and ate it so I could absorb her memories and wear her skin. You are so gullible! This was almost too easy," Tei finished with a booming cackle. He grabbed Jack by the foot and dragged him to the back door, tossing him out by the garbage can.

Tei began hauling him again by his foot. He was heading to the apartment building where he had been living, overlooking Main Street and the water from the top floor.

"You don't have to kill me. If you want me dead, I'll take my own life," he mocked in a girlish voice followed by a thunderous evil laugh. When his laughter fell quiet, Tei got the unsettling feeling that someone was watching. He looked around, but the alleyway had too many dark corners.

He dragged Jack across the street to the side that was out of power. He rubbed his fingers together and muttered an incantation, setting his fingers ablaze to light the way into his apartment. Dragging Jack up the stairs, the armor clinked and clanked, bouncing off each step.

Tei began sneering again as they ascended the stairwell.

"I thought you were dead," he said in a girlish voice. "Ha! I am dead, because Tei killed me! Dumbass." Speaking in his normal raspy voice, Tei created a whole conversation by himself to torment Jack, who was forced to listen without being able to reply.

Tei continued in his girly voice. "Tei took everything from me! Blah, blah, blah, and blah blah, all the whining and crying." He cackled at his own jokes. "Aw, is that right? Did your buddy Gavin die in that car accident? Maybe he should grow a pair and drive over the people who want to kill his little student."

Finally, they reached the top floor. Tei kicked in the door to the apartment he now called home and kicked back in his chair on the balcony after tossing Jack's limp body into a corner like a businessman would his briefcase after a long day of work. He was feeling good about himself; the taste of victory was sweet. In his conceited, ignorant, and foulest humor, he turned and looked back at Jack in the corner.

"Hey, bud, how's it feel to be lost in pain?" He turned back in his chair, tilting his head back and laughing for a moment. Then his face went sour and he began mumbling, "Stupid little boy. Thought you were going to defeat me? Ha! Who's lost in pain now?" He laughed once more before returning to the view from his balcony.

Epilogue

The car crash had severely injured Gavin, but he wasn't dead. When he regained consciousness, Jack and Tei were long gone. He stumbled on his peg as he fetched three plastic vials of the health potions he'd thrived on over the long years of battling beside Peter and now Jack. After drinking the magical liquid, he spent fifteen minutes pulling glass from his face and shoulder. The potion helped heal the wounds once the glass was removed, but it did not dull the pain.

Less than a half hour after the crash, Gavin followed the path Jack had left behind. When Jack had run through the woods he had been glowing, but hadn't realized his unstable emotions lashed out, pulling bark from the trees and leaving a blue scar. The air chilled his lungs as he breathed heavily in pursuit, the ground crunched and snapped under his stumbling footsteps, his peg continuously catching on bare roots.

As Gavin ran through the thick trees, he could hear the unearthly fireworks and saw the sky above lit up in a radiant blue. It took Gavin much longer to get through the woods at a natural jogging speed, but eventually he arrived at the same dead-end street. As he neared the edge of the forest, he felt surges of pulsating energy forcefully pushing against his every step. The thunderous fireworks and curious sapphire flashes were almost constant now. Instead of emerging from the woods, he climbed a tall tree to overlook the battle. Gavin knew if he were to step in now to help Jack, he would only be slaughtered. There were far too many of the undead creatures, who luckily had not caught his scent. Gavin assumed Tei was commanding them to attack Jack with his magic.

He sat in his tree, amazed at Jack's elegance with his weapon, following every step Gavin had taught him. The tree shook every so often with the force of Jack's magic. Gavin watched with great pride. Toward the end of the battle, Jack started moving so fast that blue streaks lingered in the air; Gavin could only catch a glimpse of a human body in the collage of light. It was the most beautiful and frightening thing he had ever witnessed.

As Jack dropped to his knees, the last of the creatures fled. When Gavin felt they were far enough away, he dismounted the tree carefully so he could assist Jack, but paused when he heard a woman's voice speaking. Immediately, he knew it was a trick. Tei had already fooled Gavin in the form of his oldest, dearest friend and adopted father, Peter. Jack would fall prey just as he had. Thoughts of failure flowed steadily through his mind as he blamed himself for not emphasizing Tei's trickery to Jack. He should have known Tei would use Jessi against him as the sirens had.

He pulled out his shining pocket watch and gently traced its elaborate woven vine design with his fingertip. He turned the nob and popped open the watch. Instead of a clock face, Peter somberly stared back at Gavin. He leaned back against the tree shielding him from view.

"I need your help, old friend. Everything we have fought for and everything we have built is crumbling. Jack is in dire need of rescue, and I lack the strength to do it," Gavin said apologetically, feeling sorry not only for the tragic circumstances but for summoning him. He was under the impression that it wasn't enjoyable for the spirit.

"I have been watching through your actions. Today is not lost, my dear friend. You were wounded yet nearly sprinted through a vast forest on a leg made from a chair. You are loyal and brave," Peter said with confidence. "Steer your emotions; you must survive this night."

"And leave him here with Tei and your Immortal Trap? How can I? Being lost in pain is worse than hell. A prisoner of your own mind listening to the world carry on without you, unable to react or respond. All while sopping with adrenaline from the excruciating pain, with no escape."

"*My* Immortal Trap! That is blasphemy! I stole it from Teiwaz on our last journey to Farion. I brought it back and hid it in the training room. My plan was to trap Teiwaz in the event he were to ever find a way to this realm."

"Not your—I am so sorry, I thought you had created it as one of your many inventions. I was the one that brought it out in the open, I handed right over to him." Gavin's face hung with disappointment in himself. "I must go and save Jack from the fate I bestowed upon him."

"If you go now, Tei will smite you down and have his way. Jack is extremely weak right now, if Tei wanted him dead—"

"He'd already be dead!" Gavin exclaimed, but his excitement immediately stifled. "But that doesn't change the fact that he will end up lost in pain."

"It is there he will see what is to come. This is just the beginning, son." His words echoed in Gavin's head as Peter's face misted into the watch, revealing the clock face once more.

Cautiously, he emerged from the woods and snuck through the parking lot. He ducked behind a car and beheld the destruction traced in glowing blue, the residual damage of Jack's battle.

He turned to proceed down the alleyway and spotted Jack, watching him enter the diner slumped on the shoulder of a shadowy figure.

"You stupid boy! How can you not know that is Tei?" he grumbled to himself quietly.

Keeping to the shadows, he moved to a place where he could see in the back door of the diner. He moved forward, attempting to determine where Jack had gone, but he was around the corner, out of sight. Tei, in Jessi's form, stuck his head out the back door, looking for him. Gavin was petrified. He thought for sure Tei had seen him leaning forward into the light. Luckily Tei didn't pursue him.

After the door shut, Gavin snuck back around to the front of the diner, trying to stay concealed. Without Jack, Gavin was simply a bug for Tei to squash. Trying to get a glimpse of anything through the low corner of the window, he could only see Tei pretending to be Jessi, yelling at Jack. Jack sat out of sight from the window.

Then Gavin heard the gasping and the gurgle of blood in Jack's lungs when the spikes pushed through his heart. Tears filled Gavin's eyes. Even if Gavin could save him somehow, Jack would never be the same again after enduring this pain, unable to do anything about it, living forever with a literally broken heart, spikes in his eyes, and blades through his throat.

After a few more minutes, Gavin heard a loud sound of metal hitting pavement, clanging as it bounced into the side of a dumpster. He moved back to the side of the building away from the front window and listened to the blood-curdling scrape of the armor being dragged across the ground around the opposite side of the diner from where Gavin stood. Tei was now in his own form. Gavin peeked around the front of the diner. He watched Tei mock Jack, cackling as he dragged him across the street and into an apartment building.

Gavin crossed the street when he heard the banging of the armor up the stairs. He entered the front door and looked up the center of the stairwell. The flickering light of a flame moved along with a voice still teasing the poor young man while singing songs of victory. Gavin stayed at the bottom until the light reached the top of the stairs and Tei kicked a door open.

Gavin knew Tei was in the building straight across the street from the diner, on the top floor, first apartment at the top of the stairs. Unsure of his next move, he retreated for the night. He would have a twenty-mile journey back to Hollow Wood on foot from here, and he only had a few health potions remaining in his cloak pocket. "I will come back for you, Jack," he swore under his breath. He pulled the hood over his head and disappeared into the darkness.

About the Author

Born and raised in New England, J.J. Dice's vivid imagination was strongly impacted by Stephen King novels, above all the *Dark Tower Series*, and Robert Frost poetry. He attended Southern New Hampshire University and enjoys supernatural and sci-fi books, movies and video games.

With a lifelong interest in all mythological things, 38 Studios' *Kingdoms of Amalur* motivated him to create a magical universe filled with hero tales of legend.

Bursting with magic, wonder and mystery, the Legend of Hollow Wood and Legend of Farion book series intertwines the fate of two realms. A frightful warlock has unleashed boundless power, ripping through dimensions to dominate over all. Heroes must join forces to defeat the spread of great and terrible evil.